For The Love Of
DOG

Tree of Life Publishing

Copyright © Maggy Whitehouse 2016

A CIP catalogue record for this book is
available from the British Library.

ISBN: 978-1-905806-48-5

Tree of Life Publishing
Devon, UK

*To Mark
with great appreciation*

Maggy Whitehouse

For The Love Of
DOG

Maggy Whitehouse

Acknowledgements

Excerpt on page 174 from *Honorary Dog—Being Some Anecdotes and Reflections from Fifty Years of Living and Working with Dogs.* Dora Wright, W. H. Allen, London, 1983.

Excerpt on page 236 from *All Over The World* by Françoise Hardy and Julian More released by Pye Records in 1965.

Author's Note

This book is set in 1999, when internet access was still dial-up, and just before the advent of the Pet Passports scheme for Europe and the UK. Since then, the pet scheme has been extended so that dogs from the USA as well as Europe can fly directly to Britain. Before this, animals had to live for six months in quarantine because of the fear of rabies.

The narrative is entirely fictional as are all the characters featured—apart from Frankly. Frankly is based on Didcot, my own beagle, who was the first dog into the UK from America on the Passports for Pets scheme in 2000. Our story was very different; my husband met me when I flew from the USA to Malaga and, together with a friend, drove to meet me at Calais when I returned to England.

Other fiction by Maggy Whitehouse

The Book Of Deborah (Tree of Life Publishing)
Into the Kingdom (Tree of Life Publishing)
Leaves of the Tree (Tree of Life Publishing)
The Miracle Man (O Books)

Chapter One

I AM THIRTY-NINE years old and I am out of nice.

I have done nice all of my life. I have been an angel. I have looked on the bright side. I have compromised and helped. I have done pathetic. I have done the tears.

But I ran out of nice about six weeks ago. It's gone, vanished, simply disappeared. I don't know where it went and, of course, as I don't have it any more, I don't give a toss about losing it. It's quite comforting really. Not in a *nice* way, obviously. It's simply different.

There is not a cell in my body which has not felt the pendulum swing.

That is why I am currently holding up a queue of perfectly pleasant people at Heathrow airport and refusing to get on an aeroplane. Yes, they are going to miss their take-off slot; yes, they are all going to be inconvenienced and yes, quite a few people are getting seriously irritated. But they cannot go without me without even a further delay because my luggage is on board.

What is not on board is my dog. And I am not going without her.

I am a strange phenomenon in this world of possessions. I have no keys, no car, no job, no money and no home. All I have is two suitcases, a holdall, a laptop computer and a beagle. Logically, these are all fairly important to me—not least the beagle.

And Heathrow appears to have lost her.

Even if I were not already out of nice, I would be running dangerously low by now.

The idea is that my dog and I are transiting through London on our way from Denver, Colorado to Malaga, Spain, to live for seven months in a tiny village in the mountains south of Granada. We lived in Colorado for five years, in the days before my husband

Alex decided that I had outlived my usefulness and left me. The problem is that Alex is the one with the visa. And to remain in the USA without a visa (or, for that matter, the income that goes with it) is not a good idea. So, I have to leave.

Of course, it is far more complicated than that. It always is. But to go home to England is not an option for me right now for it would mean months of hell in confinement for a very spoilt little bitch. And the dog wouldn't like it, either.

Anyway, I'm not sure if England is my home any more; I left it, willingly enough, five years ago and never expected to return except for holidays. In fact, I'm not sure of anything. I'm going to live in a house I've never seen in a village I don't know, in a country whose language I don't speak and where I don't have any friends. Except Frankly.

So, I am not boarding this aeroplane without her. I am being perfectly pleasant about it—pleasant is different from nice. You can be pleasant and obstinate; pleasant and firm; pleasant and downright bolshie; pleasant and adamant. I am all of those.

'Well, I suggest that you find her,' I say calmly when the airline clerk says that they have lost my dog.

And I smile sweetly. It is not a nice smile.

'I can wait,' I say. 'I have all the time in the world.' And I have. I have the rest of my life and nothing whatsoever to do with it. So, standing at an airport departure gate being obstinate is as good a way of passing the odd hour or two as any other.

Frantic telephone calls are being made. To do the airport staff justice, they don't want to lose a dog either. It would be pleasant for all of us if they could discover where Frankly is and get her safely on that plane.

If I could have flown her directly to Spain from Colorado, I would have. It's bad enough for an animal to have to fly, in a box, alone in darkness with all those strange feelings that they can't understand without having to do it twice over in one day.

But there was really no alternative and, when I arrived at Heathrow and went to the Information desk to check that she was okay, they told me that she was being loved and petted and fed and fussed over by a whole load of people in the kennels.

'She's probably being far better looked after than you,' they said.

Yes, probably—but it is my first time in England for three years and, even if it is only an airport, it is good to see the old familiar shops and hear the (lack of) accent.

It is also so peaceful to be able to buy a meal without having to have a relationship. In the States I could not open my mouth without the response: 'You're not from round here, are you?' or 'Gee, I like your accent.'

Even so, I loved Colorado. Beautiful, beautiful Colorado.

Alex, Frankly and I were happy there even after such a huge transition. Frankly was the best friend you could ever want when starting a new life. She pottered through everything in her own comfortable manner, moving from chasing squirrels to chipmunks and from rabbits to raccoons with no effort whatsoever, and she was always there and comfortable and furry whenever I felt worried or upset. And she made friends for me, too. So many American people every day stopped and petted this sweet and sassy tricolour beagle, falling in love with her kohl-ringed brown eyes and soft white muzzle with the dash of white running up between her eyes. 'So cute!' they said. '*So* cute!' And from there, conversations could start and friendships be forged.

I once asked a friend if Frankly were spoilt. She thought carefully for a long time and said: 'No, she's not spoilt, Anna. She's *ruined!*'

The trouble is that beagles are as addictive as cigarettes, alcohol, chocolate and drugs. You think you can handle it; that you can quit any time you like; but the truth is that you are hooked. Fortunately, beagles don't like cigarettes, alcohol or drugs but from then on it's a fight to the death for the chocolate.

I know I should add here that chocolate is bad for dogs—can even be fatal—and shouldn't be fed to them. But I only learnt that long after a lifetime of beagles all of which had, at some stage, stolen vast amounts of chocolate without any bad effects. Lily scoffed a two-pound box given to me for my 18th birthday and littered the lawn with silver-paper-coloured dump for days. Never turned a whisker.

It's traditional to blame your mother for any problems and my mum certainly initiated our family beagline addiction when I was very young. It was after Dad had left; Richard my brother was eight and I was six so it was entirely understandable. Aromatherapy was not readily available in those days and hugging was not then fashionable, let alone accepted in Mum's family circle. Beagles, on the other hand, were very paws-on and definitely smelly. But, despite the infinite furry rewards, the eager wet noses and the soulful eyes, it was a long and exhausting life of beagledom. In fact, Mum told me once that she thought that raising children had been a piece of cake in comparison. Richard and I had come when we were called; rarely stolen from the larder, never chewed her shoes or clothes, slept in our own beds and went off to obedience school five days a week for fourteen years.

I did not even have an adolescent rebellion; I was too awash with beagle puppies to fall in love with pop stars or ponies. But when Richard and I both went away to University, some kind of Cosmic Law took a hand. The last beagle went to the happy hunting ground and Mum was left alone in the house. It was not an easy time for her but, with the help of friends, a little alcohol and quite a lot of chocolate, she made it through. She was over it. She was in recovery. She got a Cavalier King Charles Spaniel.

It is said that whatever you do, you will eventually end up like your mother. I did not believe it myself but ten years after the last childhood beagle went chasing celestial rabbits, Danny died in that stupid accident and I decided to get myself a puppy. I was working from home as a cookery writer and part-time in the evenings as a pastry chef so it was feasible.

'Mum,' I said, casually over Sunday lunch at her place. 'If I got a dog, would you be willing to look after it one or two days a week while I'm at work?'

'What sort of dog,' said my mother suspiciously.

'Oh, a beagle,' I said airily.

There was silence. I looked at Mum and she looked at me. A long struggle was going on inside her. Finally, she spoke.

'Three days a week,' she bargained ruthlessly.

Frankly arrived six weeks later. She had a worried little puppy brow that wrinkled when she tried to think and she did a lot of thinking; almost as much as she did sleeping (and that was mostly on a cushion next to my computer keyboard).

She followed at my heels, snuggled into my arms, whimpered when I left her and made it totally and abundantly clear that she was mine for life as long as I obeyed her every whim. We compromised on that after a battle of wills that brought on my first grey hairs. I won a few points and Frankly learnt to sit, stay, beg and shake hands. She never, ever walked to heel.

But she was there in the evenings when Danny's pictures spoke of the love and laughter that we had shared. She was named after him in a way—Danny had had a habit of saying 'Frankly, this' or 'Frankly, that' and we had made up an invisible friend and a private joke that 'Frankly' always had an opinion on anything.

The furry Frankly was only downstairs in the kitchen and could be fetched and held tightly in the nights when Danny's ghost was not there to comfort me and the tears would not stop. She was someone to care for when there was no Danny to kiss me or tell me that he would be perfectly safe and it was just another, normal, diving trip.

She was there too, when the anger finally surfaced; the anger at Danny's carelessness and bravado and belief that he was immortal. His disregard for my fears as he went diving ever deeper and longer in the cold, hostile waters of the North Sea. She was there when my memory haunted me with the bitter hours when they searched for his body; when people tried to be hopeful and I knew full well that Danny's oxygen would have expired. It took three days to find him and they would not let me see his body.

One day, I threw Danny's clothes and equipment into black plastic bags and took them to Oxfam but, when I got back, Frankly was curled up in the now empty wardrobe. Danny's clothes and fading scent had been part of Frankly's life, too, and she did not understand why they had gone. We sat in the wardrobe together and I cried and Frankly licked me and then we decided to eat a pot of ice cream together. It was Frankly's idea.

Slowly, life rebuilds itself. When someone you love dies, part of you dies too. But there is a resurrection. I recovered. I met Alex and I loved him.

And now, here I am, waiting at Heathrow and an adapted quotation from Oscar Wilde is running through my head: "To lose one husband is unfortunate. To lose both looks like carelessness." But Alex has gone and he, too, is not coming back.

There will be time enough in Spain to go over and over what has happened. Just be aware that I am not going to be nice about it. I am not going to be understanding; I am not going to see Alex's point of view. I tried all that and it didn't work.

'Anna, are you running away?' asked my mother when I told her of my plan.

Yes I am. It is easier to be honest when you don't have to bother being nice.

'Oh look!' The nice (*really* nice) female flight attendant is looking out through the window. 'Is that your dog?'

I jump up and, together, the three airline staff and I peer down at the tarmac. A wooden 'sky-kennel' is being transported towards the plane on a hand-pulled trolley. The end with the wire grill is pointed towards us and a little brown and white face is peering out anxiously.

'Oh! How cute!' say the airline staff and my heart melts too. It is Frankly and she can do cuter than cute without even trying. As we watch, two stewardesses on the tarmac run up to the kennel and start trying to stroke her through the wire. How could anyone resist such a sweet little dog, especially one that pathetic?

The relief is so great that I can feel a slight edge of niceness warming my fingertips. I even smile at the officials as I take my boarding pass and walk down to the plane.

It doesn't last: I am so tired and there is so much more to do. I can feel the strength seeping out of me as the aeroplane begins the slow taxi to take-off. Deep in the bowels of the plane, Frankly is probably wondering what is happening to her and why it is happening again and I am looking in a tired and confused way at the last of England, not knowing what I feel.

Take off is achieved. I unfasten my seat belt and sit back in the narrow seat. A drink would be wonderful: a gin and tonic or even a whisky. But I daren't have a drink because I will have to drive more than 150 miles once we have arrived in Malaga. Numbly I ask for a tomato juice and eat as much as I can of the in-flight snack because I will need to keep my strength up.

There is a stewardess on the flight who reminds me of Ella. She has the same height and dark striking looks and the same proud way of walking. In the past she would have intimidated me but seeing her now brings a rush of warmth to my heart.

Ella the Californian has been my best friend these last three years. It was Ella who taught me how to be strong and where the borderline is between being reasonable and a doormat. It was Ella who took me to task over packing up Alex's things.

'Anna, the bastard has left you!' she said. 'He has walked out leaving just a letter behind him. He has left you alone in a foreign country without a visa or money. He has dumped you like a worn out old mattress *and you are packing up his Dresden china!*'

'It was his grandmother's,' I say, rather sheepishly. 'It's not her fault.'

'She's dead, right?' says Ella.

'Yes, she's dead. But his mother's still alive and it's not her fault either.'

'There I disagree,' says Ella, picking up the box which I have just finished packing and sealed with tape. 'She raised him. And it's not like he hasn't done this before, right?'

While I ponder this, Ella has walked to the front door of our lovely colonial house with the wooden porch and white railings. She stands at the top of the steps and looks back at me.

'Anna, watch and learn,' she says.

The box arcs upwards as it leaves her arms and everything goes into slow motion. I am on my feet with my mouth open and my hands out as if to try and catch it.

The sound of the smashing china is astonishing. It is so final; so destructive; so utterly vengeful. I am awed.

'Your turn,' says Ella, once the last tinkle and crunch has died away in the gentle wind that ruffles the broad-bladed grass by the sidewalk.

'My turn?'

I could not have done what Ella has done. But the worm did begin to turn. Niceness has no place in my life now. 'Quite right,' says Ella. 'Be wonderful, be kind, be loving, be horrible, be outrageous, be unreasonable. Just never be *nice*. Nice is just nothing.'

'Can I get you anything else?' says the stewardess who looks so much like Ella.

'No thank you,' I say, smiling. 'You have already done more than you could possibly know.'

It is dark when we arrive in Spain which, for some reason, surprises me. I think I'm expecting it to be tomorrow morning. But the air is very different and foreign, filled with the buzz of activity and strange scents. What will Frankly think of it? Or of the different language spoken by the people who will be unloading her from the plane?

But there is no time to worry about that; the worry is reserved for getting a beagle, hand-luggage and two suitcases through Spanish customs simultaneously when I hardly speak the language. But I have a phrase book and I have learnt a few simple syllables so I can just about manage '*¿Donde es mi perro, por favor?*' to the fierce looking woman at the information desk.

The trouble with speaking a foreign language is that people reply to you in that self-same language and then you are buggered. Because, for all the sense it made to me, her reply could have been 'Where you left it.' There is an impasse where a tired and confused British woman looks hopelessly at bored and irritated Spaniard but the woman at Information relents. She is pointing towards the baggage carousel where the suitcases are—and, sure enough, there is the sky kennel jolting through the rubber flap along with a pile of other cases.

Frankly is on her feet inside, squeaking loudly. You get superhuman strength when you need it and I dive across the hall and lift the whole contraption off without even thinking. At once, I am surrounded by customs officials demanding the documentation which is strapped by tape to the kennel with duplicates (and triplicates) inside my holdall, just in case.

Six pages of information in English and (bad) Spanish and they want to look at everything.

Frankly is still whining so I call to her lovingly, trying to be reassuring. My two suitcases lumber past behind my back but they don't matter. Knowing that Frankly's paperwork is clear is far more important.

Oh God! How much longer are they going to take? They are obviously searching the documents for one in particular. Is it there? The authorities in Colorado scarcely knew how what was needed to get a dog to Spain and the Spanish Embassy in California was curt to the point of hostility when asked for help and advice.

I rustle through my bag to see what else there might be. Here is the health certificate, stamped and ratified by everyone I could think of, the export certificate (ditto) in triplicate with its Spanish translation. Here are the various vaccination certificates—what else could they want?

Nervously, I proffer the last little letter hand-written by the vet and painstakingly translated by Ella's friend, Carmen the Mexican, from the taco house on Main Street. It certifies that Frankly is a household pet and not being imported for show or breeding.

The officials share it around between them, nod wisely and beam at me. That is what they wanted! They all put the documents on top of Frankly's wooden box and stamp them vigorously, making the little beagle jump.

I feel the relief flood through me like a river of heat.

I make gestures asking if I can open the cage but no, not until I have shown the papers to more officials at the exit, so I am dragging the kennel across the floor with Frankly crying inside, showing the papers to yet more officials and then, worst of all things, having to leave her outside, in the box, while I run back to grab the cases.

I had a trolley—but it has gone, so both cases must be pulled simultaneously across the floor and through customs back to where Frankly is. And now there is a crowd of kids around the sky kennel banging on the roof. They think it's funny.

Before I have even thought, I have boxed the ears of two of them and shouted at the rest. They scatter like ninepins and I almost fall at the door, snatching at the locks and letting my little beagle out. She jumps into my arms and wails with delight.

'Oh Frankly!' I gasp and let the tears come because we are here and we are safe together and nothing else matters.

Until the next bit.

The next bit is getting all the cases and the dog (not forgetting the holdall and the laptop which have been on my shoulders all the time) down to the car hire area. The only way to do it is to abandon the sky kennel for the moment. Luckily, this is Spain and nobody comes trailing after me shouting about it and, even luckier, all my car hire documentation is in order too. Within twenty minutes all the cases are in the Fiat Punto, Frankly has found something similar to a dandelion in the open-air car park which is of sufficient quality to merit the depositing of a huge puddle of pee—and I can breathe again.

There isn't any room for the sky kennel anyway so I'm not going back.

Okay.

That was easy enough. All I have to do now is drive for two and a half hours in the dark in a strange car, on roads I don't know with only meagre instructions to guide me. And I'm heartbroken, jet lagged and exhausted from a sixteen-hour journey. Should be a piece of cake.

For five minutes I sit with my face buried in Frankly's fur, stroking her back and stomach and listening to the beagle's snuffling, huffy noises as she paws at my face and licks me. Then I take another deep breath, start the engine and drive out into the Spanish night.

Malaga is busy tonight. The bright lights strobe across the wide, vehicle-filled roads and cars weave back and forwards in a dance they know intimately. I am a good driver and I cope—as I always do—but it helps to swear and curse as I swing the wheel to dodge another overtaking car that cuts in front of us too close. I squint at the signposts that are approaching too fast for comfort, looking for the road to Motril. Ben's voice echoes in my ears with the directions. Whatever I do, I must be in the right hand lane or I will end up in Cordoba.

When people back in England heard that Alex had left me they said things like 'Well you're so strong, you'll cope.'

Thanks a bunch, I thought at the time, hearing '*Oh good, I don't have to do anything to help you*' in the background. But what could they have done to help anyway? I was in Colorado and, by then, Alex was back in England. Friends in Colorado were different— but Americans are another species.

Rather homesickly, I think back to my friends: beautiful Ella and circular Gilbert the failed restaurateur. In days when I thought I would never laugh again they had me in hysterics and not always because they intended to. Ella, particularly. Now that's a strong woman if you like.

What do people mean by strong anyway? Does it mean that you don't just lie down and die? But who does? Does it mean that you just don't act like the half-destroyed mess that you are? Did the people who say I'm strong think that because I was able to talk to them on the telephone without crying that I didn't weep and howl and hate and *want* to die? That I didn't care that much?

Who knows? I'm too tired to think. I have a long drive ahead and a beagle who is frantic for company and reassurance, trying to climb onto my lap. Poor love, how can I expect her to understand anything?

'No, Frankly! Not now.' Not now that I am trying to negotiate a Spanish dual carriageway in the dark. Around me the drivers from hell are holding a competition to see who can shave the most paint off the hire car's bodywork without actually leaving a dent.

Frankly puts her ears down and looks pathetic but I can't afford even to put out a hand to stroke her. The traffic is vile and, despite everything, I still want to live.

There must have been an angel somewhere because suddenly we are on the right road and out of the city. It's virtually motorway and I can relax a little. My hand goes out to the soft, furry head and Frankly sighs as I massage her ears. By rights she should be in the back but there's no room for both the suitcases in the boot.

'We are going to a lovely village,' I tell her. 'A place where we can stay for seven months. Then we can go back together to England. Frankly, we're going to be safe.'

Frankly whiffles at me. Where's My Supper? she is saying and I realise that I, too, am starving.

Twenty minutes later we are sitting outside a little café in some unknown Spanish town which has been carved in two by the main road. I am eagerly eating fried chicken and rice and sharing it with Frankly who has forgotten everything except the lure of food. This place smells different and that was all very interesting until the waiter arrived with chicken. Now it is of no importance whatsoever. Food is food and it is Frankly's god.

I have ordered a bottle of wine and another of water and the one glass of alcohol that I am allowing myself is rough, red, warming and comforting. The temptation to have more must be very firmly resisted, though, and I re-cork the bottle with a presentiment that it may be needed later when we get to Los Poops.

But for now, this is lovely. The café is too close to the road for real comfort but the four little tables on the pavement are gaily covered in red and white check tablecloths, helping me to feel festive. The waiter doesn't care who I am or how I might feel and serves me with the panache of a sulky sixteen-year-old but the food is good and fresh and every mouthful brings back strength.

As I sit back, replete and happy with still half a glass of wine to savour, it is safe to think back to Ella and Gilbert without too much homesickness. I am in the middle of an adventure now and adventures are fun. Ella would enjoy this.

It is a good road to Motril, thank God, and the traffic is dying down by the minute—but that has its drawbacks because now I have time to think. It is too dark to enjoy the scenery and there is no radio in the little car to distract me. Alex's voice starts talking in my head, justifying, telling me that it is all for the best and that he didn't leave me for Suzie. Suzie was only ten per cent of the reason; ninety per cent was the bad state of the marriage, he is saying—just as he said in the letter.

Yes, I remember, the marriage that was so bad that he made love to me on the last morning that we were together, before he met her; before he ran away from everything we had ever built together as if it had never existed.

And I am lost in that hideous downward spiral of self-justification and pain which is so real that it feels as if there is nothing else. My whole body is heavy with anger and grief and I am not concentrating on the road.

The car weaves slightly across the central line and an oncoming lorry blares its horn, making me jump and sending a rush of prickling sensations of fear down my arms and back. My attention is snapped back to the present. Before I know it I am in a tunnel and, because it is night and there are no lamps on this road, there is no light at the end of it. It could go on forever. Oh great. Wonderful symbolism. Thanks a bunch! 'Cut it out!' I shout at any passing deity that might be listening.

Then the car shoots out into unexpected moonlight, then back into another tunnel. There is a dance of darkness and shadows for mile upon mile but then the mountains recede and the tunnels are over and we dive into the night itself—a world of deep velvety blue and grey. To my right the sea is dark and calm and wide, dominated by a great silver three-quarter moon. Its light glitters across the water, drawing a magical luminous pathway, and a beloved memory slips into my mind dispelling the echoes of both Alex and of fear.

It is of a book I read as a child, *The Princess and the Goblin* by George MacDonald. Irene, the little princess, could always escape danger by looking for the lamp burning in her grandmother's room high in the turret of the castle. It was a magical lamp which could be seen through rock or wood and it always guided her safely back home.

When Danny died, I saw that lamp in a circular globe of light through a neighbour's window as I sat in my darkened bedroom staring blindly down the garden with no hope and no future. It lifted me then as it does now.

Grandmother's lamp. We must be nearly home.

Ben warned me about the turn-off to the village so it is fairly simple to spot it in good time and I only miss it twice and have to do dangerous U-turns which wake Frankly from a deep and peaceful sleep on the front seat beside me. She sits up, scenting the end of the journey and sways from side to side, looking at me resentfully as I negotiate the final ten kilometres of potholed concrete track up into the mountains around what seems to be a hundred hairpin bends. Turn after turn, I swing the wheel backwards and forwards as the headlights arc out over echoing nothingness. I can feel myself dredging up a few prayers from nowhere.

At last, I can see the village lights ahead. 'Thank you, God,' I say in relief—then swear violently as another hairpin takes me by surprise.

The road swings off to the left into yet more mountains but Los Poops is to the right and I can coast gently into the small village square surrounded by tall whitewashed houses with big, closed, dark wooden doors glowering at any stranger who might pass.

We are here. I stop the car and lean forwards to rest my head on the wheel in exhaustion and relief. Ben's soft voice giving me directions to the little holiday home that he has lent me indefinitely echoes in my sleepy brain. 'As soon as you turn into the village, there is a doorway with two steps to your right. Park just beyond it because the street to the house is too steep for a car.

'It is called *Calle La Era*. The house is two thirds of the way down, next to the village shop; there is a little courtyard to the left and the door is there, on the right.

'The light switch is to the left of the door. Don't worry if the lights don't go on; the fuse may have tripped. There are candles in the kitchen drawer and the fuse box is next to the cooker. Enjoy, Anna. *Mi casa es su casa*.'

Oh joy. Bed is just another twenty yards away. Frankly shakes herself, eager to get out and explore. There are lights on the sides of the houses so I can see my way.

'Come on, Frankly.' I open the car door and she follows me out, flopping down onto the cobbles, her nose twitching at all the strange and humid smells.

There is a lamp showing the name "*Calle la Era*" plainly but the street itself is virtually perpendicular. With laptop and holdall swung on my shoulder I make my way downhill, my legs almost buckling in exhaustion. Frankly follows cautiously. This Road's Wrong, she says. What Have You Done To It?

'Nothing, honey,' I say. 'It's what happens on mountains.'

I have a habit of answering Frankly's alleged thoughts. Now we will be living alone together that will probably get worse. Still, it's better than talking to yourself.

This must be the courtyard. This must be the door. A great dark wooden slab in the white wall with great metal bolts all over it. And the great, old key, sent so lovingly to me in Colorado by Federal Express, must fit into it somewhere.

It takes an age, for the lock is loose and old and it is an art form to open it. Amusement turns swiftly to irritation as I jab it, push it, bully it, coax it; but eventually it turns just before temper gets the upper hand—and the door is open.

Frankly stands nervously at my feet as I fumble for the switch. Are There Dragons? she asks with a nudge of her nose on my leg.

'Probably,' I say. 'But not the sort that eat beagles.'

That's All Right Then.

Click.

Nothing. The darkness doesn't even flicker. Oh God. Now I have to find my way to the kitchen in the pitch black and find the fuse box. Stumbling, I feel my way along rough walls. My sight is clearing and I can see both the cooker and what looks like the fuse box. Yes, one of the switches is down. I flick it and light floods through the house.

In a haze of relief and exhaustion I slide down the wall to the floor and sit looking around me while Frankly has a good sniff around.

No Dragons So Far, she reports, nose quivering with interest.

'Oh good. I'm glad to hear that.'

It is so pretty. One complicated open-plan little room comprising kitchen and living room with whitewashed walls, French windows and a red tiled floor. Old wooden beams loom above in the roof and there's a huge arched skylight above them. The far wall is completely covered with books so old and dusty that you can hardly read the names. It looks as if no one has been here for months, if not years. All the plants around the window are dead and plaster is flaking off the walls.

Never mind. A shower, a drink and bed are all I need (a bath would be better but I have been forewarned that there isn't one). Ben has told me how to light the immersion heater which gives constant hot water so that's the first important thing.

Seven attempts and a glass of wine later, the immersion heater lights. Only then do I discover that there isn't any water and I sit down, suddenly, on the floor again and start to cry with great sobs of hopelessness. It is too much.

Frankly paws at me as I sit in the dust on the floor with hands on my head, sobbing and rocking myself like a child. The cold wet nose pushes into my face and she starts to lick the tears but that only makes me cry the more.

The cases in the car must wait. Everything must wait. I must get to bed and finish this day. I have had enough. In the tiny single bedroom by the front door, there is a double duvet packed in polythene. I pull it roughly out and throw it onto the mattress.

Lock the front door. Go to the kitchen and drink down another glass of wine in the hope that it will make me sleep and pour a little of my precious bottled water into a bowl for Frankly. She drinks it thirstily. Now, get into bed in your clothes because, guess what—oh perfect!—the duvet is damp and unaired. I am totally miserable, lonely and lost but within minutes, a warm little creature has clambered up beside me and curled up against my stomach.

Frankly doesn't mind the squalor, my dirty body, the tear-stained cheeks or the damp bedding; we are together and that is all that matters. She sighs contentedly and falls asleep.

In books you would sleep well, but this isn't a book, it's real life and I sleep appallingly, even with my own personal bed-airer and hot water bottle snoring rhythmically beside me. Thoughts circle in my mind until I think I'm going mad but, when dawn approaches and the first glimmers of light creep across the floor, things begin to feel better. Together, Frankly and I have aired the duvet with our bodies; the first light is wonderfully encouraging and, when I get up to go to the loo and pull the chain with an automatic reflex, it flushes.

Hallelujah!

Yes, the taps are working—and there is a pile of towels in the bathroom cupboard. I am in the shower as fast as can be and the instant-heat immersion works! Oh this is so pleasant! There is even a scabby bit of soap.

So I wash Colorado out of my body, fill several saucepans with water in case this wonderful flow is purely temporary and brew a cup of black tea with a very old teabag from a jar by the cooker. Then I sit by the French windows, wrapped in towels and eating the last of my chocolate and watching the colours of the sea far below. The waves, so distant, are alive with silver, as the setting moon sends ripples of light across the water. Above in the barely-brightening sky, there's a wispy pattern of cirrus clouds, luminous with the very first touches of the pre-light of the coming dawn. I sit, silent and still to watch this slow, clear beautiful luminosity as it first echoes, then touches and then spreads across the waters to Morocco. Entranced, I forget my stiffening legs and cooling body, lost in a cascade of flowing beauty. It is one of those times that imprints itself in memory as a treasure forever.

I'm going to be okay. I really, really am.

By the time I have woken again it is nearly 11 o'clock and Frankly is scratching on the front door to go out. Sunshine is flooding the little house and I feel much better. I scramble into my crumpled clothes and go outside for a stretch in the bright light while Frankly sniffs around and does what comes necessary—with some reluctance.

Where's The Grass? I Need Grass! she grumbles, wandering around on the cobbles and concrete. Luckily there are some weeds across the tiny courtyard which belongs to this funny little home and she can sink her bum on those with a canine sigh of relief.

I put her on the lead to go up the road to bring the suitcases down from the car. Once they are in and unpacked I can start to organise myself.

So far, Los Poops is just a jumble of white buildings and cobbled streets. I do know, though, that I'm in a good location: the village shop is just opposite the little house. In fact, it makes up the other side of the little courtyard. This morning, the shop is open and inside the trailing metal fly-guards over the doorway a queue of chattering women is waiting to be served. Frankly looks, hesitates and I stop her before she can barge in to say Hello, Where's My Breakfast? Even so, a barrage of stares is turned on us through the metal strands and my feeble '*¡Hola!*' is not returned.

It is hot already and the road is very steep. It is also very populated. By the time we have reached the top, we have met three feral cats, two hostile dogs and a very bored mule as well as being perused by more eyes than I can trace into the darkness of a dozen opened front doors. It is unnerving—but breakfast is the great priority and I have food stashed away in those all-important cases. Coffee, biscuits, long-life milk, a can of baked beans (with tin opener—I'm not stupid!) and even a loaf of bread which I packed frozen and should still be edible.

There's a jar of my mother's marmalade, too, which has travelled all the way from England to Colorado and back—and I stole some airline butter on the flight which might still be recognisable. There's Frankly's dried food too.

Ten minutes later we are both fatter, stickier and happier. Thank God I drew off the extra water in the night, because the supply is off again.

Obviously the sensible thing to do would be to unpack properly, check what supplies Ben has in this funny little house, do some shopping, air the rest of the bedding, tidy up and check my email. So, I get changed into clean clothes, put Frankly on the lead and go out to explore the village instead.

It's a long haul back up the path to the car for the sun is blindingly hot, reflecting rivers of heat off the white walls of the houses each side of *Calle La Era*. Inside the dim recesses of the shop another cluster of women is debating something furiously. It sounds as though someone's character is being ripped to shreds but they are probably discussing the weather. Everything sounds as if it might be so much more interesting when it's in a foreign language.

There is an unfamiliar feeling in my stomach as Frankly and I make our way up the hill again and I can't work it out. I think it must be freedom. For the first time in years no one's decisions matter except mine. I can make a complete and utter fool of myself and there is only me to judge.

Loneliness appears to be having an extra-long lie-in so I might as well make the most of it.

At the top of the cobbled street is the little square where the car is parked and the rest of the village appears to be to the right. It's a mixture of houses, nearly all painted (whitewashed?) white, some beautifully well-kept with window boxes of flowers and others derelict. The face of a soft-nosed mule looks out of a broken stable-door only one room removed from someone's front door and the stench of its bedding wafts cheerfully around attracting flies by the dozen. Above and below the village there are almond groves twinkling as the sun strikes through the powder-blue sky, to bounce across the leaves and, miles away down through rounded hills, the sea is deep blue, stiff and crinkled.

It is very hot. Already Frankly's tongue is hanging out and I know how she feels. Mad dogs and Englishwomen… But still I keep walking.

There is a brief altercation with a couple of village mongrel dogs which were resting in the shade of a broken-down wall. They look at me suspiciously, then roar at Frankly in derision and outrage. A Dog On A Lead! Pathetic! She bounces back at them on stiffened legs, belling as the true hound she is, and I drag her round the corner into three more dogs which, fortunately, are slightly less vociferous. Serious bum-sniffing ensues and I wait politely while this time-honoured ritual is carried out to the satisfaction of all.

This must be the main square. The road has opened out into a paved area with a few bedraggled evergreen trees rather like Scots Pines. There's a three-storey building calling itself *La Posada* which, presumably is an inn. The sign on the solid black wood door says "*cerrado*" and there is a scribbled note added saying "*retourno a seis.*" Further on a church, surprisingly painted pink, sits almost apologetically between an official-looking building with notices pinned to the door and a load of cars parked haphazardly where the hillside climbs in a way that is almost perpendicular. On the other side of the square is a railing that guards a slope bearing an unexpected sliding pile of rubbish that extends under a bridge below the village's lower road. An odd place to choose for the local tip, I think, peering over and dissuading Frankly from investigating the possibility of food.

There is a small herd of people in the square, mostly elderly, dressed in black in the case of the women and grey in the case of the men. They don't seem to be doing anything other than hanging around. All of them are looking at me rather suspiciously but there is a cautious response to my '¡Hola!' as we go past.

Another five minutes of wandering through narrow, cobbled streets takes us to the far end of the village and onto a narrow mule track into the surrounding hills which fall like a series of cleavages into darker, greener levels below. I let Frankly off the lead and wander cheerfully along, looking at the strange flowers and trees and enjoying the feel of the sun on my back.

Just around the second corner, perhaps 300 yards from the last house, is a tiny concrete and stone reservoir which looks as if it was once part of the village's natural water supply. It's shaded and surprisingly cool and consists of a network of different channels and troughs filled with dark water. If there is water here, why is the supply cut off? Ben said that there were Britons living in the village so perhaps I can find out from them.

I sit on the concrete, scratching at the mosses and lichens with a stick and looking over the terraced hills until Frankly catches up with me. She is pootling and sniffing and snorting happily in her own sweet way. The new smells don't seem to bother her at all but she is grateful for a long, cool drink.

I catch her by the collar and put the lead on again, for there is a mule coming down the track towards me with a rather crumpled rider swaying comfortably on its back. The man is dressed in faded red and grey, gnarled like an olive tree and is whistling tunelessly to himself while slapping the beast rhythmically on the neck.

'Hola.' The man and I greet each other casually as he guides the mule up to the water troughs so it can drink. The mule is unimpressed and stands, stolidly, completely ignoring the ripples and bubbles of the spring beneath its nose. 'Aha,' I think to myself. 'You can take a mule to water but you can't make it drink.'

Thump, thump, thump go the man's heels against the mule's

side. It lowers its head and sniffs the water and then blows out thoughtfully. It is bored.

Thump, thump, thump. No response. I think that the mule is falling asleep. Its long-lashed eyes are half closed and it seems to be snoring.

Thump, *thump*, THUMP, THUMP.

I am beginning to laugh. It's rather a strange feeling as amusement has not figured too highly in my life lately. The muscles at the side of my mouth feel rather stiff but it's a good feeling all the same.

THUMP, THUMP, THUMP!

The mule sighs deeply, lowers its head and begins to suck up water noisily. It sucks and slurps and sucks again, drinking what must be whole pints. I can hardly believe it. Giggles are suffusing my whole body.

The mule stops drinking and turns its head to look at me thoughtfully. His rider looks too, nods and smiles.

Thump, thump, thump, go his heels and the mule lowers its head to drink again.

When it has finished and the odd ensemble sets off slowly back down to the village and I sit, still laughing, wondering how much else that I have been taught in my life is totally false.

Chapter Two

IT IS NIGHT time and I am sitting by the French windows that overlook the lower village with the fall of the mountains below and, in the far distance, the sea. Frankly is asleep on a rug at my feet, her nose whiffling as she chases rabbits in a dream. We are surrounded by lighted candles to enhance the dim, dusty bulbs of a wooden four-branch chandelier hanging over the dining table. There is a book in my hands but I am not reading, rather sitting in a quiet dream, assimilating the day and enjoying a deep and unexpected feeling of peace.

You see, nobody in the world—except the owner of this little whitewashed house—knows exactly where I am. Not Alex, not my mother, not my friends.

Nobody has the telephone number and, unless I call out, there will be no calls in. I was going to keep in touch with a few people via email but Ben's phone is old-fashioned Bakelite and the plug cannot be removed. I don't have a mobile and, even if I did, it probably wouldn't work in the nooks and crannies of the Alpujarras.

Even the BBC World Service is having trouble reaching Los Poops and that's via short wave radio. It would appear that there is trouble in the Middle East again and that some African president is holding a peace conference without inviting anyone who dislikes him but neither of these appears exactly relevant to someone like me who is living in a tiny and remote Spanish village.

There is no one to tell me anything; what I should do, what I should feel, who I should be.

I like that.

I have achieved a lot today and that brings its own contentment, too.

Probably most importantly, I have braved the shop next door

and bought three huge bottles of water, frozen fish, fresh chicken, packaged rice and a basketful of beautiful, locally-grown brightly-coloured and delicious vegetables.

It was a slow process. Luckily, I learnt patience in Colorado even if I lost my niceness. The motto in the rural areas there might as well be '¿Mañana? Why so soon?' So I was suitably patient with the Los Poops shop.

It looks as though any foreigner has to wait for a regulation twenty minutes before being served, not because the queue is so very long but because, from the moment that the shop opens until the time it closes, it is filled with gossiping women.

My slightly apologetic presence was not regarded as even vaguely important. As the voices soared and fell it reconfirmed what my phlegmatic English psyche suspected. It must be a plot. Surely such enthusiasm or rancour cannot just be being voiced over the price of fish? Something drastic is being planned. The village shop is, without doubt, a hotbed of vice.

Even now, at 9pm, as I sit here musing, the urgent tones of the protagonists are echoing out through the shop's still-open door— and in through my bathroom window. If I look out, I can see the shadows of a vast Mafia of women (or is it a Mafia of vast women?) perched on every available protuberance—both of the shop's and theirs—gesticulating, nodding and making up their own private language as they go along.

For this is not Spanish. The Los Poopians speak their own particular dialect. I had to buy my purchases today by pointing and smiling for my Spanish phrase book and its companion CD are virtually useless and my attempts to voice what I have learnt so far met with blank incomprehension all round.

Perhaps it's not a dialect. In fact, I think it's a secret code. Something like adding an extra 'g' to every third syllable on alternate Thursdays. The Enigma code machines of World War Two are probably secreted at the back of the village church and people go and swot up on the latest enhancement to the language after service on Sundays.

The shop itself is a tardis—seeming far bigger inside than out— and it has quite enough variety of food for anyone to live on but no fresh milk nor eggs. Ben told me that you buy those, together with goat's cheese, from individuals in the village. I shall look forward to that. The idea of bringing home a jug of fresh, warm goat's milk is wonderfully appealing. Only one of my purchases has proved to be a total waste of time—but it could have been a lot worse. On one dim shelf I saw a pile of small packages called 'nouget.' Assuming that it was nougat, I added one to my pile of purchases but when I brought it home and looked more closely a tiny but nonetheless explicit picture of a skeleton chasing rats put that faint hope to rest. It is obviously rat poison.

It is up on the top of the fridge freezer in case Frankly can't spell either.

I have explored the house, including its cool lower floor with two extra bedrooms and a stiff double door that goes out onto another little courtyard lower down on *Calle La Era*. The downstairs walls are pock-marked and brittle with what must have been a cowboy plastering job, most of which has rearranged itself over the red, tiled floor. Maybe it's just too damp down there for the work to hold. Whatever the cause, it has deposited itself all over the floor. I swept it all up but, five hours later, more has fallen. I think I will leave the lower floor be and live upstairs as much as I can.

Frankly agrees with me. She has decided that we are to sleep together from now on and is resolutely ignoring the rug I have placed for her on the floor of the living room.

This Is Nice, she says, clambering up on the bed possessively. I haven't the heart to turf her off. She looks so cute and she knows it. There will be battles ahead.

I have dusted and swept the little strange-shaped, five-walled bedroom with its curtain-covered wardrobe space half-filled with Ben's clothes and now completely filled with mine. As I look at Ben's clothes I remember that I must call and thank him for letting me stay here. He obviously needs a maintenance man as well as a cleaner but it is the least I can do to try and clear things up.

God knows what I would have done without him.

Ben was a friend of my father's and I haven't seen him since Dad's funeral three years ago. He is a lovely man; inexpressibly kind and with an eye for the ladies and, when Dad was still alive, he was often there when Richard and I made our awkward duty visits. He helped to make them more bearable. It was not that Dad was a bad man or a difficult one; he just did not know how to cope with children and never had done and, once he and Mum split up, he became even more uncertain about it. We made friends again once I was grown up but those early years were never comfortable.

Once I knew that I had to find somewhere to stay in Europe, Ben was the only hope I had. Even so, it had taken some courage to telephone him from Colorado after all that time. I had no excuse other than a favour to ask. But Ben remembered who I was and his voice softened at the sound of my name. Yes, he had heard that I had moved to America and, after telling me three stories about his time over there, he wanted to know what he could do to help me.

'Ben, do you still have a house in Spain?' I said.

'But of course! A lovely little place in the Alpujarras,' he answered. 'Why? Do you want to go and stay there?'

How much easier could it be?

I explained that I needed to bring Frankly home and that meant taking her to Europe for seven months so that she could become officially European and come into the UK on the Pet Travel Scheme when it started up next year. I could not put her through quarantine, I said. My cousin Jim's beloved mongrel Billy wasted away and died in a kennels near Folkestone after a lifetime in Canada. He was cared for perfectly adequately but he never understood why his life was suddenly confined to four walls and no walks. The kennel people discouraged visits—and Jim was living in the north of England anyway.

I went to visit Billy once and wept all the way home. He was confused and aggressive, nipping my hands while simultaneously wagging his tail and asking for attention. I stayed half an hour and, in the end, he just went back to sleep in his bed so it was useless to be there. He was the same age as Frankly is now and he simply lost interest in living.

'I understand,' said Ben. 'But why is your husband not helping you?'

So I told him.

There was a silence for a moment. Then Ben's voice took on the timbre of an angel's.

'Anna,' he says. 'You are a brave and admirable woman. *Mi casa es su casa*. As long as you want, whenever you want. It is all sorted, Anna, you do not need to worry.'

'But I hardly know you!' I stammered.

'You are the daughter of my good friend David,' says Ben. 'You are a child of mine as well as his. I will do everything I can to help you.'

The floor of Ben's house is of red tiling throughout and it needs re-colouring and polishing. I will find a shop which sells the polish and make it beautiful again for him. It is now, at least, clean. The books, which cover one entire wall, will have to wait another day. They are all brittle from damp and heat and you can scrape grey dust and mould from the spines. I thought that Ben came here every year but that now looks unlikely.

The brown wooden beams across the six-foot-by-four-foot skylight above are encrusted with spiders' webs, their occupants, both alive and dead, and the empty carcasses of their prey. The skylight is above the stairs and I can't reach the beams even with a broom so there is nothing I can do there.

The fridge-freezer has been scrubbed to within an inch of its life and the few dead contents within exhumed and fumigated. There was some ex-margarine, the remnants of something which might once been a head of garlic and an opened packet of long-life milk which had evolved into a new and repulsive life form but had fortunately not yet developed the power of movement. The fridge itself stank, as they will if kept closed.

I have done some washing (by hand) and hung my travelling clothes out on an airer on the roof. There are steps by the front door up onto a perfectly barren square of whitewashed concrete with walls of barely a foot high around it. The view is magnificent across the roofs of about fifty other houses below me and down to the sea. The houses behind, higher up the hillside, can probably watch me as I can watch others but it's still a lovely space to sit and think. If it gets too hot inside, perhaps I can bring a mattress up at night and sleep here under the great canopy of familiar Western stars.

I know how to use the calor gas-powered immersion heater and cooker—and I know that we are dangerously low on gas and that the shop does not sell it. I know that the water comes on, briefly, only twice a day and that I am going to have to live with the constant companionship of flies.

I know that there is no television, let alone satellite or cable, no hope of the internet and that there is no one to entertain me but myself. No one to comfort me either.

However, the telephone is there and I can activate half of England in a network of communications from one single phone call to my mother if and when I want to.

But for the moment, it is enough to sit in the candlelight with a stomach full of home-made fish and lentil stew and a half-drunk glass of rough Spanish wine sitting on the floor beside me. I have gathered kindling from the fields to make a fire in the open hearth if I want one and there are enough logs under the awning below the steps to the roof to last for most of the winter.

There are no sounds apart from the echo of the voices of the women in the shop and the soft sound of Frankly's breathing and there is nothing to do but immerse myself in one of Ben's old and fragile books.

I once heard someone say that pain, grief and anger were caused by too much past and that fear was caused by too much future. My past and future are dormant and all I have is now. It is enough.

Of course the following morning I am miserable as hell and howl all over Frankly and the World Service. Fortunately the morning's serialisation is *Madame Bovary* and I am so irritated by Emma Bovary's insipidity that the grief turns to anger and I stomp furiously out of the house for our morning walk rather than whingeing and whining my way up to the top of the hill. I hate Alex and all that he stands for. I hate his lies and betrayal and his sanctimonious words that it is 'all for the best.' I will be better off without him but I don't need him to tell me that. Today I turn left out of the village, still on a mule path but a more arid one with less vegetation. Frankly is wheezing a little in the heat with her tongue hanging out but she is happy enough pottering along and sniffing. The steep climb up means that I am soon looking down on Los Poops and I cannot help noticing that there is a gathering of people around one particular house. As I watch, a coffin is brought out and a small *cortège* begins to make its way up the street. I discovered yesterday that the graveyard is just around the corner ahead of me—so I hurry on to avoid getting caught up in the way. We can always loop around the back of the hill and return to the village from the other direction. As I walk, I can see two police cars winding their way up to the village. Ben told me something about some ex-police commissioner living here. Perhaps he is the one who has died and old colleagues are coming to mourn him.

The graveyard is a neat affair, firmly fenced off from the rest of its surroundings and with a high wall cut into the hillside for mini-crypts holding the bodies of about half the graveyard's residents. The more ordinary graves are scattered around below, each one looking fresh with flowers. They are plastic flowers but it's the thought that counts.

I chivvy Frankly on and she grumbles to herself, complaining about the heat and the lack of green grass to eat for her digestion. Moments later she is distracted by being bounced on by what looks like a half-grown golden retriever that appears from nowhere. It bounces on me too so I am hardly surprised to hear a voice call, 'Tigger!' from the other side of a grove of long-leaved trees. What does surprise me is that it is obviously an Englishwoman's voice and its owner confirms that when she appears on the pathway ahead with fair colouring and a faded 1980s Laura Ashley dress.

My first delight at seeing a fellow countrywoman is tempered with some deep, long-forgotten instinct that tugs at me as she approaches with a 'Cooeee!' and a friendly wave. It is like the first day at school or at a new job when you know instinctively that the first kind soul who wants to make friends with you is going to be the one person you want to avoid for the rest of your life.

34

I have three alternatives: pretend to be a deaf mute, jump over the edge of the path or swallow hard and take my medicine. I may be out of nice but this is a very small village and it would be shooting myself seriously in the foot to make enemies now.

'Good morning. You must be Anna,' says the woman in very precise tones, holding out her hand to be shaken. I school my face into a polite and welcoming smile. Her grasp is claw-like but I'm aware that I am already paranoid. How does she know who I am? What does she know about me? However, I won't need to ask any questions; all I have to do is listen.

'Ben let me know that you were coming,' she says gaily. 'You've been living in Colorado and you're bringing your sweet little dog back to England on the Pet Travel Scheme.

'I'm so sorry I wasn't here yesterday to welcome you. I wasn't sure which day you were coming. Ben is so naughty; he really doesn't keep in touch as much as he should.

'Let me introduce myself. I'm Stella Collins and I live in *The Bay House* over on the top up there.'

She waves her hand airily at the village but, as I am in the process of being bounced on again by Tigger who nearly winds me with a two-pawed attack on my stomach, I am more concerned about being half knocked backwards against a tree.

'Careful, Tigger,' says Stella absently. 'Silly boy! He's such an enthusiastic dog. I can't bear these repressed little animals that don't express themselves, can you?'

'Ah,' I say wisely, getting my breath back while my own repressed little animal vanishes quietly behind an olive tree.

Stella is a striking-looking woman in her sixties with a deeply lined face and a wide mouth. Her hair is naturally blond turning grey and, from the tightness of the dress, her figure has obviously seen better days.

We walk on together and it is clear that I have been adopted. Frankly glowers at me from behind her tree when I call her to follow on and she is bounced on the moment she emerges. Seeing that there is no alternative, she bears it with stoicism bordering on saintliness. I foolishly try to distract Tigger and get a terribly friendly little bite on my hand.

Meanwhile, Stella is twittering on. I am prepared to be determinedly reticent about the reason why I am in Los Poops but Stella is so pleased to have an audience that she doesn't allow any space for any of her questions to be answered and instead regales me with details of village life and its occupants. Within the space of ten minutes I go from being paralysingly ignorant of Los Poops and its inhabitants to having rather more information than I really wanted to know.

In a nutshell:

David and Stella moved to Los Poops six years ago when they both took early retirement from their publishing business. They own two houses, one of which they rent out to visitors. Two of their dogs have been poisoned by the villagers: 'It's the hunters that do it,' she says cheerfully as I look at Frankly in horror. 'If the dogs take any of the game they're systematically poisoned. Often, they just put down rat poison everywhere.'

Tigger bounces on me again from behind without any attempt of restraint from his mistress and I wonder whether it's just Stella's dogs that get poisoned. I know already just how easy it is to get rat poison.

Also living here are Rani and Sylvia who have an open marriage. They lived on a commune somewhere once and Sylvia has a tendency to take lovers much younger than her.

'Except there aren't any young men left in the village any more,' says Stella, not noticing my slightly bemused expression at being told the intimate personal lives of total strangers. 'They've all gone to look for the bright lights in Malaga. So she has to look further afield now.'

There's Katherine, too, who takes care of *La Posada* since George and Emily, his wife, moved down to the coast. George comes up three days a week and, as Katherine is a widow, there is quite a lot of talk about that.

I suspect that there isn't much talk that doesn't originate with Stella.

The rest of the Britons are visitors—and five or six are present in the village at the moment. I haven't seen them? Oh, they're out and about. I'll bump into them soon enough.

The Phillipses are here and Klaus and Marketa from Poland who speak excellent English but let their children run wild. Sarah hasn't been here for about six months now and her house desperately needs a new roof. She really ought to attend to it. As for Ben, well it must be a year since he turned up and that was with really the most unsuitable girlfriend.

Stella has a long and elegant neck but unfortunately it is not long enough for me to tie a knot in it on behalf of all these people who might actually have a life.

'And there's the Risboroughs, of course,' she says, with what I know will become a very irritating little laugh. 'Well, they're American really. Such a silly idea to buy a house here. They thought they were going to be living in England and decided on a holiday home in Los Poops. My dear, they completely gutted it and put all sorts of unsuitable things in. But the job didn't work out—and she never liked it here anyway so it's all wasted. He's visiting at the moment to put the house up for sale but it's far too grand for anyone round here to be able to afford it now.'

I am getting dizzy from all this unwanted information but there are some things that I do need to know so, as Stella draws breath, I ask about the water situation. Is this rationing going to last? She doesn't know but there's a long diatribe about how inconvenient it all is and how inefficient the Spanish authorities are. Where do I buy calor gas? Oh, there's a man who delivers once a month. When would that be? Oh, sometime soon but he's not very reliable. Great.

'So who died?' I ask, wondering if Stella knows as much about the indigenous Los Poopians as she does the immigrants.

'Aldo the builder,' she says. 'No loss. A wife beater. Oh, my dear, everyone knows it. Sanchia was perpetually covered in bruises. Heart attack, I expect.'

'I wondered if he had been in the police.'

'The police? Why?'

'Because of the police who were driving up the hill to be a part of the funeral.'

'What?' Stella's nose goes pinched when she is excited. It gets two white marks on the side of the nostrils. She is avid for more details and tries to insist that we return to look at the funeral to see exactly who these policemen are. With some difficulty I decline but only escape after agreeing to go round for a drink with her and David tomorrow at seven. At least I haven't been deemed worthy enough to be asked for supper.

Tigger is called and cajoled into turning back and Frankly stands, looking at me doubtfully. I stroke her soft ears and make the clicking sound that means 'come on' and she looks pleased. Frankly is deeply unimpressed by puppies, particularly those that bounce. She is even more unimpressed by unfairly curtailed walks, no matter how hot it may be.

We wander on, noting how the landscape is softer and greener where the crumpled hills meet—evidence of hidden streams which must flow in the spring. I am trying to work out how to circle the village without walking too far but my attention is caught by what looks like a ruin just a little further on below us. It's just a house without a roof but it is surrounded by little walled gardens which show how much it was once loved. There are pink and yellow climbing roses running wild and what looks like lilies, as well as fruit trees and a vine which has over-run everything. I find myself working my way down across the parched earth between almond trees to take a closer look but, before I am near enough for my footsteps to be heard, a figure appears from behind the house. It is a man, silver-grey haired, definitely not a local Spaniard by his height, his colouring and the quality of his clothes. He is in jeans but they are very smart jeans—probably designer label—and they are topped by a businessman's crisp blue and white striped shirt. I can't see his face—he has a hand raised to his eyes. Oh my God, he's crying!

I stop dead. Whoever he may be, he does not want a stranger to see him like that. There is a clump of bushes to my right so I move swiftly behind them and duck down to hide.

Frankly, however, trots happily on down the hill.

He sees her just as she sees him and Frankly stops with one front paw slightly raised looking unbearably cute. The man hastily changes the positioning of his hand so that it looks as if he is shading his eyes before he looks around to see if the dog's owner is present. Seeing no one, he drops into a crouching position and stretches out his hand.

This is the kind of behaviour that Frankly usually ignores but today she trots on, cautiously, until she is close enough for him to reach out to stroke her. Man and dog regard each other with close attention for some moments and come to a mutual understanding as to the necessity of Frankly's ears being stroked.

'Hey, fella,' says the man, identifying himself as the American Mr. Risborough. 'How are you doing?'

He has obviously owned dogs because he knows just how to scratch ears properly and Frankly knows that she has found a friend. She sits down and puts her head on one side while raising a paw with which to entreat him to continue.

'So where are you from?' says the man looking at the tag on her collar which still has our Colorado address. This evidently surprises him (as it would) but it seems to distress him slightly too.

'What are you doing here?' he says putting his head right down to Frankly's. 'Why aren't you at home?'

Then he pushes back the silvery hair which is falling over his forehead and sits down with his back to me, on a piece of broken wall, still stroking Frankly's ears. I think he is crying again.

Now what do I do? I can't just stand up and walk down. I could edge away back to the path while his back is turned and pretend that I just came round the corner but if he is crying he won't want anyone to see.

'Coo-eee Aaaaannnna!'

Oh bugger, it's that interfering old bat.

She is not in sight yet but her voice has had an electrifying effect on the man. He virtually dives back into the ruins, leaving Frankly on her own. At least that problem is solved.

I turn, reluctantly, back up the hill, trusting Frankly to follow me, just as Stella comes trotting into view.

'Oh there you are!' she trills. 'Oh my! Such a shock! The police! Aldo was murdered!'

We walk back together into the village. I am a realist and I know that no one could ever escape a woman such as Stella when she is so big with news.

Just my luck to move into a village which has a murder within forty-eight hours. So much for peace and quiet.

Apparently, the funeral has been stopped and the coffin taken down to Motril, the nearest coastal town, for a post mortem. On the contents, I hasten to add, not the coffin itself.

'So they don't know that he was murdered; they just suspect it.'

'There must be a very good reason for their suspecting it,' says Stella grimly. 'The doctor certified natural causes on the death certificate so someone must have reported something suspicious. Obviously Sanchia would be top of the list—it must be poisoning. But she wasn't here; she's been visiting her mother this week and she only got back just in time for the funeral.'

'Surely they would have waited?'

'Oh goodness me, no. Not in these temperatures. You can't just leave bodies lying around in this heat! It's just not done.' Stella must have been a prefect at a private school. They are the only ones who learn how to talk like that.

It would be tough to hear that your husband is dead and not be able to get home in time for the funeral. Or would it? Does a funeral really help? Did Danny's? I ponder this as I walk home, having managed to escape Stella at last.

It's a good question and I think generally that the answer is yes. And it would be important to have the burial before you knew that your loved one's body had deteriorated. I didn't have that option but then I didn't really believe that it was Danny inside that coffin. In a way he left me just as Alex has. Just went away one day with a goodbye kiss and never came back.

I never thought of it like that before.

However, this is not a line of thought that I want to follow.

Fortunately (although it does not seem so at the time) there is a distraction right ahead of me.

Just as I am cooking lunch, I find out that the police really don't suspect Sanchia.

They suspect me.

Two short, grey, middle-aged policemen turn up at my door and Frankly roars at them like the good guard dog she is. I can do nothing but let them in politely—and the questions begin.

But of course they speak no English and I speak virtually no Spanish. For all I know, they could be asking me if I dance the can-can.

'*No hablo Espanol, Señor,*' I say, smiling apologetically and making a hopeless gesture with my hands but they don't appear to believe me. I can catch the words 'Ben Taylor' and 'casa' and several others which sound familiar but it is a hopeless task.

Then I spot the word "nouget" and my eyes stray to the pack of rat poison on top of the fridge. The great detective with the moustache follows my gaze and almost leaps to impound the clue before I can move. He is standing with the unopened packet jabbering away to his companion excitedly. Then they both start looking through the rubbish in the pedal bin.

'Hang on a minute!' I say angrily but I am of no account. I am told firmly to sit down and be silent (and you can understand those words in any language) while they examine the contents of my store cupboard and the rest of the kitchen.

This is surreal. Am I supposed to have poisoned a man I have never even met with an unopened pack of rat poison? Dear God, don't let them arrest me and take me away. I suppose they would have to find me an interpreter but what would happen to Frankly in the meantime?

One of the officers turns back to me and speaks with gestures and I work out that he is going to try and find someone who speaks both Spanish and English. At least, I hope that's what he said. Otherwise it could have been 'I'm going to fetch the handcuffs and you're nicked, Madam.'

The other officer and I are left, looking slightly awkward. He has a gun in a holster and he puts his hand on it warningly. Of course, I had already considered wrestling him to the ground and making my escape but I think I'll put my faith in the power of the spoken word instead.

It is a surprise to see who the first officer brings: it is the American man I saw at the ruined cottage. He is speaking in accented but what appears to be fluent Spanish as he comes in through the door but he pauses to smile at me and nod. His face has a slightly blurred look about it—some people might have suspected him of being a drinker but I know why his eyes are not as clear as they might be.

I'm a little distracted but I still notice that it's a good face with distinctive laughter lines around his eyes. He would once have been quite dark haired but the silver suits him well. It's a bit long—he looks like some kind of ageing rock star but the face is masculine enough to take it.

Frankly, who has been ignoring everything pointedly and hiding under the table, immediately comes forward squeaking a welcome and the man's face softens at once. He leans down to pet her. He is wearing cowboy boots and the jeans are definitely Armani.

'How do you do, Ma'am,' he says in a soft, cowboy drawl once he and Frankly are sufficiently reacquainted. 'My name is Watlington P. Risborough. I have a house here in Los Poops and these gentlemen from *La Guardia* have asked me if I could translate some questions for you.'

I bow my head in assent, watching him carefully. He is a strange mixture of two men in one; an urban cowboy if you like. The eyes are set wide and are of a deep, velvet brown and the chin is small but this is not a weak man's face. I would prefer this man to be on my side in a fight.

'Would you and the other gentlemen like some tea or coffee?' I ask.

'Real coffee?' he says hopefully.

'Ground coffee—from Colorado,' I say.

'That would be great.' It has worked; we are on the same side. He turns and asks the two policemen what they would like to drink but this is obviously not the way they want to play it and a curt 'no' is followed by a stream of questions or instructions.

'May I?' I gesture towards the kitchen. Mr. Risborough (I can't call him Watlington P, I simply can't! My lips twitch at the thought) asks the *Guardia* if I may make coffee and they assent gruffly. This is not turning out to be quite the keen interrogation they had planned.

Everyone watches me as I light the gas cooker with a match and put the kettle on. I take a small packet of Oreos out of the cupboard and put some on a plate and then turn to my questioner with a query on my face. He is looking at me keenly and one side of his mouth turns up in a smile as he takes a biscuit.

'The police are investigating the death of a villager, Aldo Ramos,' he says. 'They believe that he was killed by rat poison and they have heard that you were seen buying rat poison at the shop yesterday.'

That bloody mafia of women!

'Yes, they have already found the stuff I bought,' I say. 'I bought it by accident because I thought it was nougat. I gather that they think that I may have killed a man I have never met, twenty-four hours after arriving in a country I'd never visited before, using a pack of poison that hasn't been opened.'

'Ah,' says Risborough (Watlington P.) taking another biscuit. 'Well, they have to look into every circumstance, Ma'am.'

The kettle has boiled and I am making coffee in a cafétière. 'Milk and sugar?' I say.

'Just black. Thanks.'

The two policemen break into a torrent of words but I have a feeling that Watlington P. Cowboy Boots is more than a match for them and he calmly gestures to the table where we sit to drink our coffee. Frankly shimmies up to him and puts her paw on his lap.

'They would like to know your name, where you have come from and why you are here in this house,' he says, one hand going down to stroke her. 'And come to think of it, I wouldn't mind knowing myself.'

I look up at those disconcertingly warm eyes which I know have recently been filled with tears and wonder who he is and what he means. This is not a man who would easily cry nor flirt unnecessarily.

'You have a real cute dog,' he adds with a smile.

Frankly, the little trollop, is all over him, in bliss from prolonged ear scratching.

'My name is Anna Marks,' I say. 'I am English but I have been living in Colorado, USA. I am here because I don't want my dog to go into quarantine before I return to the UK so I am registering her as a European dog so that I can take her into the UK on the Pet Travel Scheme. Ben Taylor, the house's owner, is an old friend of mine and he has lent me his house to stay in.'

'No, that won't do,' says Risborough. 'They won't buy any of that. Except the name, of course.'

'What?'

'*La Guardia* need things simple. That is just way too complicated for them. Can I tell them that you are Taylor's girlfriend come out here before him to clear the place up? They'll understand that and it will help. Taylor's real respected around here.'

'But it's not true!'

'Ma'am, that is of no relevance whatsoever when it comes to Spanish law!' His face is set but there is a twinkle in those brown eyes and I can't help but twinkle back.

'Okay,' I say. 'Tell them what you think will work. Just save me from the hangman.'

'Oh it wouldn't be as bad as that,' he assures me. 'Just a few years in prison with time off for good behaviour. Nobody holds much of a brief for Aldo around here.'

Then he turns to the police and speaks in swift, impressive Spanish.

The conversation goes back and forwards for a few minutes and I can see that he is winning them over. Risborough (Watlington P.) seems to have a knack of winning people over. I feel myself backing off mentally. The charm offensive is not going to work on me!

Frankly, on the other hand, is trying to climb up on his lap, boss-eyed with bliss from his talented ear-scratching.

'No,' he says firmly putting his hand on her head. Frankly obeys instantly and sits, leaning against his leg. I am outraged. She would never obey me like that.

After some more discussion, during which both the policemen become quite agitated and there is sufficient hand-waving for me to fear for the crockery in the wooden rack over the sink, the two men nod to me and turn to leave.

'Is that it?' I say. 'Do they still suspect me? What's going on?'

Risborough (W.P.) waits until they have left before answering.

Then he leans back in his chair as if he owns the place and smiles. 'Nope,' he says. 'They just hoped that they would be able to pin it on a stranger. It's only natural.'

'Why? Who do they suspect?' It is a silly question—I don't know anyone in the village so the answer won't make sense.

'Every single one of the women,' he says. 'Is there any more coffee?'

'What?'

'Coffee. Is there any more?'

Now he is teasing me and I feel irritation rise. For God's sake, I don't need a week like this last one has been, culminating with police coming round to arrest me and now some smart-arse American playing games.

'Ah,' says Watlington P. Risborough (God how those initials annoy me. Trust some stupid American to have a pretentious name like that). 'You're mad at me. I'm sorry. I should be more thoughtful. I don't know who you are or why you're here—apart from what you've told me—and I'm treating you like some kind of friend. I'm sorry.'

Well that one's a facer!

Silently I pour him some more coffee and take my feelings out on Frankly by grimacing furiously at her. She totally ignores me. Watlington P. Pretentious's right hand is caressing her head again.

'Thanks,' he says, drinking the coffee and taking his time. He must be a Mid-Westerner; no East- or West-Coast American would take so long about anything.

'What seems to have happened is this. Every single Spanish-born woman in the village bought rat poison yesterday. Every single woman called in on Aldo sometime yesterday and now every single woman only has an empty packet left and a completely spurious story about what they used it for.'

'What?' I sit down, amazed. 'You mean every woman is under suspicion?'

'Yep—that is, nope. The police know perfectly well that somebody killed Aldo. He was a bad lot and his wife had trouble with him. He would beat up on other guys too. I guess he drank and they say he took cocaine, too…'

Cocaine? Conspiracy? Murder? What kind of hell-hole have I come to?

'But they're not going to be able to prove a thing. There are just too many suspects. The women have obviously conspired together to get rid of him while his wife was out of town. Maybe she knows about it; maybe not. One thing's for sure: nobody's going to say a thing.

'I think they're going to call off the post mortem and let it stand as natural causes. Not a lot else they can do.'

'Oh my God!' I remember yesterday and the women in the shop. Were they planning this then? Was my joking thought about their plotting real?

'But one of them must have done it! One of them must be a murderer.' Or maybe all of them are! This is like *Murder on the Orient Express*.'

'Yep, but there's nothing the police can do but arrest the lot of them and that wouldn't stand for a moment. I guess they hoped that it would turn out to be you. Why did you buy that poison again? You said you'd only been here a day.'

'It was a mistake. I misread the label. I was going to take it back today.'

'Well I wouldn't do that!'

'Er, no. Perhaps not.'

We sit together in silence for a minute. God, Alex would have found this funny. The real Alex that is, the one who… No! Stop it. He doesn't exist any more. There, now I'm angry again. Better. Not good, but better than the grief.

I am surprised to find that the hand which had been stroking Frankly is now resting on my fingers. It is a strong, powerful hand with well-cut fingernails and dark hairs on the back of the wrist and a small gold signet ring on the fourth finger.

'Are you okay?'

'No, not really.' I hang my head and pull my hand away.

'Anything I can do?'

'No. No, thank you.'

'Well, if you ever need to talk something over, I'd be glad to listen.'

'No, it's okay, thank you.' I am quite sharp now. I wish he would leave me alone. The whole day has been ruined and I need to have some time to myself.

'Right.' Watlington P. Stupid Name stands up. 'Well… I'm, er… leaving tomorrow for a couple of weeks but I'll be back here at the beginning of next month. Will you still be here? If so, would you have dinner with me?'

'I don't know. I mean, yes, I'll probably be here but…' I look away.

'I'm not asking you to sleep with me, Anna; just dinner.'

My jaw drops. Our eyes meet. He is still talking.

'I'm married. I'm not trying anything on you. But I'm out here in Spain quite a lot at the moment and I just think it would be nice to have some female company sometimes. Especially somebody who knows the US, particularly Colorado. I have a place there.'

He would. Probably a whole mountain. Those boots must have cost $500. But now I feel a fool.

'I'm sorry,' I say. 'I guess I'm just a bit fraught. Life has been a bit challenging lately.'

'Yeah,' he says. 'I understand. Well, I'd love to listen sometime. Really I would.

'I'll see you around.'

If he had a Stetson, he would be doffing it now.

'Thanks.' I get up but he is already half-way to the door. In the movies, the hero always looks back at the heroine at the last minute and says something incredibly cool like 'my friends call me Sundance.'

'Oh, by the way,' he says, looking back. 'My friends call me Jack.'

The heroine would just say ''Bye, Jack.'

I sit down, miss and fall off the chair.

Just like cowboys do, he walks back, asks if I'm okay, helps me up, ignores my giggles and smiles.

'Why Jack?' I say once I have recovered a modicum of equanimity.

'Well I reckon Watlington's a bit of a mouthful.' He looks

slightly sheepish. Interesting. Most Americans with ridiculous names are proud of them.

'There's the "P".'

'Ah. Yes. No, that won't work either,' he says.

'Go on. What does the "P" stand for.' I can't resist this.

'Perivale,' he says and my face creases up involuntarily.

'Your parents really didn't like you did they?' I say.

'Well… Nope, it's not that. It's just the way things are done in my family.'

'Then you must come from a very interesting family,' I say, somewhat shakily, realising that I've been hideously rude.

'Well, I guess,' he says. 'If anything good ever came from Nebraska.' Then he grins because he is amused by my trying not to laugh.

'It's even worse than that,' he says. 'It's not just Watlington Perivale Risborough, it's Watlington Perivale Risborough III.'

We are both laughing. 'Oh I am sorry!' I say with my face splitting in two. 'That really is tough.'

'Yep,' he says. 'So it's just Jack. I'll see you.' And he is gone.

Chapter Three

I KNOW QUITE a lot about cowboys. Real cowboys, that is, not the pretend ones. Real cowboys are gentlemen, even if they do have some very odd ideas. Real cowboys can handle powerful women. You could tell a cowboy that you were a NASA scientist with two Master's degrees and that you were a hundred times richer than he could ever dream of being and he would still understand that he is a man and you are a woman. He would be appropriately impressed but he would still doff his hat and hold the door open for you and he would still want to take you to bed.

Let me tell you a story about cowboys—and about the people who live with and around them. Then you may understand a little how much I loved Colorado.

I was visiting Los Angeles. Los Angeles, Colorado, that is. It consists of four streets, three bars, a grain silo and a railway line—a far cry from its namesake to the West. It was a day out just to celebrate life and a way of filling a lonely weekend without Alex.

I was planning to go horse riding at a dude ranch to the West of our home in Unityville and I left Frankly with Ella for the day.

Beautiful Ella lives in a trailer. I hadn't known her for very long then and it was the first time that I had visited her so it was so strange seeing someone so elegant living in a trailer crammed to the gunnels with gunk—box after box of healthy cosmetics and assorted vitamins and just a corner for Ella's bed and clothes.

All the washing facilities and the kitchen were in the nearby farmhouse which she shared with the owners. It suited them; who was I to comment?

Frankly was sufficiently intrigued not to mind being left behind. She was certain that there was something edible under the second pile of boxes to the left and by hook or by crook she was going to find it. I left Ella catching flying boxes and saying 'Down Frankly!' in the kind of voice that beagles learn to disregard automatically about five hours after birth.

It was a beautiful morning for a fifty-mile drive and I was good and early so I thought that I'd stop and have breakfast in Los Angeles, which is about half way between Unityville and the ranch. So I parked by the railroad in the shade of a grain silo and, as it was getting hotter by the minute, I took off my cord over-shirt and put it in the boot. Then I shut the boot.

With the key in it. And I had locked the car doors.

It was one of those moments when you just don't believe it. My first thought was that I was so thankful that Alex was not there; he would have been so angry with me. Not that I was entirely thrilled myself but at least there was only me to worry about. What the hell was I going to do?

Los Angeles on a Sunday morning is shut; and I mean shut. I took a brief look around but there was nothing open but the *Broken Arrow Bar* where I was planning to eat. The whole town looked as though it was abandoned twenty years ago.

However, four cowboys were walking rather oddly down the main street as I returned rather nervously to the car. They were my only chance, so I asked them if they could help. They were not exactly sober, having been on a stag night which hadn't stopped yet, but they were charming and all introduced themselves in the usual grave and polite way of the sober Colorado cowboy.

They just got all the words mixed up.

Luke was the bridegroom and Hal, Lee and Red were his staunch supporters. They were planning to steal a boat for the day and take up piracy on the Silverfish River but they had the time to help a lady in distress. Particularly one as pretty as me.

'Yuh not from round here, are yuh?' asked Red perspicaciously.

I told them that I *was* from around there; that I was from Unityville; but this turned out to be a very confusing statement for them and one that I had to withdraw. The destruction of several million brain cells overnight seemed to have removed any possible facility to allow foreigners to live in Colorado, so there really was no alternative but to move myself back to England. And as London was the only UK city known to the amount of brain cells still available I gave up on Manchester, let alone Warrington.

The cowboys then turned their attention to my dilemma. Could have happened to anyone, they said—although not to a nicer and prettier lady, oh no!—after all, Luke once left his horse behind after going visiting and only realised when he needed it the next day.

The dynamics of that having been argued out (because Luke could not remember which particular horse this was and it was vitally important, all of a sudden, to work out how many white socks it had) the cowboys offered to break the car window for me so that I could get in. When I politely declined they took me into the *Broken Arrow* and, with great good sense, told the barmaid, Corrine, all about it. She introduced herself to me with a big smile, commented that I wasn't from round here, was I?—and handed me an old Bakelite telephone on a cord which stretched from the wall behind the bar, suggesting that I call the local cop at home. Corrine and the cowboys said that the cop can get into cars, no trouble, and he'd come right round.

No he wouldn't. Of all the people I met in Colorado, that cop was the only one who did not want to help. He was fairly curt (after all, it was still pretty early on a Sunday morning) but he did give me the number of a local man who had a garage and said that he would gladly help.

The cowboys were outraged that the cop wouldn't come and help and offered to start a fight or a riot so that he'd get called out anyway. I said that this was an impressive idea but in sorting out the riot, the cop probably wouldn't have time to deal with the car. They agreed, sagely, and offered to buy me a drink.

A brief but spirited debate on why I did not want a beer with a whisky chaser followed and, to distract them, I told them that in England it is customary, after a stag night, to put the bridegroom on a train to the other end of the country or to tie him, naked, to a lamp post. They all thought both of these were excellent ideas. There were only two problems. Not having a station, they doubted they'd manage to get the train to stop—and Los Angeles doesn't have any lamp posts.

I called the guy from the garage and he was lovely. He was mowing his lawn but it was not a problem and he would be round in five minutes. It all seemed rather unreal that I was sitting at a bar surrounded by cowboys who were being so incredibly sweet and helpful (in a sweet, unhelpful sort of way) and a barmaid dialling the numbers for me on the phone on the wall at the back of the bar and then handing the phone across the counter. She had to duck underneath it all the time as she went back and forwards serving drinks and food to the dozen or so people in there.

All of them by now had sussed that something unusual was happening. The general consensus of opinion was that I wasn't from around there.

Randy arrived very swiftly with his car-breaking equipment which comprised of a load of wedges to get down inside the window seals of a car and coat hanger-type things to hook the locks. We walked out to the car together and he said it would not be a problem and set to work. But he couldn't do it, try as he might. He suggested I phone Unityville Ford and ask if they'd got a spare key. They might bring it out, he said. It is only twenty miles. I said I doubted it, even if they were open on a Sunday, and was there a taxi in Los Angeles?

'No,' said Randy. 'But someone might drive you there. I would be happy to.'

And he meant it. So, I went back into the pub and looked up the Unityville Ford number in the phone book and the cowboys talked about getting into the car through the sunroof. 'There isn't one,' I said. 'Well we can make one,' they answered with inescapable logic. Red, who was by far the drunkest of them, introduced himself for the third time. 'You're not from round here, are you?' he added thoughtfully.

There was someone at Unityville Ford but he said no, they didn't have spare keys, though they would have been happy to bring one out if they had. He suggested that I call a locksmith. My heart sank but I was grateful that he gave me a number and I went out to tell Randy that I really appreciated his time and kindness and what did I owe him? And he wouldn't take a dime. Not a dime. He just smiled at me and touched his hat and wished me luck and a better day and got into the truck to go back and finish mowing his lawn.

Inside the pub the cowboys were back to their discussion on taking up piracy on the Silverfish River to get themselves a little extra cash. As I dialled up the locksmith's number Luke, who by then was the most charmingly drunk, came over and shook my hand for the fourth time and offered to lend me his horse to get to wherever I was going. I could bring it back tomorrow, he said.

The thought of borrowing a horse to get me to the place where I had planned to go riding for the day was fairly surreal.

I tried to answer him and talk to the locksmith at the same time, just as someone turned up the juke-box so loud that you could hardly hear yourself think, and I totally confused some very pleasant lady who'd never been a locksmith in her life, nor been married to one, and couldn't for the life of her think why Unityville Ford should have given me her number. She hoped that my day would get better.

And Corrine the barmaid danced back and forward under the wire serving the cowboys with beer topped up with tomato juice (I'm not joking) telling me that it was a preventative cure for hangovers.

Distracted, I accidentally let go of the phone and it shot back across the counter, missing her by inches and ricocheting up the wall, smashing into a hundred pieces.

I apologised profusely, almost in tears, and Corrine said, really nicely, that it didn't matter a bit and she would get me another phone in a minute but the other waitress hadn't turned up and she'd got to take orders for breakfast.

The guys took deep and appreciative draughts of their pale crimson-coloured beer and asked me what I was planning to do today, so I told them and they said that I shouldn't ride up at that particular dude ranch just then as it was rattlesnake season. I said that it didn't really look as if I were going to ride there anyway, thanks all the same, and realised that I had better call the ranch to cancel. Then I remembered that I broke the phone.

Then Corrine brought me somebody's mobile phone with a big smile and I considered recommending both her and the owner of the phone for a sainthood. Who it was, I had no idea; I turned to wave at the anonymous benefactor who was seated in the alcoves at the back of the pub and fourteen people waved back at me.

There were three locksmiths in Unityville and they all opened car doors. I picked the one I liked the sound of best and dialled the number. As it rang, someone turned up the juke box again so I took the mobile outside and talked to him on the pub doorstep. His name was Dave and he said he'd come immediately. For $60. Pretty much the cost of a three-hour ride at the dude ranch. He was actually quite pleased to come as he was going to have to paint the guttering otherwise.

So I called the dude ranch and told them what had happened and cancelled the riding and they told me to have a nice day and then it was time for another spirited discussion with the guys about why I wouldn't have a beer. Their plans for piracy were beginning to form nicely so they were fairly easy to distract. I chose my moment when they were all fiercely debating whose boat they were going to steal (Jed's was nicely painted but it wouldn't deal with the rapids so that was no good. They thought that perhaps they'd steal the cop's as it would serve him right for not helping me) and I slipped outside to wait for the locksmith. He was kind and told me, just as the cowboys did, that I hadn't done anything that anyone else doesn't do and got out all his official lock-breaking equipment and started work.

'It won't take long,' he said.

Three quarters of an hour later, I asked him if he had any optimism left, and he said 'enough,' and I really admired him for that. We had a brief discussion on how inconvenient it is that they make cars so burglar-proof nowadays and I went for a walk.

Up and down the leafy streets I walked. All four of them. At the end of First Avenue there was a little church and far more people who could ever have got into that little wooden building were flooding out onto the surrounding grass. One of them, a large and suspiciously blonde lady of indeterminate age, bumped into me and apologised. My reply elicited the usual comment as to my lack of local ethnic origin and, before I knew it, I was gathered up into the heart of the community.

'This lady's locked her keys in her car and can't get in,' said my new friend the large blonde to the even larger, blonder female preacher. 'We must pray for her.'

'Oh no!' I thought with a flood of embarrassment washing over me. But it was too late.

Yes! They must pray for me! Of course they must! Where was the car?

'Over by the railroad,' I said nervously and suddenly there was a great rush of people surging down the road towards the car, almost carrying me in their wake. In fact, there were only about twelve people but most of them were women and all of them were large and they surely knew how to surge.

The preacher, being the largest of all and prone to shouting 'Praise the Lord' at regular intervals, led the way in a manner which would have halted a herd of charging buffalo. You got the distinct feeling that God would not want to mess with her and, if He did, the outcome would be in some doubt.

They spotted the car with Dave still working on it and surrounded it with the kind of motherly love that means you have a third piece of pudding because you would not dare not to. You just know that it would break their hearts if you didn't eat it all even if it was going to take you a lifetime to remove the result from your hips.

Everyone was holding hands and praising God but Dave did not turn a hair. He had lived in Colorado all his life: this was perfectly normal for a Sunday.

'Let us pray for Anna's car!' The preacher's tones echoed out over the other voices. That resonance must have reached every home in the town. It must have reached Unityville. Passing eagles a thousand feet up fell stunned into the nearby fields.

'Lord, we ask you now to open the doors to Anna's car, just as you broke through the walls of Jericho for Joshua in the Promised Land. And so say we all. Amen.'

'Ay-men!' echoed the congregation.

I screwed up my face and added a little prayer of my own, even if it were only for everyone to go away. Quietly and quickly.

Then Dave gave a shout and the car door was open.

'HALLELUYAH!'

What could you say? The Lord came through. The power of prayer really worked. I am not sure if God was simply outnumbered or if the power of prayer is so great that really it can move mountains. Everyone was delighted and everyone got hugged. I felt as if I was being embraced by a series of bouncy castles.

I had to go back with everyone for a post-Church breakfast. It was the least I could do and I was so grateful that I didn't mind at all. They gave me the address and made me promise to come as I explained that I had to pay Dave and take the phone back into the *Broken Arrow* first. Once my solemn promise was extracted, the Surge of Faith moved off down the road like a hovercraft.

I gave Dave the $60 which was going to pay for my ride and he drove off wishing me a wonderful day. For a moment, I stood in the sunshine, leaning against the car and being thankful. I talk to God myself now and again and I made a mental note then to do it a little more often (if not quite that loudly).

Then I went back into the pub to tell them that all was well and return the mobile phone and fourteen people gave me a round of applause and shook my hand in turn and the cowboys made me promise to come and be honorary female on the pirate ship when they finally got her rigged out.

This afternoon I decide to have a thorough turn-out of Ben's house. I call him first, just to check that it's okay to mess about with his things—and he's there, as kind and helpful as always.

As I am no longer nice—and because it is a good idea to let people know if there's something slightly wrong in their holiday home so they can expect it and deal with it next time they come—I mention some of the slightly less convenient things, such as the fact that the kitchen sink is almost permanently blocked and the strange vagaries of the cooker which will quietly go out without a word of explanation and present you with a half-cooked or raw dinner just when you're totally starving. Ben chooses not to hear me and tells me again how happy I am to be there.

This is, of course, true. Perhaps I was just being ungrateful.

We don't really have much else to say to each other once I've him that Aldo is dead as I have no other knowledge of the village gossip. I make sure that he knows that I am suitably grateful which is balm to his heart, for Ben is the kind of man who lives to help others. And I *am* grateful. Learning from experience, I don't tell him about nearly being arrested for murder but he chuckles when I mention Stella and suggests that I take a carafe of wine round tomorrow evening.

'A carafe?'

'Have you not found my barrel of wine in the cupboard downstairs?'

'No.' I am quite excited at the thought.

'But you must find it and drink it! It is not good for the village wine to be kept for too long,' he says. 'Drink as much as you want. It is a wonderful wine. Remember, *mi casa es su casa*. Enjoy!'

So, once he has told me again what a wonderful house it is and we have said our goodbyes, I venture down into the damp basement, braving the crumbling plaster and aura of dampness while Frankly follows me, suspiciously Looking For Dragons. Since our first exploration she, like me, has ignored the concrete stairs by the bookcase, regarding them as a doorway to another planet and not one where you would wish to venture unnecessarily.

She stops dead at the bottom of the stairs, neatly tripping me up so that I cannon into a pile of blankets and boxes piled haphazardly against the wall and bark my shin on a unexpected chair that has been hiding beneath everything else.

'Monster,' I hiss at her once the pain has receded enough to allow coherence.

Not My Fault. Had To Investigate Important Smells, says the beagle with her head underneath the pile of fallen blankets. Wow! Look At This, Mum!

She drags out what, at first, appears to be part of a dead donkey and smells almost as bad. It is some kind of animal skin but, now she's found it, Frankly is not at all sure.

She sneezes and backs away, looking up at me to say, Over To You. It's Bigger Than I Thought.

Gingerly I put a finger out. The fur is very dark—and it is fur rather than horse's hide. It is also rather moth-eaten. Reluctantly, I clear the towels and old shirts that obscure the rest of this pelt and jump with shock as a pair of glassy eyes and a mouthful of fangs is revealed.

Wo Wo Wo Wo WO! bells the beagle in sympathy, backing up to the stairs in horror. Dragons! I Knew There Were Dragons!

No, not dragons. A bear. It's a very dead bear and a skinned one which someone thought might make a nice rug. Someone with very little taste and even less tanning experience.

Frankly is halfway back up the stairs and still yelling.

'Shush,' I say. 'It's okay. It won't hurt you.'

Bollocks To That! The beagle abandons me completely and vanishes round the top step still going *Gurrerr* in a last-ditch attempt to be fierce.

Thoughtfully I lay the bearskin out on the floor. It really is hideous and smelly but it's also interesting. I've seen them in Colorado, of course, but it must have been a hundred years or more since there were bears in Spain. If there ever were. I must call Ben back and ask him about it. But, for the moment, it needs to be stored somewhere safe where it won't attract insects or have spiders' nests made in it.

I give it a good brushing and pack it up in the plastic bag which housed my duvet and remember to store it with the face turned away, in case I come down again and think it's a goblin.

I don't usually have much patience but, for some reason, I clear up, tidy and sort everything in the downstairs hallway before investigating the two downstairs bedrooms. There are cupboards and everything does fit fairly well. Most of it is junk—either broken or faded and torn.

I think I'm working up to a drink. I want to really appreciate the abundance of wine at my disposal. But I must make sure I'm not sozzled to go out later. That would be a *faux pas* with someone like Stella!

Satisfied, I survey the hallway. It looks presentable now. And I am very pleased with myself as I venture into the far room with the high, shuttered windows. Sure enough, hidden behind a curtain, is a cupboard in the wall.

The door is locked. Or is it simply jammed? No, it's jammed; the bit around the lock will move.

You know how a little voice in your head sometimes tells you exactly what's going to happen and you ignore it? 'That cupboard's going to spring open and all the contents are going to fall on you,' says my Guardian Angel succinctly.

Actually, it doesn't. What does happen is that the door comes off its hinges and swings wildly round, knocking me against the wall and vomiting mops, boxes, duvets, toolboxes, a kettle, buckets, a kitchen sink, two fake Christmas trees, a dead sheep, a load of metal cans and a television across the floor.

'Shiiiiiiiiiiiiit!'

WoWoWOWOWOWO! roars Frankly, helpfully, from upstairs. I'm A Big Fierce Beagle! You Leave My Mum Alone!

Yeah, right.

I can see stars, just like in a *Tom and Jerry* cartoon. That hasn't happened in a very long time.

I was not joking about the kitchen sink. Nor the television. The sheep was just a sheepskin. But I forgot to mention the mice.

They are very much alive and seriously irritated. About a dozen of them, all as tiny as a 200-peseta piece, scurrying around in all directions and squeaking at the tops of their little voices.

They are so cute! I can appreciate that as I examine the graze on my upper arm, the bruises to my hand and wrist and the twist in my ankle. Anyway, they sort themselves out—fleeing back into the cupboard and grumbling to themselves about earthquakes and giants and the sheer inconvenience of having to build new nests.

I think I need a drink. That barrel has to be somewhere.

Cautiously, I prop the door up against the wall and switch on the light. The first thing I see is a shelf piled with tins of cardinal red polish. Wonderful! Now I can make the floors shine. Every single tin, bar one, is half-empty and completely dried up. Oh well.

The cupboard is still full, despite the debris strewn across the room. There are yet more buckets and electrical adaptors and old electric fans and fires and a pile of dusty tools and metal boxes, including what looks like an old school trunk. And lodged securely under the bottom shelf is a dark brown barrel with a tap.

I run upstairs for a jug and give my Big Fierce Beagle a reassuring pat and race downstairs again. Frankly stares doubtfully at me from the top step and *Gurrers* a little. After all, what would she do if I didn't come back? It's only two hours until her suppertime.

I reach the cupboard without incident apart from treading on a towel which has a mouse in it. Had a mouse in it. Horrified, I apologise profusely, which is of no use whatsoever to the ex-mouse and shed a tear of shock and sorrow. I make a mental note to throw the whole towel out.

God, I need that drink.

Logically, one would expect the tap on the barrel to be unturnable. But, after wrestling for about five minutes, I can move it enough to release a trickle of reddish-brown wine into the waiting jug. I let it run until I have about half a bottle, turn it back (and it works), get up, walk back upstairs, pour myself a glass of wine and sit down at the table.

It smells like sherry; it looks like sherry. It tastes like petrol.

One well-deserved cup of tea later, I discover that it is marvellous for unblocking the sink.

Chapter Four

Now I HAVE met one British ex-pat resident in Los Poops, the others turn up in a bunch, just like buses. Within twenty-four hours of meeting Stella, I have bumped into George, Katherine and Sylvia and been waved to by two other Brits in the distance. Word travels like wildfire here.

I have had coffee in *La Posada* and been shown all around its slightly lacy old-world charm and sussed out for myself that there is absolutely nothing but friendship going on between George, who is an irascible Yorkshireman with a barb for a tongue and meek-eyed, grey haired Katherine. The reason is fairly simple— Katherine is George's sister. How Stella missed that perfectly obvious connection is a mystery but then, most of Stella is a mystery. Katherine is obviously still grieving for her husband, Tom, who drove his car over the edge of the road one night six months ago. How ghastly. The subject is changed swiftly before I can say that I actually do have some idea how she feels.

It's not as if there isn't enough to talk about. Aldo's murder/ natural death is the hot topic of gossip for everyone and thanks to Watlington (Jack) P. Risborough I have the brand new angle. The rumour *has* circulated that the post mortem was cancelled and his body is being brought back up tonight for a re-run of the funeral tomorrow but nobody knows why.

It seems that I'm the only non-Spanish woman who bought rat poison yesterday so none of the others have been interviewed by *La Guardia*. George and Katherine are round-eyed with amazement at the theory of multiple murderers.

'Do you think they know themselves which one of them did it?' asks Katherine. 'I don't think I'll sleep tonight. What if they try to kill one of us?'

'Why would they?' says George, shortly. 'Aldo was a right

bastard. They just quietly took him out like a good soldier would.'

Somehow I suspect that George was a soldier.

These people do want to know my story but I am as evasive as I can be, just telling them the very basics about living in the USA and wanting to bring Frankly home. Alex is dealt with by a flippant, sarcastic remark about his repeating patterns of leaving women when he has sucked them dry and found a new full-blooded victim. Sarcasm is a useful tool; it repels all boarders lest it should be turned upon them.

Anyway, Frankly and I are welcomed into the fold and told to call by any time I want. Frankly is thrilled with *La Posada* because she can spot a soft touch at twenty paces and Katherine is soft as a feather pillow. *La Posada* also has a cushioned window ledge for sitting on. It's as comfortable as a sofa and a sofa is an essential piece of kit which should be provided for every beagle. It is appropriated the moment everyone is looking the other way and Frankly is So Cute, once she is discovered, that no one has the heart to move her. She looks at me triumphantly before settling down for a serious doze. It Has Been Noted that there isn't a sofa at our new home and it is obviously my fault.

Katherine coos at Frankly like a broody hen and fetches her biscuits just in case the sweet little dog would like one. One? Frankly leaps up, scoffs the lot and begs for more. From then on she shadows Katherine nose-to-heel, being prepared to abandon even the wonderful sofa in her rightful pursuit of food. She is showing devotion akin to worship and Katherine, in turn, is totally besotted.

She is one of those incredibly quiet women who actually rule the roost without anyone noticing. It's done through that kind of sheer, unrelenting kindness that wears you down eventually. I used to resist it as a matter of politeness but now I'm out of nice I don't care. She can cosset me as much as she wants to and I'm really not going to worry about whether it's inconveniencing her. I do put my foot down about her offering to feed Frankly each day with the meat she cooks in her pressure cooker for the stray village dogs. 'It wouldn't be any trouble and it would save you

having to go to the trouble of finding suitable things,' she purrs.
She really wants to do it.

'No thank you.' I say firmly. 'I think it's important for a dog
only to be fed by its owner wherever possible. A few treats are all
right but not the main meal.'

Katherine looks suitably abashed but bounces back with an
offer on a completely different subject and, before I have realised
it, I have agreed to keep my passport and important papers in *La
Posada*'s safe. Katherine's reasoning, that they could get damaged
by dampness, lost somewhere or even get eaten by a goat, is not
as outrageous as it seems. Loose goats do sometimes roam the
village streets. But really, she just wants to help. Bugger. And I
have just given in. I must watch out for incipient niceness. I really
can't afford it.

While Katherine makes yet another cup of tea, George tells
me a few horror stories of guests at *La Posada* and some of the
suppers that went wrong. The best one is the tale of the drunken
Austrian woman who seduced two men from the village in one
evening and caused a fight in the Plaza. I respond with stories of
The Die Happy Café in Colorado, where I did some cooking for
my friend Gilbert.

Before I married Danny I worked full time in restaurants as a
pastry chef. Since then I've worked in restaurants part time and
written cookery articles for books and magazines and I still love
to cook—*The Die Happy Café* was where I spent a lot of my spare
time these past few months.

It's poles apart from *La Posada* but soon I am comfortably back
to happy times as I describe Unityville's least-successful business
venture and I can feel myself lighting up as I talk about it. George
wants to know why it was not a success but it's fairly obvious to
anyone (except Gilbert) who knows anything about America.

There's the name for a start. America is too health-conscious
and too unfamiliar with irony for that ever to work. The new
customers who went in asked what the name meant and, when it
was explained that the food was good enough to clog up all your
arteries in one go and take you to heaven by its very taste, they
tended to look nervous and back out again. And Gilbert was not

a businessman. He was always in debt; always getting reported to the Health Inspector and always thinking up new ideas that would not work.

I love the name and the picture that it conjures up of thick dairy cream and oozing chocolate. But America does not do cream; it does non-dairy creamer. It does not do butter; it does chemical-filled butter substitute. It does not do cholesterol. Even packets of sugar have written on them: 'This is a non-cholesterol food.'

Gilbert does not do his own cooking, he has Terry to do that but even this is not a very good idea. Terry is, without a doubt, an astonishingly handsome man and he has to be one of the best cooks on the planet. However, it is generally agreed that one, or maybe both, of these attributes must have been a mistake on the part of the Universe as it obviously felt that it had to compensate for the errors by making him rude, offensive, slovenly and generally vile in every other respect.

Terry comes from the "Tastes Great, Looks Like Shit" school of cooking and his offerings, carefully laid out on doilies in the cool display area, look like the first mud pie creations of an eight-year-old. This does not tempt the passing tourist, although those few who live in Unityville and who refuse to acknowledge the word "cholesterol" in their lives have learnt that Terry's Chocolate Fudge Messy Disaster Cake is the best in the whole wide world so they don't mind scraping it up from where it has collapsed under its own weight on the plate and bled extra icing onto the tablecloth.

Second only to the chocolate cake is "Alleged Auntie Beatrice's Strangely-Coloured Soggy Carrot Cake" which lists sullenly at the back of the cabinet, groaning under its weight of glorious and very messy icing and sinking steadily into its suspiciously orange sogginess during the day. No one believes that Terry ever had an Aunt Beatrice but it could be that there *was* one and she invented the cake in a vain effort to smother her obnoxious nephew as a child. However, that is only wild speculation and, if it were true, it is sadly apparent that the cake got Auntie Beatrice first.

Also visually stunning are the Dead Pigs in Shit Cinnamon Rolls which loll contentedly on their sides with brown cinnamon syrup leaking from every orifice, delicious, tangy yellow lemon juice oozing from the base and crispy, dark caramelised sugar crumbling everywhere. Next to them in the fridge cabinet lurk the Severed Hand Fruit Scones which are piled up in a haphazard and precarious heap, bleeding scarlet and pink massacred raspberries and strawberries and bruised purple with blueberries.

Terry is mad. Simply that. He looks about my age but he is probably about fifty years old and obsessed with his own physical health to the point of having all sorts of natural hormone injections to make him look younger. He pumps iron twice a day and has a long, lean and magnificent body together with dark, curly hair, regular features and a slow grin which, until you realise that he is mad, bad and dangerous to know, could melt the heart of any poor unfortunate female. Looking at Terry you could understand the myth of Lucifer, Son of Morning. Satan would not be ugly, as people think; he would be incredibly handsome so that people would get tempted to fall for his wiles. However, the fallen angel probably has charm as well whereas Terry has a mouth as foul as a portaloo.

Terry is obsessed with sex. He does not do subtle, let alone politically correct. 'Fancy a fuck?' would be his customary greeting to some new college girl just arrived in town or even a customer, should he be allowed access to one. Terry is, generally, kept back in the kitchen but when he does erupt, his personality loses the café more custom than the sight of his cooking.

For a little cash in hand or free meals I would often lend a hand in *The Die Happy Café* when one of the long-legged "Miss America" waitresses broke a nail and went into trauma or one of the less leggy or beautiful girls overdid it on the (illegal) alcohol and (even more illegal) drugs overnight. I didn't have a Green Card but hey, Gilbert never worried about anything like that so neither did I.

Now and then, I even did a little cooking. I was there on the day that Gilbert was lamenting Terry's being picked up by the police overnight and left to calm down in the cells after a night of throwing leftover scones at people's mail boxes from his car.

'It was his second ex-wife who shopped him,' said Gilbert,

sadly. 'He's smashed her mail box before with his cooking, only that time I think it was stale pumpkin pie from Halloween.'

The display cabinet was horribly sparse of food that day and, on an impulse, I offered to make some scones and flapjacks—if they had the ingredients. I had been going into the café regularly for about three months by then and everyone knew me because of the (lack of) accent—but I had never let on that I used to be a professional. Gilbert and I had struck up a bit of a friendship and, as he had never been outside Colorado, let alone to "Yurp," as they call Europe, he liked to talk over any foreign news with me as if I would understand what was going on in Uzbekistan, Germany or Iceland. I was still grateful because no one else in Unityville had much perception that the rest of the world actually existed.

Unluckily, flapjacks in Colorado are a description of a poor man's pancake and my offer went down like a lead balloon but, even so, later that day at home I did some baking and took a couple of cakes (and some flapjacks) back downtown. Gilbert was thrilled and so was I, sitting with a complimentary mocha and watching people buying things that I had made again.

'Of course, it's illegal,' said Gilbert later on. 'You have to have a Health Department Certified Kitchen to cook for the public. But we won't say anything about that.'

So, on the regular occasions when Terry (or one of the girls) slipped into some other dimension, Gilbert would give me a call and I would see what I could do.

Both George and Katherine are thrilled that I have café experience, asking if I would be willing to be called on if they get particularly busy. Looking at the state of the place—there is a stillness to unused rooms which is unmistakable—I can't see that happening but I'm certainly willing to earn an honest crust.

I could have stayed at *La Posada* all evening—and it is with hugs and kisses that Frankly and I leave for our date at *The Bay House*.

Drinks at Stella and David's is a very different kettle of fish consisting of a very civilised gin and tonic with ice and lemon and some rather old cheese and onion crisps. These are regularly knocked to the floor by Tigger and are snatched by Frankly while everyone pretends not to notice. I have already been bounced on by Tigger several times and have managed to explain to him— by judicious thumping with an elbow when eyes are not trained in my direction—that this is not appreciated. He bounces on Frankly instead, so much so that she does her very rare beagle *yowp* which is a kind of cross between a snarl and a whimper. Tigger thinks that this is incredibly exciting and tries to bonk her instead.

A short but vigorous altercation follows which confirms Stella in her previous suspicion that Frankly is a very badly behaved dog. Not that she would say so; it would not be polite, but the accusation remains hanging in the air.

Frankly, having won the bout on points simply by firm repetition of her opinion of Impudent, Ill-bred Furry Bastards, has now gone to examine the cooker in the kitchen. She is quite convinced that there is some food underneath it and spends a happy ten minutes lying on her side, stretching alternate paws underneath the appliance to try and dig the delicious morsel out. I have to explain what she is doing and this, of course, adds to the already heavy air the imputation that Stella Doesn't Clean The Kitchen Properly.

Tigger, meanwhile, is so enamoured of his new-found sexual prowess that he is bonking my left leg instead. With cunning timing, I push the Retriever away with a hefty shove just as Stella says; 'Tigger *dear!*' giving her the completely erroneous impression that her dog is obedient.

In fact, both Stella and I deserve full marks for not scratching each other's eyes out within ten minutes.

Once things have settled down a little, Tigger has turned his attention to David (Who? Oh yes, the man in the corner) and Frankly has found a deceased pea which is eaten with appropriate relish, I am interrogated about the rat poison and the latest rumours. Much is said about the devious character of peasant peoples along with speculation about whose idea it must have been (someone called Blanca is the prime suspect). Stella is of the opinion that they should exhume Aldo's body (I forbear to mention that he isn't buried yet) and *insist* on the post mortem so that the women do, at least, know that their crime has not gone un-noticed.

David doesn't appear to think at all. Poor man, he has been bounced to death by a series of uncontrollable dogs whose pictures adorn the walls. Tigger is now sitting on his lap. He really is a beautiful creature of great pedigree and no manners whatsoever. Tigger that is. David is just faded and grey but his manners are impeccable.

We play that so-common-among-uncomfortable-strangers game of trying to find what things we have in common, even if it's things we don't like. There isn't much apart from dogs and Stella, perhaps foolishly, takes the step towards politics by asking what Sunday paper I read. I've never been a fan of those—for me, Sundays have always been special times for extra-long walks and outings, not days spent reading other people's opinions and, in the USA, the Sunday papers are ridiculously enormous.

I say, 'I don't read a Sunday paper, I'm afraid,' and Stella stares at me aghast.

'Then how do you know what to think?' she says.

I have absolutely no answer to that.

In the ensuing silence, David suggests a tour of *The Bay House* which saves the day. It is enormous. I think they live in about a quarter of it and the stark empty bedrooms which are waiting for tourists to visit are as cold and empty as those at *La Posada*.

'We have people to stay at our other house, *Casa Blanca*, all the time,' says Stella but I don't believe her. This is a hidden, forgotten village as far as tourists are concerned.

David tells me some interesting things in a quiet voice while Stella attends to dinner (to which I am still, mercifully—but also insultingly—not invited). Los Poops is officially the least important village in Spain, he says. It was the last place to receive an automated telephone system and is constantly forgotten by the hierarchy in Andalusia—which can be useful.

'You watch your water tomorrow,' he says. 'It'll be on again. And from then on, there'll be eight hours a day instead of four.'

'How do you know?'

'Because the villagers are disconnecting the official supply tonight,' he says. 'They were forced into having the municipal water supply two years ago to come in line with the rest of the region but the farming industry is so intensive now that there are always chronic water shortages in the summer. The village men have had enough and they are re-connecting the original supply from the artesian wells tonight. There's far more water in the hills than can be provided from a reservoir.'

I can see that David is a mine of information but, as Stella returns to her seat, he retreats behind Tigger again.

While she chatters on I sit, half listening, slightly high on gin and wondering about this extraordinary place. I have been here just two days and already I am surrounded by mysteries—and I have been offered work by two people. Stella could do with help in cleaning *Casa Blanca* and she is willing to pay. I'm happy enough to clean the house for her before and after any time tourists are due to arrive. I don't have a problem with the idea of being a cleaner—and obviously Stella does. Oops, I didn't mean that… it just floated down from the over-charged air above me.

David walks part of the way back with me when I leave as he has to exercise Tigger and supper is going to be another ten minutes (to make sure that I don't have to be invited to stay). He gives me a spare key to *Casa Blanca*. 'I'll leave the pilot light on so you can heat the water to have a bath if you need one,' he says. 'I know Taylor's place is a bit basic.'

I could hug him.

Just as we part, a silver BMW makes its way cautiously down from one of the higher roads of the village. At the wheel is Watlington P. Jack. David waves at him but he does not see us in the shadows. The car crosses the Plaza and disappears along the road down to the coast.

'That's Risborough, the American,' says David forgetting that I have already told them how Jack (P.R) had already saved me from a fate worse than death that day.

'Yes, I've met him.'

'Nice chap.'

'Yes, he was very helpful.'

'Flying back to New York tonight. Expect he'll be back in a month or so. Shame his wife doesn't like the place.'

'Where does he work?'

'Anywhere he wants to. He's a millionaire. Does consultancy here and there.'

'I thought he worked in England and bought a place here and then lost his job or something.'

'No. That's what the Old Girl thinks,' says David peaceably. 'But it's not the way of it. Truth is, he's got places all over the world. Thought his wife would like one here and did it up as a wedding anniversary present but she didn't take to it. He likes it though so he comes and spends a few days here when he's working in Europe. It's officially up for sale but he doesn't seem to be worried.'

'Funny lifestyle.'

'Ah, the rich and famous!'

'Is he famous?'

'Well-known in his field, I think.'

'Which is?' I feel embarrassed now at being so curious but David doesn't seem to notice.

'Internet, I think,' he says. 'Venture Capital or the like.'

'Ah.' We both nod wisely, neither of us really having the slightest idea what that involves.

Frankly is ecstatic when I get home because she has remembered The Oven Game and can spend the next hour scrabbling underneath Ben's old gas oven for remnants of food that departed this world last year if not before. I cook myself some pasta and write a few emails because George says I can use *La Posada's* modern phone line to send and pick up mail tomorrow. It's been a fairly odd day but part of me is very happy knowing that I have companions here: people who will help me and teach me how to live in the mountains of Spain for as long as I need.

I hope that Gilbert and Ella have been in touch. I have so much to tell them already.

But this is dangerous ground, for thinking of Colorado makes me think of Alex which I have so far avoided doing—and it is only the repeated kicking of a perfectly innocent doorpost which makes me feel a little bit better.

* * *

In my dream, I am walking Frankly among the Sagebrush and Indian Paint on the hillside above our lovely home in Unityville, watching for the first slivers of silver sunset that will soon engulf the enormous Rocky Mountain sky. Following the silver will be pink and orange, crimson and vermilion, purple and gold; all the colours spreading, dancing and weaving themselves across the great arc of sky above and settling below to give the Sangre de Christo mountains their name.

The people of Unityville come out of their houses each evening just to watch it, night upon night. Never was anywhere so beautiful to them or to me.

I throw my arms out as I walk, drinking in the spring air and rejoicing that the harshness of winter is through. Even in April there is snow on the ground but only in little pockets here and there on the higher ground. It still falls in the night now and again but people go to work in shorts (even wading through a foot of snowfall) knowing that it will melt in hours and the temperature will be up to seventy degrees by noon.

Alex will be on his way home now, walking back from the campus, and we shall all reach the house at roughly the same time, with Frankly scampering ahead to greet him with squeaks of joy.

So, it is time now to make our way down from Amity Park and walk back along Granville Street to our 1920s wooden home at 626 South Fifth. I call to Frankly, who ignores me on purpose just to make the point, and set off back down the narrow path. She will follow in her own good time; there is never any point in hurrying Frankly. She drives Alex crazy with her bolshieness but it rarely bothers me. Frankly knows on which side her bread is buttered and it is suppertime at the end of this walk. By the time I get to the edge of the road, Frankly will be right by my feet looking as if it were entirely an accident that we should meet just there and it was Nothing At All To Do With Supper.

I always look forward to seeing Alex. He isn't handsome as such—tall and lanky with dark wavy hair and brown eyes—but after Danny's death, Alex was the first man who made my heart sing again. He is the kind of man you can't help being proud to be with and I love him with a passion that almost frightens me.

He is already home. I call out a greeting as I walk in through the unlocked door (no one ever locks their doors in Unityville). Frankly clatters past me on the wooden floor and goes to investigate in case Supper has already, magically, appeared in the kitchen. Alex is making tea.

But when he turns to face me the beloved eyes are cold and accusatory and his voice is charged: 'You chose the dog over me, Anna. You are not fit to be my wife.'

I wake shivering and sweating. The light of the moon is shining straight through the thin curtains across the bed, making me blink in added confusion. There is an eerie light everywhere as ghosts of the past haunt this room.

I must get up. Lying here will only make it worse. A cup of tea and some kind of distraction may take my mind off it.

The distraction turns out to be a piece of buttered toast and, deep in her sleep, Frankly's powerful nose scents the essence of food. I hear her get up, shake her ears and flop down onto the floor. Then the clatter of claws across the tiles and a cold wet nose is pushed into my hand.

Alex did not really say the words he spoke in my dream. But he might just as well have.

Frankly interrupts me by trying to steal the last mouthful of toast.

'Get down, you shark!' I say and my face creases into a laugh. 'You are a bad beagle.'

But no, she is a very good beagle. It's her job to steal food, just as much as it is to be furry and comforting and impossible.

She is a substitute child, of course. Neither Danny and I nor Alex and I ever had children. With Danny we were young and there wasn't that much time—and Alex already had two from his first marriage.

Alex did not leave his first wife for me. But the "blame" was transferred in his first wife's mind. Picking the children up for weekends or evenings was a minefield of closed faces and clipped

FOR THE LOVE OF DOG

words and, when the visits finally stopped, I was grateful, even if
Alex's anger increased.

In fact, come to think of it, Alex was quite enough to look after
without even thinking about children of our own. Funny how
you don't realise these things until later.

Stop it, Anna! Think of the good times. Think of Gilbert.
Think of the drag review.

That's better. I can feel my mouth curving up in a smile. Oh,
dear Gilbert! I am back in time again but this time I am laughing.

You can't miss Gilbert. He is tall, circular and he wears shorts.
That alone catches the eye but they are good legs; brown and
hairy and well shaped. That particular day, as I sat outside *The Die
Happy Café* with Frankly, sharing a scone, he came out to talk to
me about the iniquities of the coffee delivery man. As I listened, I
was struck by something rather odd.

'Gilbert, what has happened to your eyebrows?'

Gilbert's eyebrows are thick and dark like the rest of his hair.
Usually. Except this day they were thin and shaped like a woman's.

Was I mistaken, or was Gilbert blushing? The eyebrows were
fantastic but I was sure there was something even odder about
him, too.

Three things actually. One, Gilbert had suddenly got blue eyes,
two, he had plucked his eyebrows and three, he had shaved his legs.

The first is easy to explain: coloured contact lenses. The
eyebrows I'm not too concerned about. The legs, however, have
me beat.

'Why Gilbert? Why?'

'Can I trust you?' Gilbert looks hopeful. The answer, really,
was, 'That depends. If you have just killed your mother with a
chainsaw, then no'.

'Yes, of course,' I said.

'I'm taking part in a drag review tomorrow night,' he said. 'And
I need some female advice. I can't think what to wear.'

I always knew that Gilbert was gay—it was fairly obvious. It
was also fairly brave there in redneck country where men were real
men and women were grateful.

In the café it didn't really matter, as it was not a beef and burger

73

place and those were the kind of people who were more likely to ride the gay-boy out of town.

From there on, life started to get somewhat surreal. Ten minutes later, Frankly and I were inside Gilbert's apartment around the corner from the café.

It was a tiny little place filled with caged finches which started a cacophony of cheeping as soon as they heard his key in the door.

'There there, my darlings,' said Gilbert, going from cage to cage to greet each and every bird. Frankly followed him curiously, wondering what on earth was going on and standing on her back legs to stare at these fluttering things through the sides of each cage.

'Oh you're so cute!' said Gilbert, trying to hug her.

'Bugger Off!' said the beagle, backing away at full speed. 'Mum! A Barrage Balloon Is Trying To Abuse Me!'

I wandered around the apartment while Gilbert went off into his bedroom and I tried to work out why I felt like a mother who has been invited to the school play by a six-year-old.

'Come on through,' Gilbert called and I did, wondering what would meet my eyes. Red leopard skin wallpaper? Good grief! Gilbert's bedroom was a deep blue, decorated with photographs and paintings of beautiful young men, and the curtains and bedspread were in pale blue and pink chiffon. I blinked a little.

Meanwhile, Gilbert was rummaging through the wardrobe, bringing out enormous bras, high-heeled shoes and what looked like a box full of wigs.

'Well, it's an experience,' I thought, marshalling a group of thoughts that were running around in all directions and trying to hit the 'Emergency, please panic!' button in my brain.

But now he was standing in front of me, asking which dress I thought he should wear for the review. He held them up in front of him with an expression of mixed hope and embarrassment. Not that he was embarrassed about the idea of wearing a dress. Oh, no. It's just that he thought I might criticise his seamsmanship.

'You made them yourself?' I asked, amazed. One of the dresses was spangly royal blue with sequins and the other a deep, rich gold. They were of very simple but classic design—flattering to the woman of fuller figure.

'Well it's not really a good idea for a boy to shop for dresses in Unityville,' said Gilbert. I nodded wisely. He had a point.

We decided upon the gold one which was less sparkly and more classy. Once Gilbert had tried it on, it was obviously definitely the right choice. But it was a good thing that he shaved his legs.

Then it was the matter of which wig. The blonde, the red or the black. Each was tried on for my opinion.

All this felt like working with my computer: 'Please insert disc and close gate... No disc in drive A.' I had no suitable disc for this. My ego was frantically searching for a familiar, similar drive in which to file what my eyes reported seeing.

'Well?' said Gilbert.

'It's hard to judge,' I said tactfully. 'Without make-up on anything other than black looks rather funny.'

Gilbert gave me a big grin. 'The beard doesn't help, does it?' he says.

I do realise here that I have not mentioned Gilbert's beard before. It sort of slipped my mind as I was so used to seeing him with it. But come to think of it, it really wouldn't do with the dress.

We both giggled together. Gilbert's beard, like his own hair, was a rich natural black. It was wonderfully trimmed and shaped but it certainly did not do much for the image. He was planning to shave it off later.

'I think I prefer the black wig anyway,' he said, trying it on. And he was right. The long, straight tresses did suit him, beard and all. Gilbert would make a very pretty woman.

But the boobs. Oh boy, the boobs. Gilbert has two sets of boobs: one is a simple padded bra manufactured for cross-dressers and the other is one he made himself. The professional bra was good, he said, but there was no weight. I handled the vast expanse of nylon which was broad and deep and at least a DDD cup.

'It's a bit outside my scope!' I said, pointing to my own B-cups and laughing.

'Well I've got to dress up to my size,' said virtually circular Gilbert. 'They suit me this big. The problem is that they ride up and they just don't move properly. Your breasts move properly when you walk.'

'So I should hope!'

So, he showed me the second pair of boobs. These were just spheres which he fitted into a separate black, lacy bra. The boobs were the perfect weight, had wonderful movement and were encased in nylon stockings with a beautifully made nipple to show slightly through the clothing. I took them in my hands and scrunched them slightly, just about to make a comment on never having handled a woman's breasts before. Then I fell about laughing. The boobs were made of bird seed.

Gilbert joined in. 'I know it's ludicrous,' he said. 'But it works!'

'Gilbert,' I said. 'Thank you for this experience. I can't tell you how much I am enjoying myself.' And I meant it. This was pure joy in its own funny way.

'Thank *you*,' said Gilbert. 'There aren't very many people who can handle it.'

I was sure that he was right.

We moved on to shoes—and that was a fairly easy task. But I had forgotten Frankly. After examining the kitchen and the rest of the house for food (including the now famous lying on her side and stretching a tentative paw underneath the cooker), my would-be vacuum cleaner had decided that she wanted a game. After all, her walk had been rather curtailed. And what more exciting new toy could there be than a nylon boob filled with bird seed? Swiftly, she snatched it by the nipple and threw it across the room. Gilbert shrieked and leaped after her, forgetting his three-inch heels, and time slowed down as he flew impressively through the air, a look of comic dismay on his face. Frankly flinched, dropped the boob and backed away as the barrage balloon descended inexorably towards her.

Crash! Gilbert hit the floorboards and the boob simultaneously. Great swathes of birdseed exploded out of the nylon across the floor and Frankly dived away from the shrapnel of sunflower seeds just in time. I was torn between concern and amazement at the quivering of the golden mound on the floor as the shock waves flowed through the flab. Then Gilbert sat up gingerly, wig askew and one contact lens missing.

'Bummer,' he said, one brown eye and one blue eye blinking simultaneously. 'Got any spare pantyhose, darling?'

Chapter Five

THERE'S A PIG outside the front door, trying to kick it down.

I wake up to the sounds of snuffling and banging—it sounds as though two people with sinus trouble are having sex on the doorstep. Frankly, being underneath a pile of blankets, hasn't heard a thing.

So, I get up and walk rather uncertainly to the door, pulling my wrap around me.

'Hello?' I go, somewhat cautiously.

The banging stops for a moment—as does the snuffling. But just for a moment. Then a series of grunts splits the air and the door is very soundly kicked.

This, Frankly *has* heard. Now she is right behind me, peering round my knees at where the door is vibrating.

We look at each other rather uncertainly. Should I Bark? asks the beagle.

'Yes, I think so.'

'Okay.' She checks my knees for solidity and begins to bell as only a hound can.

'*WoWoWoWo*! Go Away! This Is My House!

'Or Else,' she adds, rather uncertainly.

The kicking stops. For a moment. Then starts again just as firmly.

'Frankly, stay!' I say kindly, so she doesn't have to pretend she's brave.

It must be some kind of animal. Logic says, with the snorting and grunting, that it would be a pig.

And so it proves to be.

I open the top half of the stable-type door and peer over it.

The pig looks up at me with bright, twinkling eyes. '*Grunt*!' it goes expectantly. And kicks the door firmly with one neat cloven hoof.

It's a fairly big pig. The sort that could knock you over with one barge. And, having got my attention now, it's really rather excited.

It rears itself up on its hind legs and I just have time to back off before a fairly friendly but decidedly assertive head with snout and bristles pushes itself forward. Both front hooves are locked over the top of the door and the grunting intensifies.

Frankly goes ballistic. 'What The Hell Is That? Bugger Off You *Thing* You!' She is roaring at the top of her lungs but the pig is ignoring her completely. Instead it looks at me interrogatively, nodding its head and smacking its lips. It obviously expects some food.

I back away and fetch the crust of yesterday's bread. This is probably stupid, as the pig will realise that it's onto a good thing and may kick all the more, but there seems to be no alternative. I hand the bread over cautiously and the pig takes it with surprising grace. Then with one final grunt, she drops down to four legs again and, to my immense relief, trundles off.

'*Wo Wo Wo!*' Frankly is still belling, horrified. Not only has this monster attacked her house, it has actually been fed! This is a national disgrace.

With a big grin, I placate her with her breakfast which she eats in ravenous snatches, tail clamped to her backside and looking around as if she expects a monster to steal it from her at any second.

She takes a little encouragement to go out into the little courtyard for a pee (and I'm a bit wary myself). But I peek up and down the steep street at the end of the house and there's no sign of the pig.

'Come on Frankly,' I say. 'Let's go and find out.'

We climb our way up the steep cobbles, avoiding the fresh goat and sheep dung, and make our way along to *La Posada*. Katherine is there with her wonderful ability to provide tea or coffee at the drop of a hat and to explain whatever vagaries the village has thrown up overnight.

The idea of a pig trying to break my door down doesn't faze her at all.

'Oh! Is Rosina back?' she says in tones of delight. 'That's wonderful. Everyone will be so pleased.'

I ponder this as the tea is made and Katherine fusses around, offering dry Spanish biscuits and some Cadbury's chocolate sent by her son in England. Frankly is already on the cushioned window-ledge but the chocolate is just too tempting. I swat her automatically as the nose looms over the table and she retires resentfully to the furthest edge of the window seat.

'Rosina?' I say with a slight inflection meaning 'Who or what the hell is Rosina and just how dangerous is she?'

Katherine sits down peacefully with her own coffee and begins the story.

Rosina is the village pig. Obvious, really, but there it is. However, she doesn't have a sty or a home because she is communal property. She was given to the village by the mayor last year and everyone feeds her. When the fiesta comes in two months time, there will be a raffle for Rosina and she will be slaughtered and roasted on a spit. The winning family gets half the meat and the rest is shared by the village.

Except that two weeks ago she vanished.

There was a frantic search, then uproar and people from the next village up the mountain were accused of stealing her. Nothing but bad-will transpired from that but Rosina had just vanished.

Now, if she's back, the whole village will be delighted. Apart, that is, from the dogs and cats which she bullies in a firm but friendly manner. If there's food in the street and Rosina has seen it, anything that gets in her way is in for a butting.

For once, my visit to Katherine's is curtailed as she wants to go out and spread the good news. Frankly and I go for our morning walk along the path with the century plants and past the little spring and the reservoir where the mule drank.

The century plants look like mutant aloe vera: huge cactus-like things, bigger than me, that flower once in a lifetime, throwing out what looks like a tree of dull flowers on a huge trunk. Once that is done, the whole of the plant is exhausted and it dies. It's not pretty but it's getting to be a familiar and friendly sight as we walk.

I have put my hair up—it's the only thing to do in this heat. The light breeze is pleasant on the back of my neck but the heat is still searing. Sweat is the norm out here.

As we walk, swallows and flocks of pigeons dive past and continue their flight below us, just above the morning mist that is rolling out towards the sea revealing terrace after terrace of almond trees interspersed with prickly pear, tangerine trees, the pale, bright green foliage of spruces and patterns of broken dry stone walls.

Lazy wasps buzz around the fallen prickly pears on the path. In the first days I would almost dance along these pathways to avoid the fallen pears, the mule dung and the sheep droppings. But now I find that the pears are very satisfying to step on—a crunch and squidge as the fruit spurts out into the dust. A bit like ex-husbands' brains really.

The rocks that show through the earth are a strange combination of rusty red and deep blue slate with the pale beige soil scattered all over it. Wonderful colour combinations merge and match with the dark green of the olive and almond leaves, the grey and brown stumps of dead trees and bushes and the glorious colours of the fading autumn flowers. The bright morning sun slants down from the sky forming beams through the branches of tall, unidentifiable mixtures of spruce and oak. From deep inside the coolness of the branches a still, silent green lizard watches me with an unblinking eye.

As we turn the corner past the reservoir, I can look back at Los Poops snuggling happily into the hillside. From here it is all white walls and red terracotta roofs, an idyllic view. The vines in the fields above the village are neatly laid out and heavy with fruit as are the many roof gardens in the village. They show bright splashes of colour where the clumps of grapes are covered with plastic bags or pieces of rag to keep away the insects.

There is Cosima, walking slowly along the street above the church to her daughter's house. Every morning at this time she takes that exact route with a gift of grapes or home-made bread. Her daughter is a high-flyer by Los Poops' standards, with a job in Motril five days a week, and her mother tidies and dusts the house for her and is always there when seven-year-old José comes home from school. There is no husband and I don't know if there ever was one. That kind of question would be completely out of order until I have lived here for at least six months—always assuming my Los Poopian Spanish develops enough to be understood. However I am, already, learning a little of life here. There is no husband now, therefore it is irrelevant who or what he might have been. I have no husband now either and the white mark on my wedding ring finger is already beginning to fade.

How light that hand felt without those three rings: the simple gold band which was once my greatest possession in the world; the ruby engagement ring and the seven-stone eternity ring.

I stop on the path and laugh out loud. Eternity ring! How ridiculous! Eternity indeed! If eternity exists it is in the landscape around me, not in a man's empty promises.

Here or there, by the path where there is some land that has become uncultivated—perhaps the owner is dead?—there are also vines, some of which have run wild but are still thick with fruit dotted and marked by everyday life in the wild. Dusty red stems and strong leathery leaves and the inexpressible sweetness of sun-kissed fruit stolen from the wayside.

I stop for what must be five whole minutes to look at the beauty of just one fallen vine leaf which could have been made from suede. It is chestnut, gold and green; mottled in such a perfection of design that it could be the most expensive *cloisonné*. On the other side, it is amber parchment with darker veins and still a touch of green from when it had full life.

Across the rift valley before me I can see parallel paths and terraces, burnt-black shafts of almond tree trunks and grey landslips mingling with tiny valleys where rivulets run in spring.

The sound of children tap-dancing in clogs creeps into my consciousness. Frankly hears it too and raises her head from an interesting smell at the base of a century plant. A couple of soft 'clonks' reveals the sound to be the village sheep and goats approaching along the path. They are in sight before I can catch Frankly and my heart sinks. What if she tries to chase them?

The first sheep sees her and, I swear, its ears flatten like those of an angry horse. It is a venerable beast; a huge, sheared ewe with mad eyes and a great roman nose. Before I can do anything, it has marched up to Frankly and lowered its face to hers. Frankly stands transfixed as the sheep appears to lean against her, forehead to forehead, daring her to move. Cheerfully, the other sheep trot past with barely a look in Frankly's direction. They know that the Alpha Sheep has the situation in hand.

The two scruffy sheep dogs too, take no notice. Usually they threaten and roar at Frankly on sight but, today, everyone is doing their job.

The shepherd comes last; a young man burnt almost black by the blinding sun. He is dressed in an outfit that could have come from centuries ago, including a thin and ancient sheepskin over his shoulders. He smiles at me with white, almost perfect teeth and the deep brown eyes are friendly.

'*Hola.*'

'*Hola.*'

He says something else but I can't catch it; something about *la perrita*'(the little dog) but it sounds reassuring so I just smile. I think we hold eyes just a second too long, if you know what I mean. Then he is past me and the great, old ewe is backing away from Frankly, who still stands as still as she can. The sheep snorts, scrapes a cloven hoof on the ground and trots after her herd.

For a moment Frankly doesn't move and then she airily sniffs a nearby bush, darting me a quick look to see if I have noticed how coolly she is taking all this.

'Oh Frankly!' I say kindly, sitting down on a rock and holding my hands out to her. She is there at once, letting go of the cool façade. I stroke her face and scratch her ears and she is whiffling in response.

Mum, I've Been Assaulted By a Sheep And A Pig! All In One Day. It's Not Fair. When Are We Going Home? she says.

'We are home darling.' And, for a moment, with the warmth of the sun on my shoulders and the clear, warm breeze caressing us both, I believe it.

But we are not home. England is home, whether I like it or not. And there are things to be done.

If I am going to take Frankly back to the UK, I have to get her a passport. Which is why, later that day, we are sitting in the offices of a very pleasant young vet in Almeria, about thirty miles from Los Poops. Or at least I am sitting and Frankly is cowering.

She has, in all honesty, had a bit of a day. But even if she hadn't been beaten up by a pig and a sheep it would still be important to Frankly that she should be seen to cower in a vet's office just to let people know how cruel I am in Constantly Submitting Her To Abuse.

It is similar to her I'm Not Loved And Not Fed pose to virtually anyone who has food anywhere on their person. And the vet's receptionist has got an open jar of dog biscuits. I would bet serious money on at least three of them finding their way into Frankly's stomach before we have left.

I once saw Frankly charm a cocktail-size raspberry pavlova from the hand of a hardened Hell's Angel simply by turning those great, pathetic brown eyes on him. It may be that he wasn't sure what to do with a raspberry pavlova himself but he was as helpless as a baby once Frankly had achieved eye contact.

So it is with the receptionist. The sheer cuteness of the little foreign dog, together with its obvious deep misery, charm her into a hypnotic trance and biscuits find themselves fulfilling their true destiny in Frankly's tummy.

I can't blame her for not being happy at the vet's. What dog is? And, in recent years, Frankly has almost been right about Constant Abuse in that she has had to be examined right, left and centre by a series of vets in order to get the appropriate certificates for emigration, not to mention being like a pincushion from all the rabies jabs. There was one to leave England for America, regular ones out there and another to fulfil the regulations in order to be able to come from America to Spain—and the law says she has to have yet another to get into the UK. No matter that the previous two are still valid—the appropriate authorities live by the letter, not the spirit, of the law.

As I wait for the vet my mind goes back to the horrors of getting Frankly out of Colorado. You'd have thought it would have been simple, but no. The only thing that was simple was human error—and through my mistake she was nearly left behind.

The problem was the Spanish Embassy. They required a health certificate and an export certificate (in Spanish) and official ratification of the two from the State Vet. Both of these had to be obtained fewer than ten days before departure and sent to California for further verification. Which meant getting them to San Francisco and back to Colorado in eight days. You can do that—there is a UPS service which will deliver and pick up—but I forgot to enclose the fee. The fee was $3. And because I forgot it, the Spanish Embassy stuck the certificates at the bottom of the pile and forgot about them.

Without Alex being in Colorado I had no right to stay on—and no money to re-book my flight—so this was a true emergency.

Ella had a friend who spoke Mexican Spanish so we did get everything translated—and Carmen phoned the Spanish Embassy two days before I was due to leave to ask what had happened to the certificate.

So, they wouldn't release it without the $3. And there wasn't time to send the money to them (which would cost $25 to do by FedEx or UPS). So, they said, there was nothing they could do. Frankly could not be permitted to go to Spain.

'Time for lateral thinking,' said Ella as I sat, white-faced and shaking, on Carmen's sofa. Frankly was lying peacefully on the carpet, dozing in the sun.

First Ella telephoned couriers in San Francisco. If she placed an order with them, would they bike round $3? No, they wouldn't.

She phoned a florist. If she ordered a bouquet of flowers to be sent to the woman at the Spanish Embassy, would they put $3 in? No, they wouldn't.

She phoned an old acquaintance. Would he go round to the Spanish Consulate and give them $3 which she would pay him back? Sorry, he's really busy right now; maybe tomorrow.

Carmen, Ella and I sat quietly for a moment. I remember having that strange feeling of unreality.

'Anna, you know I'd take her if the worst came to the worst,' said Ella. 'I could bring her over later on.'

I smiled weakly. What a generous offer. But leaving Frankly at all would be like losing a limb.

'Carmen, did the woman at the Consulate speak any English at all?' asked Ella.

'The woman with the forms does,' said Carmen.

'Anna, talk to her yourself,' said Ella. 'But pray first.'

'Pray?'

'There isn't any better option,' said Ella. 'Remember the evangelists who got your car open in Los Angeles.'

So I nodded and sent up a prayer to who or whatever is the patron saint of getting dogs safely to Spain.

Carmen phoned again and used her Spanish to get through to the right department. Then I was speaking to the woman who held Frankly's future in her hands.

And she was helpful. She suggested that we got a money order, photocopied it and the FedEx order and sent it to her and faxed proof of that to her that day. Once she had proof that the money was on its way, she would release the forms and UPS would get them back to me the following morning.

I thanked her very quietly, took the fax number and put the phone down with my hands shaking.

Ella and Carmen did the rest. I didn't even know how to get this money order but they were out in the car within minutes and all Frankly and I had to do was wait. Frankly yawned a lot and scratched some imaginary fleas.

In an hour they were back, saying it was all done. We phoned the Spanish Consulate again and the woman said yes, she had the fax and yes, she was releasing the forms.

I cried then and cuddled Frankly who was, frankly, pissed off at such an unnecessary show of sentiment.

The Pet Travel Scheme for the UK requires her to have a microchip then a vaccination and then a blood test. If a rabies microbe came within a mile of Frankly already, it would expire in a puff of smoke.

It has been an interesting challenge finding a vet who has all the equipment for microchipping and who has the knowledge of what we have to do. That's why we're in Almeria and not in one of the local towns near Los Poops.

Even so, Juan does not want to do it. I am in complete sympathy with him but I am trying to explain that it has to be done. I have even shown him the Ministry of Agriculture website to show the instructions but he is digging his heels in all the same.

Please God, not another problem. Please.

Thank God Juan speaks English. I dread to think what this would be like in my Spanglish.

'She doesn't need a vaccination,' he says for the third time. 'She is immune.'

'Yes I know. But it has to be done. Then we have to wait a month and have the blood test taken.'

'But it is a month since her last vaccination in America. Why not give her the microchip and take the test now?'

'Yes, that would be very sensible…'

'Then we will do it.'

'We can't. It's against the rules.'

'Pah! The rules are stupid!'

This is a very Spanish attitude and it is such a tempting one.

'Why do you want to spend unnecessary money?'

'I don't,' (believe me, I don't!).

'Then we will give the dog the microchip and the certificate and send her blood off today.'

'Without the vaccination? But…'

'Yes. I will give you the certificate for the inoculation without the inoculation.'

'But it has to be dated after the microchip.'

'I will date it after the microchip.'

'Okay.'

Suddenly I am beaten. This perfectly pleasant man is prepared to perjure himself in order to save me money and Frankly from having more holes than a sieve. What the hell. It's his soul and surely any benevolent God would forgive this act offered from the heart of kindness? All I need is the documentation.

So Frankly is microchipped. It takes just a second and she is distracted by a dog treat so not even she can complain about it (much). Then comes the blood test and she watches in complete fascination as Juan draws blood from her front leg. It can't hurt or she would be whingeing. Instead she is looking at the syringe and then at me and back at the syringe.

What The Hell Is He Doing Mum?

The brow is wrinkled with puzzlement. Once it is over, she leans forward and sniffs the plastic cautiously and only starts to fuss when Juan tries to put a pad of antiseptic on her leg. This Is More Like It. This Is Real Abuse, she says, wriggling and complaining loudly.

The blood test is packaged up while she is still grumbling and pretending that she doesn't want the chew that Juan has given her to make up for the horrendous pain of having her leg swabbed. And now all we have to do is wait for a month for the test to come back from the laboratory in Santa Fé.

That was simple. Totally anti-establishment but simple. Delightfully, confusingly, Spanish.

We stop for a walk on the beach on the way back and Frankly remembers to limp for a whole two minutes. With the wrong leg.

Tonight I am having supper with Rani and Sylvia. They are the ones who (according to Stella) have an open marriage. I haven't met Rani yet but Sylvia wafted up to me in the main square yesterday and introduced herself.

She's one of those pleasantly vague women who would wear a kaftan if anyone still made them, who doesn't seem to wear a bra and whose skirt has tassels on it. Her hair is faded brown and her eyes a clear and surprising blue with a mass of laughter lines around them. She takes my arm, which is a little off-putting, and coos a bit much over Frankly who takes no notice whatsoever but I have a feeling that underneath the New Age appearance she is what we Brits would call 'a good egg.'

Rani and Sylvia live in a deceptively small-looking house right in the heart of the village and, from the point of view of smell and flies, worryingly near to a mule stable. I have left Frankly at home tonight—because Rani has asthma—and, having discovered that the door to the bedroom will not shut properly, I can be fairly sure that I will go home to find a furry canine hot-water bottle halfway down my bed.

I gather that Sylvia and Rani are vegetarian but I am confident that you can't get tofu or bean sprouts anywhere around here. Then I check myself and realise that I am thinking Alex's thoughts, not mine. He is the one who is fiercely carnivorous, not me. I shake my head in surprised disgust; how much more necessary disentangling of body, mind and spirit is there to come?

They give me a lovely welcome with a glass of local wine from their own private barrel. It tastes like appalling sherry but it is obviously lethal and supplies are going to be ample. The house is lovely, very open and simply decorated with the traditional blue and white tiles of the area and curtains and a cloth on the large kitchen table which try very hard to match and fail in a way that is utterly charming.

We will be eating in the kitchen where Rani is chopping vegetables and throwing them skilfully into a huge cauldron full of steaming beans and lentils. It all smells very good. He is a tall, painfully thin man with hollow cheekbones, abundant black hair in a ponytail and a carefully shaped beard which encircles his mouth but leaves the cheeks bare. For all that, he has a magnetism. My hand is shaken vigorously, if briefly, in greeting and I sit watching his obvious joy in cooking while I sip my wine and listen to Sylvia's discourse on how they found the house derelict and fitted it out on a shoestring.

This is a nice place. These are real people. I could spill my supper down my front or on the floor and neither of them would mind.

It may be the wine talking because the excellence of the evening is certainly tempered by the ample availability of wine—together with the universally acknowledged delight that in Los Poops nobody has to drive home.

And even if they did, they would probably find the local cop even drunker at the wheel of his patrol car.

Sylvia and Rani did live in a commune once—at Findhorn in Forres, Scotland. They are pleased that I have heard of it and even that I had friends who used to go to workshops there. It broke up their marriage because the husband loved it and the wife never really took to it. Lorraine always blamed the New Age for the break-up—and pretty well anything else after that.

The man's name is winkled out of me and Rani gives a snort of derision.

'Lucky woman,' he says. 'I hope she realised her good fortune.'

I am fascinated, having expected some New Age guff about the marriage not being what was needed to take the couple into (or up to) their higher selves.

'No, she didn't. She took it rather badly,' I say, remembering that I, myself, have taken Alex's leaving rather badly.

'Well, he's left two other women in exactly the same way since,' says Rani. 'He's one of the ones who gives the New Age a bad name. Spouts the theory right left and centre…' he waves a ladle around slightly wildly, spilling drops of casserole over the cooker. 'But can't apply a sodding word of it in real life.

'You know the type—talks a lot of bollocks about community and partnership and honesty and can't even love the woman who's right in front of him.'

'I hope he isn't a particular friend of yours,' says Sylvia, tactfully.

'Not now he isn't,' I say, rather enjoying this and taking another sip of wine.

It emerges over supper that Rani and Sylvia aren't 'together' at all. They are just two good friends who share a house in Los Poops. This rather kyboshes Stella's idea that they have an open marriage.

'So why aren't you together, if you like each other enough to set up home together?' I ask (the wine has been flowing). 'It would seem like a sensible next step.'

'Never even considered it,' says Rani and Sylvia smiles. I believe it's true.

'But doesn't it stop you finding someone you might want to set up with?'

'Probably. Maybe that's a part of it,' says Sylvia. 'We've both had relationships; both been married. I think we find this a lot more peaceful.'

'Almost like a celibate marriage?'

'Oh no!' They are both very clear about that. I can't say that I am but I am enjoying their relaxed company.

'What about you?' says Rani. 'What will you do? Do you want to marry again?'

Golly, I don't know.

'Yes,' I say, tentatively. 'But I don't quite know how that could happen. It still seems really odd that vows I made for life are just discounted now. I was raised a Catholic. That probably has something to do with it.'

'Are you okay to talk about this?' Sylvia is clearing plates. 'We have a nice, stodgy comfort pudding if it would help!'

It would help.

'Nursery food?' I say hopefully and they both laugh.

'Oh, do you remember? The days when your mother was the best cook in the world!' says Rani.

'Oh yes. My mum made the best treacle pudding and chocolate cake. Nothing out of a packet,' I say. 'What kind of things did your Mum make?'

'Indian kulfi,' says Rani. 'But she did a mean rice pudding too. Crammed full of cream. We were very much a colonial family. We did the cholesterol. Big time.'

Sylvia approaches the table with what looks like a chocolate cheesecake. It isn't—quite—but whatever it is, it's utterly delicious. We have a brief but spirited discussion on what you can and cannot buy to eat in Los Poops and the surrounding areas. Marscapone, for example, is seriously not on the agenda and you have to drive all the way to Motril for fresh milk, let alone cream.

'Long Life milk rules,' says Sylvia with a sigh. 'But the fish is good—if you eat fish of course—and if you've got transport. There are still fishermen who bring their boats up on the shore down on the coast and if you're waiting for them, they'll sell you the best of their catch for what they think is a ridiculously high price but is well worth it.'

'What time would that need to be?'

'About half-past six in the morning.'

'So do you ever do it or do you not eat fish either?'

'Bit of a moot point,' says Rani. 'I don't, Sylvia does.'

'How long have you been here?'

'Six years.'

'And did you "live together" before?'

'Oh yes, at Findhorn.'

'Oh—of course. It just seems so ironic that you're not "together" but you've lasted better than Alex and me who were supposed to be in love.'

'Will you get divorced?'

'I suppose so—but Alex wants me to pay for half the divorce costs—and I won't. I didn't get any choice in the matter, not even a discussion that there was anything wrong with the marriage. I knew there were problems but I didn't have any part in the actual ending of it.'

Fiercely I take another mouthful of cheesecake. It is scrumptious.

'I wonder,' says Rani, thoughtfully. 'Perhaps, you just outgrew him.'

'Me? But I didn't leave him!'

'No, but you may have created his leaving you because you didn't need him any more. Because he was holding you back. That's what I mean.'

'How on earth would I do that?'

'Well, you wouldn't do it on earth. It would be a spiritual thing.'

'Ah.' I don't see and I don't think I want to see. Rani looks at me with a smile.

'I'll shut up,' he says kindly. 'Coffee?'

But walking home, I find I rather like the idea that I outgrew Alex, not that I failed him. Because there is a part of me that worries that I did fail him—he said that I didn't understand enough; that I was too stubborn. But perhaps I outgrew him and he knew that.

I try a little skip across the square. It's after midnight and the stars are glittering above me. I am happy. Drunk, yes, but happy. I have friends and I feel safe here.

Chapter Six

DEAREST ANNA,

Where are you? Did you get to Europe? Is the house okay? Have you found a wonderful Spanish lover to heal your heart? Is Frankly still as stinky?

Do get in touch, darling. I'm worried.

Business first:

The Bastard has been in touch. He phoned the real estate broker to see where you were (the new folk have moved in to your old place by the way—they have a cute three-year-old little girl and a black lab) and they put him on to me as we agreed.

Hey Anna, I don't think he'll be calling me again! What an asshole. Mind you, you were right. He could talk a racoon round. He almost had ME believing that you knew all along that the marriage was over. And he tried that pathetic line that all men do that 'it's all for the best.'

'Sure it is,' I told him. 'Anything that gets an asshole like you out of the life of a decent, honest woman is for the best.

'The one thing that's really important though,' I said, 'is that you aren't such a crap-head as to be the one that tries to tells her that. She has to work it out for herself.'

I told him, too, that sending you a letter saying that the marriage was over was just the behaviour of a moron. And a cowardly one at that. You know what he said? He said that Phil Collins sent his wife a fax to say their marriage was over and he couldn't see any problem with it at all.

'Alex,' I said. 'You can always learn from a master. So, now you know and, when the time comes, as it surely will, that you dump this next poor woman, you can do it by fax.'

He didn't like that. Can't imagine why. I also told him

that you didn't want anything more to do with him (as if he hadn't noticed that!).

'Alex,' I said. 'Insanity is doing the same thing over and over and expecting a different result. This is number three in the identical self-same pattern, isn't it? You could try learning something next time, hey? The rest of the planet is getting bored.'

But Hon, he wants that divorce. I know you don't want to cite him (and I don't quite get the rules in the UK but I gather that if you don't cite, he can't get a divorce for two years. Is that right?). Anyway, he wants out. Are you sure you want to stay tied up to such a loser? Why not just get out yourself?

Okay, it's easy for me to say but what's the point? He ain't coming back, Hon. And frankly (!) you don't want him.

So, anyway, he still doesn't know where you are. And I could tell him perfectly honestly that I didn't know either. For all he knows you could still be in the States. Good thing you changed your email address while you were here.

Do get in touch, Hon. I miss ya!
Love and hugs,
Ella.

Anna Dearest,

Well, it's not the same without you! God I wish you were still here. I need a new chef. We had the Health Inspector round on Friday. Oh my dear! You know how awful they are—I took a sink out and one year that was fine and the next year they threatened to close me down if I didn't put it back. And the year after they threatened closure again simply because I hadn't had it plumbed in!

So, anyway, the inspector comes. Some total anal-retentive called Diane Williams. I'm in the office and by some dark angel's decree, Terry is out the front.

'The fucking bitch is here now!' he shouts and walks back into the kitchen.

Ooooh! I could have died!

Even that's not as bad as what he said to her later on. I asked him to take care of her for a while when I ran out to the hardware store to get the seals she demanded for the fridge (I know, I know, Anna darling, but really there wasn't anyone else around).

Just as I left I heard him asking her if she gave good head.

I don't think she understood. After all, she is from Iowa. But I don't think that we will get a good report.

I'm closing down for a week. There's a 'restaurateur's convention' in Missouri and I simply have to go. Actually it's just a group of old Queens like me getting together to sing and dance. Wow! There's no one to leave in charge here and I'll lose less trade by closing than just leaving it with the girls.

Let me know the news. Any cute cross-dressers in Spain?
Gilbert

Dear Anna,

How are you? Grace and the children send their love. We were so sorry to hear about you and Alex splitting up.

How is Spain? I gather that you are staying at Ben Taylor's house. Do you need anything sent over? Do you want visitors? We'd love to come out and visit sometime. Haven't seen my little sister for more than two years now!

In fact I have had an email from Alex, asking me to forward it to you. Do you want me to? The gist of it is that he wants to meet you for 'candid but amicable talks' to resolve the situation and get a divorce going.

Whatever you want. Of course, he doesn't have a leg to stand on—no grounds against you whatsoever so it's completely up to you. He has given me the name of his girlfriend so you can name her if you do decide to file. That is necessary because otherwise the suit might not go through or, at least, there would be delays.

We are all fine. The tree house fell down in the last

*storm—luckily no one was sleeping in it at the time!
Perhaps Grace will be less keen on me putting up the
shelves in the dining room now she has confirmation of
my workmanship.*

*Mum sends her love. She was over for the weekend and
told us your news.*

Love,
Richard.

Dearest Anna,

*No, you don't want to do that! Dumping crockery is
one thing… I know you want to boil Alex in oil. Quite
natural. But, believe me, the revenge sites on the Internet
are not the answer! Sending him dog poo or stinky fish—
or even arranging for someone to smash his windows—
sounds great at 3am but, Honey, it wouldn't work out for
you. Trust me.*

*Let me tell you about when I left Rob. I found out that
he was sleeping with this little tart from Saratoga. She was
about 18 and of course she didn't care. They don't. They
operate on the 'a hard man is good to find' theory. This
Suzie of Alex's will be just the same. She'll be editing the
story he's told her in her head to make it everyone else's fault
but his. I'm sorry, Hon, but for the moment you are just
categorized as 'bitch ex-wife.' It's tough but there's nothing
you can do right now. You'd have done the same at her age.
Imagine if you met Alex now; after this experience, you'll
take any man's story with a pinch of salt.*

*Anyway… I went round to Rob's place and peed on his
bed (honestly!). I smashed his beer and whisky bottles all
over the furniture. I tore his clothes up. I smeared cat shit
all over his kitchen.*

*Then I went round to where the girl worked, in the
middle of the night, and painted a message on the door
saying what she was.*

*And believe me, Hon, it didn't help. All that happened
was that I felt dreadful the next day and other people*

thought I was a psycho and that he was well out of it. The sympathy vote is useful. Use it, don't lose it!

In haste,

Ella.

P.S. I've heard of Watlington P. Risborough. His wife is on pretty well every social committee in Washington— and most of the ones in Denver. Seriously rich. Seriously married! Careful, Hon. Remember that they are basically all bastards, after what they can get. If you do go for dinner, don't tell anyone; go out of the village to somewhere really public so no one can say it's clandestine if they see you— and watch yourself. You're seriously vulnerable right now and you know what those cowboys are like.

Dear Anna,

Thank you for your message. I have passed the gist of it on to Alex—basically that you refuse to cite against him because doing that would mean that you had to pay for a divorce and, as he was the one who ended the marriage without consulting you, you think that he should be the one to pay.

I don't mind acting as a mediator for you—but I have to say that Alex isn't keen. He thinks that I would be biased towards you so he is going to come back with some suggestions of mutual friends.

Hope this is okay.

Love,

Richard.

Dear Mrs. Marks,

Thank you for your communication of 27th August. However, I'm afraid that I cannot help you in this respect. The $320,000 balance from the sale of your house in Colorado, USA, was paid into your savings account as arranged with the agent. As you are both individual signatories on the account, Mr. Marks was perfectly entitled to transfer the money to another account.

With reference to your joint accounts, we need a letter signed by both parties to change any of the details, including taking one party's name off the account or closing it.

Therefore, in both instances, I am afraid that you will have to take the matter up with your husband.

I am sorry not to have been more assistance.

Yours sincerely,

Rebecca Phelps,

Mid-West Bank.

Dear Anna,

I'm so sorry but I haven't had any joy with Alex over the money for the house. I telephoned him yesterday but he was adamant, saying that he would give you your half when the divorce is through.

Obviously, he can't do that legally but sorting it out may be difficult with you in Spain. Do you want me to get a friend of mine who's a solicitor to take a look at the case? I think that if it goes to court, you would have to come over; but hopefully it won't get to that. Can you write out an account of the situation together with all the agent's details and the bank details and I'll pass it on to Joe Kenton for you. He'll be able to advise you.

Are you okay financially for the moment? Let me know if you need to borrow any money in the meantime.

Incidentally, Alex has suggested William Johnson as his preferred intermediary. He was best man at your wedding, I think. Apparently you have his email address.

Love,

Richard.

Dearest Anna,

Yes, it's perfectly possible that Suzie is pregnant and that's why he wants a quick divorce. Oh God, darling! This is just such shit. But we don't know it for sure. We don't know anything. He may just want just to get the whole thing over with.

Even an asshole like Alex has feelings and he can't be feeling very good about things as they stand. Okay, he thinks it was fine to leave you—and to do it the way he did—but he doesn't like the way it's worked out or the way people are reacting to him.

He just wants to get it all behind him so he can pretend it never happened.

I don't think your old friends will be rushing to his door but then he'll be in with Suzie's family instead. They do that kind of thing.

God, we are so blind. I let Ross do that to me (my first husband). He kinda adopted my whole family and it wasn't until we split that I realised that he wanted my folks because his own had seen through him and he couldn't get away with the charm offensive any more.

Damn good thing Alex doesn't know where you are.

Incidentally, where the hell are you? I can't find Los Poops on the map. It sounds a real cute place apart from all the animal crap.

Perhaps we should tell Alex that you're a suspect in a murder case. That might scare him a little!

Much love,

Ella.

PS. Yes, I hope she dumps him too. Sadly, not likely. Not the pattern is it? Anyway, if he charmed someone with as much sense as you, he can do it again. It sucks but it's the way of the world.

PPS. Who the heck is Jack and why did you want to look through the windows of his house??!

Dear Mrs Marks,

Thank you for your letter. I have written to your husband about the joint monies from the sale of your house in Colorado and hope to have the matter resolved soon.

Yours sincerely,

Joe Kenton

Kenton, Phillips and Jones, Solicitors.

Dear Anna,

Hope you're fine. The convention was great! I finally met up with Dane! He's the guy I've been being having cyber-sex with this last year. And he is faaaaabulous! We had a drink together on the first night but he was real busy the rest of the time, having set up a load of meetings in advance.

Gee, I think I'm in love. I haven't heard from him in a week so I've sent him a long letter telling him just how I feel and asking him to come and stay. I can't wait! The real thing would be just amazing.

Love,

Gilbert.

PS. Terry took one too many the other night and got into a real serious fight. When he's out of hospital looks like he'll be in jail. Something about some woman I expect. The other guy will make it but it was close. Looks like I need a new chef. Wanna come back and take over?

Chapter Seven

It's Too Friggin' Hot. The reproach exudes from every pore of the beagle as she lies spread-eagled on the cool stone flags of the kitchen of our tiny home.

Bloody Flies! She adds with a shake of her ears and a filthy look thrown in my direction. A noxious fart will follow, as sure as eggs is eggs. And bad eggs at that.

The trouble is that it *is* too hot for her, especially now that even the Spaniards admit that we are in the middle of a heat wave. Frankly is fading visibly in the heat. It is actually hotter than the summer in Colorado. It is Too Hot to lie in the sunshine and steam. It is Too Hot to fossick in the undergrowth (What Undergrowth?). It is Too Hot To Eat.

Too hot to eat? Yes, Frankly is seriously off her food. Even the cunningly reconstituted Spanish *Chappi* (sic) got the no-no this morning. She backed off almost apologetically and clambered wearily back onto my bed where she posed miserably as Going To Die Any Moment And It's All Your Fault.

The trouble is that I believe it. A beagle that won't eat? Impossible!

Please God, let it just be the heat. If there is something else wrong; something serious, then I just don't know what I shall do.

Temper wins out over pathos. I shall be bloody annoyed if she expires before I've got her back to the UK. Much as I love her and much as I am running away from the whole Alex situation by being here, some of this *is* a real pain and if it's all for nothing I shall be mad as fire, not to mention embarrassed and miserable.

The other worrying symptom of Frankly's imminent demise is the running stream of sound effects with which her stomach is serenading the surrounding air. I've never heard so many gurgles that did not come from water going down the bath plug.

What if she's been poisoned already like those other village dogs? What if she's got a galloping stomach infection? What if she farts herself to death?

George is reassuring when I go up to *La Posada* for my emails. He says that Frankly is just being affected by the heat and that all dogs gurgle over ninety degrees. His certainly do.

We discuss buying chickens. His dogs are fed on chicken feet, innards and heads, all boiled up until they are gooey. The 'good' bits of the chicken are served up to *La Posada*'s guests—although I have still to see any evidence that such guests might exist.

I've heard that dogs in the wild would eat their prey's stomach contents first of all to get the essential vegetable nutrients not available in just raw meat, so it sounds good but I don't think that I have ever seen a chicken's stomach.

'No problem that,' says George. 'You get the stomachs and everything in the chickens down at the shop.'

That shop reveals more hidden depths every time I go in there. It's still a nerve-wracking experience because my Spanish is progressing very slowly and I can't make myself understood. Apart from that, I'm shopping with a bunch of possible murderers which, with the best will in the world, makes one feel slightly uneasy. What if my lousy Spanish accidentally upsets someone? They say that it gets easier to kill each time and all I have to do is accidentally mispronounce something and find that instead of saying 'Can I have some cheese please?' I've said 'Your mother is a misbegotten whore.' It could happen. Except that while *I* think that *they* are probably murderers, *they* appear to imply to anyone passing that *I* am the culprit. This could be classic double-bluff but it's somewhat disconcerting all the same.

The conversation always dies down when I go in to the shop— apart from the odd remark made in a low tone. I seem to recognise the phrase: 'That's the woman who poisoned Aldo the Builder' rather more often than I'd like.

Just call me the scapegoat. I'm a foreigner; I'll do.

Of course I don't *know* that this is what they are saying but it would explain why one of Sanchia's cousins came up to me last week and wrung my hand with tears of gratitude in his eyes.

Although I know I tend to sing rather too loudly while I'm out walking and in when I'm in the shower, I wouldn't be expecting a standing ovation for my vocal prowess and there's nothing else I've done of note.

Very strange people, the Los Poopians. Odd.

Aldo himself was laid to rest peacefully, the second time, and this time I had Sanchia pointed out to me. Personally, I'd have backed her in a fight against him any day. She is at least double the size of the coffin in which her husband went to his final rest and the set of her jaw would make Mike Tyson blench. However, I know nothing (and that's the safest way to leave it, I think).

But back to chickens. I must do something to tempt Frankly to eat. Can I actually cope with boiling up a chicken head? Feet? Not a problem. Innards? Easy. But heads? Hmm.

As I am pondering this, George is really helpful with an obviously well-worn tale of his youth in England. This time it's about his first outing with the Young Farmers to a slaughterhouse.

'Half of us fainted before we even went in,' he says. 'Another quarter were sick once they set eyes on what goes on. The rest of us coped. We didn't like it but if you're going to be a farmer, you've got to know what goes on.'

He's right of course. Most carnivores haven't a clue what happens to bring them their steak on a plate. And we don't want to know. Perhaps the chicken head will be my karma for thirty-nine careless years of chomping on dead animals. But can I cope?

Well, no.

Three hours later there's a pot on the stove with wonderful chicken stock in it. Frankly has already deigned to eat some cooked chicken innards with something like her old relish. But my goose is cooked. For there are not one, not two, but *three* chicken heads lurking under the wobbling, steaming lid.

I bought this chicken at the shop and it really did come whole and was chopped up in front of my eyes. '*Toda*' I said, bravely, meaning 'I want everything'. So Maria gives me everyone else's entrails, feet and heads as well. That's the entrails of everyone else's *chickens,* by the way.

'Gosh, aren't I Spanish and resourceful,' I think, carrying my booty home and putting it all on to boil. But a dead chicken's head is one thing; a dead *boiled* chicken's head is quite another. Let alone three.

Even in the middle of the night those heads are still haunting me. They float above my head together with the humbling knowledge that I, too, might have been one of the Young Farmers who fainted before they even got to the slaughterhouse. I expect Frankly would eat them. But what if she doesn't? Could I face picking up a half-mangled, reproachful, grey and bloated head from the floor?

Aaaagh!

The first thing I do when I wake in the morning is steel myself to get rid of them. It's hard enough fishing them out with a wooden spoon and throwing them into a plastic bag to be carried up to the municipal bin at the top of the hill. But the relief when I've done it. Oh! The palpable relief. After all, I don't have to tell George.

We have a routine now. Our morning walk around the village starts with the almost perpendicular slope of *Calle La Era* up to the main street of Los Poops. Each day Frankly grumbles at me and hangs around reluctantly as she sees me take the tortuous, cobbled route upwards and she looks appealingly down the hill to where sweeter pastures lie (together with that delicious mule dung). But at the top of the hill is the dumpster and life here is ruled by simple things such as the need to take the rubbish out.

She dawdles behind me, sniffing out the customary scents and any new visitors while I keep to the shady side of the street and greet any passing Los Poopians who may be conducting a fearsome argument about how nice the weather is today. If it is before 9am the top of the slope onto the Main Street will be encrusted with the elderly and all those villagers with crutches or limps or any kind of impediment. This is the easiest place of access for anyone who lives in upper parts of the village and they enjoy a good gossip while they are waiting for the bread guy.

The sound of a tooting horn precedes Mario's little white van each day as he tours the village, delivering the long thin loaves that are utterly delicious before noon and stale by teatime, circular loaves of the same stuff and more of the same tied round in a ring so that there's a hole in the middle. There are sundry other treats such as the identical bread, sugared and with a chocolate filling which is so contradictory to itself that even chocoholics like me can't finish it. But it's a sterling service and one without which the entire elderly section (about three quarters) of the village would crumble.

After selling his wares at the top of the village, Mario drives back down the hill away from town and turns down the lower road where he stops again in the shaded corner where the feral cats gather and the trees all lean and whisper. Then it's a dice with death along the virtually impassable back streets, reversing round corners and squeaking past the ever-rolling concrete mixer until the little van pants its way up to the main square and the rest of his customers. Once that is done, Mario drives up to the bar for his breakfast of toast and jam (presumably with his own bread) and then the little white van begins the long and winding journey up into the hills to the next inaccessible village.

I wander down Main Street and past *La Posada* and the pink-walled church. When the front door is open, I often go into the porch and gaze inside for a few minutes but, for some reason, I have never gone right inside. Perhaps it is too foreign for me; perhaps it is too much of a memory of my wedding.

We walk out across the square and I look at the famous plaque lauding the instalment of the automatic telephone system by a man who is now in jail for fraud. It is bolted to the wall of the rarely used municipal building. It doesn't actually say "To Celebrate The Last Fitting Of An Automatic Telephone System In The Least Important Village In Spain" but it might just as well, for the rancour has run seriously deep.

It is too hot already to go very far today but Frankly and I still stagger out of the village to the east along the mule path to the spring. This morning is misty so the great cleft in the hills, running down to the sea ten kilometres away, is fuzzy with a gentle white against the blue. But even so, the horizon is just visible with Africa only a few miles further on.

I'm getting quite good at the natural history of Los Poops now.

Over to the left of the path, where the earth has been roughly tilled, the plant with the spiky leaves is definitely the Lesser Yellow Whatsit. You can tell it's the Lesser Whatsit because the plant is smaller than the Greater Whatsit which you only find to the west of the town and which has slightly rounder leaves. The grey and white Whojamaflip is pretty well over now and is less fragrant than it was but you can occasionally find a clump to rub your fingers on—it's a little like Thyme. The Climbing Thingummy which likes the shady side of the path is definitely over, which is a shame. That really was a pretty one, all pink flowers with yellow centres, but it smelt a bit like cat pee.

After a while we meander, relishing the shade from the walls of the houses, down the hill to the left into *Calle La Luna* and we are at the beginning of the long and winding lower road back to *Casa Taylor*.

Big Brown is wandering around at the exit to the square, his huge lop ears and grey beard distinguishing him from his many progeny. After several weeks of mutual posturing, the Alpha dog of the village will now greet Frankly with perfect equanimity and mutual bum-sniffing and he is friendly enough even to push his nose briefly into my hand in case there may be food there. He has seen me feeding Chica, the abandoned mother-bitch, on the other side of *La Posada* and lives in hope.

David follows Big Brown down the hill from *The Bay House*. Tigger is not with him so I am safe from bounce-attack and five minutes are passed pleasantly as he tells me of how badly fed the village animals are. Big Brown is a hunting dog, and prized as such, but his master feeds him very little. He was once a bag of bones but now David and Stella feed him twice a week and he sits outside their door at the same hour every day, waiting patiently and gratefully for their charity.

David says he has even seen village cats fighting over a heel of stale bread thrown to them from a window. 'Give that to our own dogs and they'd pee on it and walk away!' he says and leaves me pondering on life and pampered animals.

The walk through the lower roads never ceases to delight. I could almost swear that the village rearranges itself each night, throwing up extra alleyways for me to wander down with different whitewashed houses and yet more sleek, basking cats to look at along the way. There are homes where the mule appears to live in its owner's house—the stable door being the window next to the front door—and on several of the roads there is the morning evidence of the passing of the sheep on their way to what pasture there is in this brown and sun-baked land.

After ten minutes of getting gloriously lost on the ever-different sloping streets, it's back to familiar ground on the Street of the Cat With Aquamarine Eyes. She must be a Siamese cross but those supernatural orbs shine out of the wise and pinched little tortoiseshell face like beacons, stopping me fresh in my tracks every day. She spends her time on the rooftops or high walls, never venturing down to risk encounters with village dogs or strange people and simply stares, blinking occasionally just when you think that her eyes are glued to yours. From there it's down the Street of the Flowers where Maria-Rosa has lined the walls of her house with dozens of whitewashed pots and containers filled with burgeoning plants. Bougainvillea and roses, herbs and daisies, lilies and ivies flood up the walls in a cascade of brightness. Then, round the corner to the Street of Ten Tortoiseshells where the bulk of the feral cats live and there is a wonderful view of the terraced slopes down to the sea; on to the Road of the Wasps where the nest lies under a crack in the concrete and they buzz lazily around, bemused by the heat—and past the Door of the Sad Mule With Crinkly Eyelids. Frankly is trotting happily behind me, virtually ignoring the cats after the first weeks of inching past them with her hackles raised. And now we are back at the base of *Calle La Era* and it's a hundred and seven paces up the perpendicular winding slope back to the house. Frankly sits down and sulks. 'One day, when we're low on rubbish we'll do it the other way round and go downhill first,' I promise her. She doesn't believe me.

It is a good five minutes before Frankly clatters in through the bead curtain on the door and throws herself down on the cool concrete floor. She drinks from her bowl while lying down and, when that part of the routine has been accorded its appropriate time, she climbs back onto my bed and sleeps the morning out.

106

I have made a resolution to read as many improving books as I can while I'm here. The house is filled with bookshelves of every book you ever should have read. You know the kind of stuff; T.S. Eliot's *Four Quartets* and *Murder in the Cathedral. To Kill a Mockingbird.* St. Augustine's *Confessions, The Rainbow, The Mill on the Floss, Never Eat Anything Bigger Than Your Head*—no, sorry that slipped in by mistake.

I'd never read any of them (including *Never Eat Anything Bigger Than Your Head)* and despite an English Literature A-level, am grossly ignorant. However, slowly and surely, I am beginning to read and to learn of the joys of literature read slowly and contemplatively with no television to bribe you away with the promise of instant gratification.

In the afternoon, while I am simultaneously trying to write an article and swatting flies, the phone rings.

Still my heart jumps. Alex doesn't even know, yet, what country I'm in but, even so, I want it to be him saying that he's sorry and that he was wrong and that he still loves me. Oh fool!

It is not Alex, of course. Instead, it is William, the best man at our wedding, who is supposed to be the intermediary between us. William wrote both Alex and me a letter after he had heard what had happened. *The same letter to both of us, photocopied.*

He said in it that we both had photocopies so that we would not think he was separating us out, showing favouritism or judging one of us as being better or worse than the other. I remember sitting aghast when I looked at it and wondering what planet William is on—if any.

I had better say here that I'm not that far off the mark. William spent seven years living at a retreat centre in the Outer Hebrides where he became a saint. I'm not being funny: he *is* a saint, it's just that saints in reality are really hard to take. William is probably one of the purest men in the world. He always does everything with love and gently corrects you when you say something like: 'I think that Alex has behaved dishonourably.' What I *mean* to say, apparently, is 'I feel dishonoured by how Alex has behaved.' Yeah, right.

Of course, William *is* right. He always is right and he's so damn humble with it that you can't even hate him for it, openly at least. Knowing William has made me suspect that Judas shopped Jesus because he just couldn't stand the perfection any more.

'Just bloody well fart will you!' he must have exploded some day. 'Just say "shit!" or something when you trip over a stone! At the very least, just *try* to trip over a stone!'

But come to think of it, Jesus did turn the tables over in the Temple and shout at the moneychangers. Maybe Mary Magdalene had dumped him in a way that he felt dishonoured about on the previous day.

There's a bit about perfection in T. H. White's *The Once and Future King* which has kept me sane through three whole days this week. Sir Galahad, being perfect, had no false modesty so if he did a great joust and someone said 'Damn good show, Galahad!' he would say, 'Yes, wasn't it?' instead of, 'Gosh, thanks… just luck really. Anyone could have done it.'

Even worse, when the knights went out to rescue maidens which were about to be ravished (or was it eaten?) by dragons, they would honour the time-old custom with a bit of benign ravishment themselves afterwards with the suitably grateful damsels. But Galahad did not. In fact he would not even kiss the maidens because it was not ethical. This behaviour did not endear him to his colleagues in any way, shape or form and it certainly ruined their fun.

But William is right. It is my feelings about Alex's behaviour that are what hurt, not Alex's behaviour itself. Any psychotherapist will tell you that it's only your own feelings that you need to process and the other person's behaviour is only a mirror to your own insecurities.

At this point, any psychotherapist who wants to go on living would be well advised to keep away from any small villages in the foothills of Granada where I might be residing.

William actually does think that Alex has not behaved well (which is a relief because, remember, William is always right) but he also thinks that I should be 'processing' things with Alex. The only thing I want to process with Alex is his penis in a liquidiser.

I think it should still be attached to him at the time.

So, anyway, William sent us both this photocopied letter, in which he says that he's 'sad for the shattered dreams.'

'So what are Alex's shattered dreams?' I ask him on the phone this afternoon.

'Oh, I don't know,' he says vaguely.

'So why write about them to both of us if it's only relevant to me?' I ask in a tone that William would recognise as dangerous if he were anything other than a saint.

'I wanted to let you know that I love you both equally,' he says.

'Well I want you to know that I felt very hurt by it,' I reply (good move—managed not to say 'You hurt me' which would have been radically unintegrated of me and you do want to remain integrated while talking to William).

But this is where William comes into his own. *I have no idea* exactly how the conversation goes from there but it keeps going in a way that lets me know that he has heard me and even listened to me *but also in such a way that he does not have to say 'sorry.'* The man is unbelievable and admirable and extraordinary and infinitely lovable—and I want to shoot him.

I am finally 'in touch with my anger,' I tell William, and he agrees with me. Then he starts off on something about the difference between anger and rage and making sure that I don't cross the thin red line because anger is a positive force for change but rage is self-destructive.

And I shout at him. I shout at the saint! I shout fairly coherently as well which is more than you could reasonably expect.

I have spent all my life *not* getting in touch with my anger, I tell him. It is time that I started to shout. Perhaps I am in a bit of a rage but hey, when you are a beginner you do not always get it just right. You have to practice. Maybe you learn to distinguish between anger and rage later. Just for now, it is sufficient to be feeling them. Either of them. And, as far as I am concerned, I think that it is William's job not to judge it one way or the other.

Oddly enough the phone call ends quite quickly after that, William having been goaded into saying that both Alex and I are fundamentalists. Fundamentalist what, he doesn't say, but the surprise of that is tempered by satisfaction that I have managed to provoke him into an unsaintly remark.

Later, as I walk to the car in order to drive down to the supermarket on the coast, I ponder this idea of anger and rage. It seems a fine distinction and one that is worthy of deep consideration.

'Bollocks,' I think constructively and kick the hell out of the wall leading down to the sheep pens.

At the supermarket I stock up on chocolate and decide to take Frankly for a meander on the seashore. There is a light wind which takes away from the oppression of heat and, although she trolls along with her tongue hanging out so far that it nearly drags on the sand, she seems to be enjoying herself. When I sit on the rocks, looking over the sea, she pootles around and then comes to lean against me for a cuddle. It seems so unreal sometimes to be sitting here in a foreign country away from all my friends and family. But the little nose pushing at my hand is a friend and there is consolation in being physically far away from the situation which hurts. Presumably, Alex is living his life happily, making love with his girlfriend and explaining to all his friends (what friends?) how unreasonable I am and how he simply had to leave for his own sanity.

No! Don't go there. Let it go. There is no point in expecting the pain just to go away but there is equally no point in wallowing in it. Nothing can be done; he is not coming back. And I am not strong enough to pretend that I don't care if I bump into Suzie and him in the street. Equally, I am not strong enough to slap Alex's face or stamp on his feet or set fire to his house. Probably a good thing, really, after what Ella wrote.

It is seriously dark by the time Frankly and I return to the car. Dusk falls so swiftly here and I was lost in unproductive thoughts for longer than I thought. But, once we are back in the car and turning up the long winding road to Los Poops, seeing a lone walker ahead in the headlights brings it home to me that this hire car has to go back next week. What am I going to do without transport? I won't be able to run down to the supermarket for chocolate, go down to the sea or drive out for a different walk with Frankly. The ready tears jump into my eyes again—and I am so tired of crying.

'Calm down,' I tell myself sternly. 'You will cope.' But frantic calculations about money start juggling themselves through my head. I can't afford to keep the car. I do know that I can hitch a lift with Katherine or Stella whenever they are going out of the village but the independence will be missing and I will feel so trapped.

Round the first hairpin bend, round the second and the walker ahead of me is just yards away. It's a young man and he puts his thumb out to hitch a lift.

Something tells me that it's the shepherd from the village and I stop. These sudden moods of pain and loneliness that descend on me are such that any company is welcome and it's not much of a risk. I've always been taught never to give lifts, let alone to strange men, but surely the shepherd is safe enough? Frankly is with me, after all, and she is now a swaggering village dog. Perhaps she would even protect me if it came to it. Sitting On His Face And Farting Should Do It, says Frankly in the back.

So, I am smiling as he comes over to open the car door and even the remnant of the mood is banished as he smiles back and climbs into the car.

But the scent of him clambers in first. It is overwhelming and my first instinct is to recoil. But no, it is not unpleasant—in fact it is the most heady of fragrances. As the shepherd sits and closes the door, the night air around us simply shimmers with the aroma of warm scented wool. No, it is more than just the wool; it is the pure essence of warmth, of life itself and of the heat of a strong, tired young man's body. Not testosterone as much as a sense of vitality and gentleness, mixed with lanolin from the wool and warm oil and herbs that have been crushed under his feet as he walked the hills with his flock. I am suddenly dizzy.

'*Gracias,*' he says.

'*¿A Los Poops?*'

'*Si, gracias.*'

And he keeps on talking, very slowly and simply because he knows who I am and that I have very little Spanish and he, obviously, has no English at all. I try to understand.

He has been down into the town to…? No, that bit I can't make any sense of. He was planning to… No, that is lost too. But as long as I listen and make an occasional acknowledgement, that seems to be all that is required—for either of us. And all the time I am inhaling this fragrance of shepherd and it is making my head swim in a lake of calm and peacefulness. I am not sure if he's been treading in some kind of hallucinogenic herb or whether this is an actual mystical experience. Maybe I am going mad but somehow I know that this is a man who would search forever for just one lost lamb.

Now he is asking me questions that I can understand; am I happy in Los Poops? Why do I live there? Where is my husband?

I am answering automatically, as best I can, while keeping my eye on the hairpin bends. As we talk, I am surprised to see that Frankly is poking her nose between the seats to be stroked. He is caressing her wrinkled forehead and making gentle noises to her as if she were a ewe in labour.

When the 'husband' question comes, I am horrified to find that tears begin to well up in my eyes. This is ridiculous; not now! Not with a perfect stranger!

'Ah,' he says—and then something I do not understand—and the hand which had been stroking Frankly reaches out to touch my tear-stained cheek.

I have to stop the car because that gentle masculine touch is too much. Too exquisite and too painful for me to go on driving.

And then this total stranger is holding me in strong young arms, gently stroking my hair and murmuring words of comfort. By rights it should make me cry more but it doesn't. The pain just vanishes as if it had never been there and I have the strangest and most surreal of thoughts: 'It must be nice to be one of his sheep'.

'Thank you,' I say, pulling away a little nervously and he lets me go with a smile and sits back again in the passenger seat. Frankly climbs through the gap between us and clambers onto his lap. 'Oho!' he says easily, helping her and stroking her worried forehead. She is in bliss, the little trollop.

I drive on, half-shaken, half-immensely calm and nothing more is said until we reach the village.

I drop him at the top of *Calle La Era* and Frankly jumps down as soon as he opens the door.

'*Gracias,*' he says again with a smile and then he has vanished down the hill. I don't even know his name.

The glorious scent lingers behind him and I think that I am okay until I am halfway down the steep path to the house. Then loneliness descends like a cloak of emptiness. There is no one to hold me or love me and the scent of nobody lingers in my bed.

Frankly follows me in her own inimitable lethargic way so I leave the house door open. After all, what does it matter if anyone hears me weeping? Nobody really cares what becomes of me. But oh God! What would I give for a bath?

Casa Blanca! Suddenly, in the middle of a hiccup of tears of self-pity, I remember the keys on the back of the door. David and Stella's house with the bath! The one that I promised to clean for them! Maybe I could get enough hot water if I turned the boiler on for just half an hour and boiled saucepans in the meantime. It would be worth it. It would be something to fill the long, yawning evening ahead at least.

I get to the door with saucepans and matches just as Frankly rolls in. The poor beagle grumbles and mumbles about having to go out again. 'Well you can stay here then,' I say callously, threatening to shut the door on her.

'Bugger That,' says the beagle, giving me the filthiest of looks and, heaving a heavy sigh, she rolls out onto the slope again.

But she is so slow and I am cursing her as I lead the way to *Casa Blanca.* Every moment is holding me back from that precious bath.

'Oh you can catch me up,' I say crossly, sprinting ahead. Frankly's 'Huk-huk' exasperated noise follows, echoing against the white cobbled walls.

Casa Blanca is dark and dusty and it takes precious minutes to find the keyhole, let alone to get in and find the light switch. But the electricity works and, glory of glories, David has left the pilot light on for the cleaning I have promised to do. Almost shaking, I try and assess what kind of a boiler it is. Does it give constant hot water? If so, it will, at least, fill the bath with some warmth and I can do the rest on the gas stove. And I'm in luck.

The bath needs cleaning but it is only dust and spiders and I've remembered to bring a cloth and the *Flash*. Once four full saucepans are settled on the stove and the water is running, painfully slowly, into the tub, I go back out to check that Frankly is still on her way.

She is walking slowly and steadily down the last hill, puffing and blowing and sounding like an indignant steam engine.

'Come on sausage,' I say, kindly, stroking her back as Frankly doubtfully investigates the doorway into another completely strange house and looks at me as if I have personally murdered all her (non-existent) puppies. There is a big broad chair where we both can sit with a book while the water boils and, after a preliminary sniff around, Frankly is quite happy to be hauled up for a lap and a cuddle. She even stays there when I get up to pour the saucepans into the bath and make a quick calculation of how much more hot water is needed. Two more—so I boil four for certain and leave two by the side of the bath for top-ups.

Oh God it is bliss! It doesn't matter that the day has been boiling and is hardly even cool now; the joy of sliding into the bath and the flow of heat feels like a great wave of fulfilled desire as I sink down into the deep, soothing water.

Frankly begins to snore and I tip another saucepan of water into the bath as my body heat lowers the temperature around me. There is not enough light here to read in the bath but just lying there is good enough.

'And I can do this every night if I like,' I think. But I won't. Somehow, I know that it has to be kept special: for the really difficult evenings and for the times when I desperately need some comfort.

And as I lie there, with this body made strangely slender by circumstance (and a general lack of chocolate) and my hair floating around my head, I start thinking of the shepherd and try to remember his scent. It is elusive but I can still feel the presence of him, the feel of his arms around me and the kindness that exuded from him. He has compassion; I know that; the cardinal virtue that Alex lacks.

No, don't think about Alex. Think about hot water and kindly

114

shepherds. And as I lie there, I begin to wonder what it would be like to be held and loved by such a man. Such a basic, earthy man who does not even speak my language. Someone who tends animals and lives with them, spending each day alone with his sheep and his fierce dogs on the edge of the mountains. It is as if the life force that I felt in him is working within me.

What does he do all day? I wonder. Perhaps he takes books or music to the hillside with him? But I don't really think so. He is pretty much the last remnant of mankind without a Walkman or a mobile phone and he would more likely stand and dream or sit and watch the sky and the earth and their movements as his sheep roam and nibble and graze to fill their bellies. What do you learn of the earth if you watch it all day? What mysteries are there for the silent watcher who has nothing to do but look and see?

I lie there, thinking of him, until I find myself wafting into dreams. Then, as the water grows cool, I manage to find some discipline, sit up, wash my hair, rinse it with the last saucepan of still warm water and, getting out, rub myself briskly dry.

But, as I let the water out of the bath my hair tumbles out of the towel, falling over my shoulder like a caress and I feel myself wanting… wanting something.

Is it desire? No, not quite. Can I even remember desire? Am I still capable of feeling it? I don't know. Desire feels dead or dormant deep inside me and no return is expected. This is a good feeling, though; a feeling of life or hope or something like that.

Time to tidy up briskly and shoo Frankly out of her deep snoring sleep. Sulkily, the beagle flops down onto the floor and makes her way as slowly as possible to where I am holding the door open. 'It's My Bedtime,' she grumbles. 'That Chair Was Nice.'

We walk home together, slowly, through the still night and I am still warm from the heaven of the bath with my hair knotted in the towel and damp on my neck. Frankly is sniffing and snorting along at the late night smells of animals and ghosts and, above us, the stars circle in their courses with Jupiter and Saturn glowing side by side. The occasional street lamps mask them a little but there is enough darkness to feel the arms of night around you.

Curled up in the hard, single bed, with Frankly snoring at my feet, I dream of the shepherd.

In the morning I cannot remember the dream but I awaken contented and able to lie in bed for an extra hour, knowing that something warm has embraced me; nothing sexual or threatening but a friendship and a compassion that I have missed for so long.

As I finally get up and tip the dozy, grumbling barrel out of the front door for its morning pee, I find myself wondering, in a very abstract sort of way, how a man like the shepherd would treat his wife.

Chapter Eight

Jack Risborough is back in Los Poops. I saw the lights on in his house tonight as I was sitting on the roof, looking at the stars. There really isn't much else to do in the evenings before bed apart from going to the bar or visiting one of the ex-pats and there are only so many evenings you can do that in a week without either your eyes or theirs glazing over with boredom. Actually, I think some of them have got used to it and are addicted to the boredom factor. We discuss the same things over and over again and eat the same food and fight over *The Independent* which George brings in from Motril on a Saturday. It isn't living by modern standards of busy-ness.

I have become contemplative and am nearly a third of the way through Ben's first wall of books. I had a whole series of discussions with St. Augustine over his *Confessions* which are fairly interesting in places and overwhelmingly patronising, arrogant and stupid in others. Just my opinion, you understand. I have sat with fascinated and horrified open mouth over Wilhelm Reich's *The Murder of Christ*, have been extremely rude to Nietzsche and am beginning to make cautious friends with Goethe.

One of the easier-to-read books is on astronomy and I can now recognise all the major constellations. I am amazed at how much pleasure that gives me. Tonight Scorpio is rising in the south, huge and beautiful.

Several nights now, Frankly and I have slept on the roof of the little house, under the silver sweep of the Milky Way that Native Americans teach is the river to heaven. Remembering the departed builds their canoe for the journey and every tear their paddle. There are thousands making their way across the sky every night, the beauty of their departed souls lighting up the heavens with hope for those of us remaining. I lie there, eyes open, adjusting steadily to the night sky and before I sleep it seems that there isn't a millimetre of sky that isn't ablaze with heavenly light. Great thoughts of the Oneness of All Things are easy when the night sky is your mirror; harder, however, under the blazing light of the sun.

I think it is only because I am desperate for some different (interesting) company but I am going to walk Frankly up in that direction before bed. What direction? Oh, to Jack's house. I can just check if it is him and not just someone who's come to clean his house or something.

Actually, it is lovely to walk this late at night. The air is deceptively fresh, as though it had not festered and crawled all over you all day, and the new crescent moon is just sinking in the west. Frankly is trotting along with her tail held high in that way she has which shows that she is enjoying herself instead of her daytime habit of drooping around with her tongue dragging on the ground.

The path to Jack's winds up behind the church. It isn't paved; in fact it's a mass of potholes. God knows how a BMW copes with it but obviously it must for there it is, silver and sleek and shiny, parked along the front wall of a surprisingly unassuming house. It's unostentatious, quite hidden and, I expect, much larger than it looks.

There is a walled section in front and around the side which is confusing—is it private or part of the communal road? It is paved and neat, so I suppose it's private which means no chance of just wandering past for no particular reason.

Behind thin curtains which move in the night breeze, Bruce Springsteen is singing about deep, dark and disturbingly sexy things. My courage deserts me; I have no option but to retreat.

Frankly? FRANKLY? The little bastard has vanished. Did she trot in front of me onto the terrace? I'd better take a quick and cautious look. There is a doorway—and it is open. Oops. What if she has wandered in with her usual attitude that everything vaguely forbidden should be investigated? Normally she is into any strange house like a shark scenting blood. I'll have to go and fetch her. But no, there she is, safely outside. Bugger.

For a couple of minutes I try, nonchalantly and totally silently, to suggest to Frankly that she might like to go visiting… but she looks at me as if I were trying to explain to her that cats are a valid creation.

Oh come on Anna! This is ridiculous. Go home! So I walk back, hesitate, turn and walk on, around the corner of the house and straight into him.

He is sitting on a wooden bench, looking up at the sky.

'Hi,' he says, still looking up.

'Hi.'

He must hear my heart thumping.

'They're beautiful aren't they?'

'Yes. Scorpio is rising tonight.'

(Smart, Anna. Intelligent even. Well done).

'Where?'

'Up to your left.'

'Show me.'

So I do but he can't see it and tries to look along the line of my arm with me pointing at the constellation. Then I try to point his arm for him until we are both falling over with laughter. Then he fetches a torch so I can use the ray of light to paint the image of Scorpio in the night sky. That's fun so we trace a few others as well and before I know it, Jack and I are having lunch together tomorrow in Motril and he'll pick me up at twelve.

I like him. I really like him.

No I don't.

But what to wear? Frankly is disgusted with me the following morning as I look through my summer dresses instead of taking her for a walk. She sulks by the front door, pretending that there isn't a perfectly good courtyard to pee in—and, when I let her out for that pee, she vanishes into the open door of the shop so I have to chase her and pull her out, apologising profusely to the disapproving Mafia there.

They all know me by now and the ice has been thawing slowly but this will not have helped. 'That's the woman they think poisoned Aldo,' echoes out behind me as a punishment. I'm getting to know the dialect by now and it's unmistakable.

I think the royal blue crinkle dress. It's supposed to go with my eyes. Alex thought…

Stuff Alex.

We go for our walk slightly later and it is steamingly hot. Even the lizards seem slow today and Frankly is almost tripping over her dangling tongue within minutes. We go out by the lower path because there are trickles of water here and there all along that route and it's the shadiest you can get.

Of course, the sheep and goats are already out and we are following in their rapidly-drying turdy trail. Frankly threatens to roll in one patch of diarrhoea and earns a cuff for her pains. She glowers at me reproachfully and lags behind so I won't know what she's doing.

The sheep and goats are meandering over the hillside ahead to our left. I clip the lead onto Frankly in case there are any strays around and to stop her from being attacked by the sheepdogs, let alone the sheep themselves.

The shepherd is sitting in the faint shade of an almond tree to my left. He raises an arm in greeting and smiles calling out '¿donde es la perra?' (where is the dog?—or, more accurately, where is the bitch).

'Ai.' (here).

'Domingo' (shame). And then something about coming to sit with him with the sheep sometime to watch nature (you see how much better I am getting at this?).

I just smile and walk on with a wave, not sure why he asked. But it would be lovely to sit in the sunshine watching wildlife without a beagle constantly routing it.

On the way home I call in on Katherine as usual for a cup of *PG Tips* tea from one of the packets sent by her daughter in England.

While she is in the kitchen making it I register, with surprise, that Terry Wogan is not blathering via satellite as usual.

'He's on holiday' says Katherine as if that explained it. I suppose she doesn't like his replacement.

Instead there is a John Denver CD playing *The Rocky Mountain Songs* and he is carolling about the beautiful Colorado skies. It catches my heart so unexpectedly that it brings a constriction in my chest. Katherine's return, with a decent cup of tea ruined by long-life milk, cuts the link before I know why it hurt so much. It's not because of Alex; is it because the dream was lost? Or an echo of that deep joy I used to feel watching the Colorado winter sunsets? I don't think I'll invest the time researching it right now; it will be sure to let me know in due course.

But I am in tears and now Katherine is fussing over me which makes it worse. I don't want to add to it—I can't go back to beautiful Colorado and there's no point in talking about it. Instead, I tell her about Danny.

In turn, she tells me about her late husband. Not the best of marriages but she loved him. They would row almost as a habit— it was just a habit—and he would storm out and go drinking and then come back and they would make up. Except the last time, he didn't come back. He drove his car over the edge of the road.

We sit silently together for a while. There is nothing I can say; she is wracked with guilt. A cuddle is all that can be offered because she will never accept that it wasn't her fault.

'It's what makes me an inveterate meddler,' she says, somewhat unexpectedly.

'What?'

'I want people to be happy so much. I want people to take care of their marriages—to love one another. I interfere to make things better whenever I can. I know I shouldn't but life is short. People should take the chance of joy when they can'

'Don't those two contradict each other sometimes?' I ask, thinking of Alex taking his joy with Suzie.

'Oh yes,' Katherine runs her fingers through her hair. 'Don't take any notice of my blathering. It's just…'

'I know,' I say gently. 'I do know. Love is so precious and we don't appreciate it when we have it.'

We both sit in silence for a moment.

Then, to change the subject, I ask her about the shepherd.

'Yiannis?' she says. 'If you mean the young one? He's a nice boy. He's not the permanent shepherd, that's his cousin Josef but Josef's been away for two months—learning something to do with sheep but goodness knows exactly what. I mean, how much *is* there to learn about sheep?'

I pass on that one.

'Josef should be back by the end of the month, I think and then Yiannis will go home. It's a shame. Josef is a brute. You'd better watch out for Frankly when he's back. He's been known to poison dogs that go for the sheep.'

Oh great.

Katherine goes on with a liturgy of dogs that have been poisoned and I stroke Frankly, trying not to listen too much. I really don't need that worry nagging at me.

Later, as we are wending our way home again, think back to when Frankly was off her food. Had she picked up a piece of poison then? No, she wasn't sick, just hot. And I put it out of my mind. I have other things to think about anyway.

It's the blue dress, basically because it's the only one that doesn't look utterly dreadful. I have put on eyeliner and mascara for the first time in weeks and stared anxiously at my freckles in the bathroom mirror. I wish I had a sun hat.

We have agreed to meet on the lower road below the village. Not because we are deliberately trying to hide anything but it's not a good idea to shout it either.

Jack is on time—and the car is air-conditioned. Oh bliss. I sit back in the leather seat that feels like an armchair and sigh deeply.

He is laughing at me.

'Surely you've driven in a BMW before?'

'Oh yes, I used to have one.'

'You did?'

And I explain about Danny's pension policy which turned up out of the blue. £15,000 in the days when you could get a BMW for that amount. Everyone said I should invest it but I went out and bought a BMW. Why not? I had it for eleven years and I loved it.

'Five-series?'

'No, 318.'

'Drastically underpowered,' says Jack with a snort and suddenly I am furiously angry.

'We're not all millionaires,' I snap.

'Ouch,' he smiles at me. 'Sorry. That was tactless of me. I guess it was a really special car for you.'

'Yes it was, but whenever I think of it now I'll remember that it was "drastically underpowered." You should think before you speak.'

'And whenever I see a 318 I'll remember how I upset you,' he says. 'And I think you've had enough to upset you lately. Unless, of course, you're one of those women who just attracts disasters throughout your life…'

God this man is *so* irritating. He has just insulted me, apologised, understood me, patronised me and insulted me again in less than a minute.

'Well I've certainly attracted a disaster now,' I say. 'Watlington P. Risborough, the man who only opens his mouth to change feet.'

'I think you need a decent drink' says Watlington P. with a broad grin. 'Too much of the village wine would sour the most pleasant of women and I don't suppose you were ever that.'

'You are an utter asshole.'

'No, it's your husband who's the asshole. Life just shines out of you for better and for worse and anyone who can't see that or want to hold onto it is an asshole of the first order.'

I am silenced.

We have reached sea level and the car eases forward onto the dual carriageway that runs all the way between Malaga and Almeria.

'We can go to Motril or we can go to a great seafood restaurant I know on the seafront,' says Jack.

'If you really want to help me make the right decision, you could add "we can go to a really tacky place in Motril or to a great seafood place I know on the seafront." That would make it really clear,' I say.

'What does "tacky" mean?' he asks, completely unperturbed.

'Cheap and nasty.'

'You think I'd take you to a cheap and nasty restaurant? Why, I would never do that.'

'Well no,' and I am laughing again. Why? He is obnoxious and, even worse, he brings out completely the worst in me.

'You bring out the worst in me,' I say with a sigh.

Outside, the sea slides past smoothly and swiftly as if the BMW were simply sitting still.

'Well, that's good.'

'Good?'

'Always a good idea to know the worst about someone first. Then the relationship can't just go downhill. So, is there anything else I should know about you that's dreadful?'

'We don't have a relationship.'

God, why am I being such a bitch?

'Oh, I think we do. I'm a millionaire who, for some strange reason, really likes you and you're a prickly, scared girl in a strange country who, underneath it all, really likes me. We make each other laugh. That's good enough.'

No it isn't. Yes it is.

'How about the really great seafood restaurant on the beach?' I say.

'Hey, I didn't say it was *really* great. I just said it was great.'

'Watlington Perivale Risborough, you are a complete arrogant pillock.'

'No, am I really? What's a pillock?'

'A mixture of a load of bollocks and a prick.'

'A prick being?'

I'm going to hit him.

'It's a penis,' I say with great dignity. 'Generally a very small one.'

'Sounds like a good enough mixture. Most men must be pillocks then.'

'Oh shut up!'

'No, you don't win the argument with that one! Aren't you even going to ask me if I really have such a small penis?'

'No, I saw you through your bathroom window.'

'Were you on stilts?'

'Periscope.'

'Ah!'

He smiles at me and I shake my head at him.

'You're incorrigible,' I say.

'Like Frankly,' he says. 'We're kindred spirits, she and I. I'm only taking you out to impress her.'

'It won't impress her in the slightest!'

'It will if I bring her back some food.'

'In that case, you must have owned a beagle.'

'Aha! You've got it. I did. Barney. He and I grew up together. He went to the Happy Hunting Ground about the time you were born. Look, here we are!'

We turn off the road and draw to a stop outside a place where there is a great canopy of wooden beams covered in vines and grapes. Inside you can see crisp white tablecloths and happy people lifting clear glasses of bright wine—yellow and white and shell-pink and ruby.

'It looks lovely.' And it does.

The service is wonderful, the bread is fresh, the wine is cool and crisp and the food is delicious. And we can't stop talking. Most of it is banter but it is so easy and it flows back and forwards without either of us having to think.

We talk ideas and philosophy and sketch in a little about our backgrounds but nothing in any depth. I talk about catering college and what we did to the dressing for the *radicchio* when the principal had just told us all off. He talks of his wife and his two daughters and how proud he is of them and how they once all lived in Australia when he worked in Perth.

'Then why doesn't your wife come to Los Poops?' I say. 'If you are in Europe so often, wouldn't it be better if she were here too? Or is it the language?'

'She doesn't want to live here,' he says gently. 'And I think she should have her choice. I ran her around the world when we were younger and she raised two children, wonderfully and mostly without a lot of help from me. I was too busy building a career. She stood right by me, rain or shine and now she wants to enjoy her life in D.C. I think she has that right.'

'I thought you lived in Colorado.'

'I do, in my heart. But the family home is in Washington now. That's where my head office is now and Karen's real happy there.'

'But she must miss you.'

'Maybe a little. I mess up the house.' He laughs. 'No, seriously, I generally go back for five days every two weeks and I make sure I get great holidays. Maybe it's not the way I'd like it to be but I'm only planning to be working out of Madrid for another ten months. Then I'll go home. But this time I'm not going back to the States for six weeks. On Karen's orders!'

'Why?'

Jack looks up at me with his face full of mischief. 'I shouldn't tell you,' he says. 'But I guess you'll never meet her. Karen's having a face lift.'

'A face lift! Is she an actress?'

'Nope, she just wants to look good. All her friends are doing it.'

'Do you think she needs a face-lift?'

'If she wants one, she needs one. But if you mean do I think she looks old—she looks just fine to me.'

'But why can't you be there while she's having it?'

'She doesn't want me to see her until it's better.'

My opinion of this paragon of wifely and motherly virtue is, mercifully, dropping. She had been so far up on a pedestal I was getting tempted to throw rocks. After all, his life can't be so utterly perfect; the first time I saw him, he was crying.

'Well people can look pretty weird after a face-lift,' I say. 'I've got a friend, Ella, who had one in Denver—and laser surgery as well.'

'You do? Tell me about it! You haven't told me anything about your time in Colorado yet. Tell me about Ella.'

He sits back with the glass of wine cupped in his hand, having done full justice to the food.

'I don't think you want to know,' I say. 'At least, Karen doesn't want you to know what she'll be looking like.'

'But I would like to,' he says. 'I respect Karen immensely and I'm doing what she wishes. But I'd really like to know what she might be going through. Help me out here.'

I am slightly high from wine and enjoyment and I want to tell the story anyway.

'It was after Alex left Colorado for his new job but before he actually left *me*—and before I sold the house so I was living on my own there,' I say. 'That's just for background. Ella lived in a trailer, which was amazing really, but it had a leak and it wasn't suitable for recuperating in. She needed somewhere decent.

'Ella is an actress. She appeared in…'

Jack interrupts me.

'Tell me as if it were happening now, Anna. Not as if it were in the past. Go right back so you can see it and tell me just like you were living it again. That way it will live for me too.'

Okay. I take one more sip of the slightly effervescent delicately coloured wine and begin.

It is four o'clock and Ella's sister, Hazel, has just knocked on the back door of the house. I run through the long, thin kitchen with its dark stone tiles and out onto the back porch where the two-seater swing creaks back and forward as if sat on by generations of ghostly children.

Hazel looks exhausted, her short blond hair unbrushed. She has two suitcases in her hands and I reach out to pull them up the steps for her. Ella is not with her.

'Try not to react,' she says. 'She looks a terrible mess. She wanted me to come and warn you first.'

I school my face into an impassive mask while I wonder what kind of Frankenstein's monster is about to get out of Hazel's car, parked just the other side of the wooden fencing. Hazel had asked if she could drive up the back way behind the houses because it is broad daylight and Ella does not want to risk being seen. It is seven days since the operation in a hospital just north of Denver and I know from my phone calls to Hazel that Ella has been incredibly sick. Hazel came up from Texas specially to take care of her because they had to stay in a motel near the hospital for six nights in order to go back and see the surgeon. 'Anyway, she was so ill we couldn't have moved her,' Hazel told me on the telephone. 'We had to call the surgeon out on the second day; she was vomiting so much I thought she might even die.'

They really shouldn't have come this far today—Ella is forbidden to travel for a couple of weeks. In fact, she could hardly walk until yesterday. But now she is here, in desperate need of a haven, love and support, for Hazel must fly back home to St. Louis tomorrow.

I hesitate by the back door. Then a sweet little space alien hovers into view wrapped in a blanket. Ella's face is a jigsaw puzzle of purple, blue, red and bright, bright pink. Her eyes blink out of clown make-up and the lasered area around her mouth looks like the jowls of a Walt Disney character. Wrapped round her head and under her chin is elastic lint to support the jaw—like Marley's ghost.

Strangely enough, she looks very pretty. Odd but lovely. Like a pixie. And her 'please don't criticise me' expression only helps with the elfin look.

I laugh. But I am not laughing at her.

'You look beautiful,' I say. 'I'm not joking. You look like a lovely space alien. You should patent it for the next *Star Wars* movie.'

Ella smiles a little (she cannot laugh because of the pain). She cannot speak easily either. Nor eat. It will be soup and purées for days and she must sleep sitting up to drain the fluids from the scars.

We hug carefully and I show her the spare bedroom where I have put her favourite Stargazer lilies and a pile of books beside the bed in case she cannot sleep in the night. After living in a trailer this is paradise to her, although it looks very little to me.

Hazel is gone swiftly to return to St. Louis, flying back to the claims of husband and children and Ella and I sit and look at each other.

'Oh Anna, it was so awful,' she says and begins to cry. Even that hurts her for the tears scald the massacred skin. But beside that, she is in such pain and can only take a certain amount of painkillers. Obviously not enough.

I dose her with arnica drops and Rescue Remedy and Frankly climbs up on the sofa and leans against her. Ella holds the beagle in her arms, glad for the physical comfort after a week of clinical touch. Is this the time to mention that if Frankly wants stroking she will paw at people's faces? Probably not.

The surgery took five and a half hours. FIVE AND A HALF

HOURS! You can get a heart transplant in that time. You can get a new liver; have your hip replaced; have three or four hysterectomies. You can die.

So, this poor, sweet woman has risked death, disfigurement and spent $9,000 for vanity.

'You have to suffer to be beautiful,' the Little Mermaid is told in Hans Andersen's fairy tale. Obviously.

I stare doubtfully at my 39-year-old face in the downstairs bathroom mirror while I am heating up some smooth chicken soup in the kitchen next door. It's a good face. The neck's getting a bit scraggy if you catch it at the wrong angle and the freezing Colorado winter has not helped what is generally a smooth, if freckly, complexion. But would I spend five and a half hours in surgery to perfect it? Would I spend $100, let alone $9,000? Would I hell!

But this is not to judge. Ella is an actress. She needs a beautiful face. She has the money from selling her business. What would I do with $9,000? Oh, how many things! My mind scrambles at the thought.

Ella drinks her soup through a straw but with obvious relish. The acute sickness she suffered after the anaesthetic has both starved and dehydrated her but even so, she will not rest. Once she has eaten (drunk) enough to feed a gnat, she starts unpacking her bags—two of them; huge. I would need less to circumnavigate the world. One is almost completely filled with beauty and health requirements including a huge package of special lotions she must use on her face, particularly on the lasered part. And which she had to pay for separately. Then she does some washing, impervious to suggestions that she should not.

I run her a bath, purée some fruit and intend to leave her to it. But Ella is a Scorpio and happy to carry on a conversation with the bathroom door open while sitting, stark naked, on the loo and complaining about what the anaesthetic has done to her internal system.

'Did you have your nose done too?' I ask curiously while I am washing up. This was not on the long list of corrective measures which Ella had considered at length and run by me for my completely unknowledgeable opinion.

'Well, you know, I think I did,' she says with great interest, moving over to the bathroom mirror. 'I didn't ask for it but it does look different, doesn't it?'

It does. It is now a cute little snub job where it was once somewhat more assertive. I'm not sure what I think about the new nose but Ella is intrigued. She stares at it in the mirror and eagerly takes the hand mirror that I offer so that she can see her profile.

I hesitate because if the surgeon has done something she does not like and did not ask for he will have deep and intense litigation on his hands. Ella is an American and has lived in California as well as being a Scorpio. She considers the nose as long and hard as the nose itself is not.

'I like it,' she says firmly. 'It's the nose I used to have.'

'Sorry?' I'm not quite up to speed on the regular rearrangement of the noses of beautiful women.

'I used to have this nose,' Ella says again. 'Then I got mugged. I had to have it re-set then because it was broken but the surgeon gave me another nose and I never liked it.'

My mind boggles at the idea of the surgeon searching boxes for new noses, but I say nothing.

This is not ideal as Ella wants and needs assurance that I think the new nose is lovely too. Well, I do, for what it is worth. It looks like a very pleasant nose.

'Does it work properly?' I ask to fill in any gaps of enthusiasm that I have not encompassed.

Apparently it works well. It is a good nose, a lovely nose. It must be admired for the rest of the evening and referred to as often as possible. In the end I just say 'Nice nose' every time she speaks and this seems to do the trick.

For all the pain and the time-consuming lathering-on of potions, Ella is still not ready for bed by 11pm. I retire, exhausted, taking Frankly with me as she may get up and try to get into Ella's bed in the night if I don't. The beagle is very pleased to have a bed to sleep on and a human being to steam against. She sighs happily, settles down and begins to snore.

At three am I get up to go to the loo and Ella's light is still on. I peer around the door and she is sitting up in bed reading.

'Are you okay?'

'Not really,' she says. 'I can't take any more painkillers for three more hours and it's just awful.'

'Have some more arnica.' I go and fetch her some and four drops in water, drunk through a straw, does seem to ease the tension that is apparent throughout her body.

We talk about complementary medicine and life in general including husbands and dogs, and Ella tells me the Apache story of creation.

At the beginning of time, the Great Spirit made the heavens and the earth and all the birds and fish and animals thereon. And last, He made the dog. This was a creature of strength and joy and loyalty and affection and Great Spirit was proud of His last and greatest creation.

So the world developed and all was well. Then one day Dog came to Great Spirit and told Him that it was lonely. So the Great Spirit made man to keep him company.

I stop, hurriedly. I have finished the story of Ella's face lift and there is no need to go on. There is a tear in my eye and it spills over and I bow my head and let it run down my cheek to the corner of my mouth. That is less conspicuous than wiping it away.

When I look up Jack is sitting back in his chair, staring out over the ocean, but the wine glasses are empty now and there are cups of strong black coffee before us on the table.

'And yet we are so cruel to our dogs,' he says, unexpectedly. 'We invite them to love us and then leave them.'

'I didn't leave Frankly.'

'No, you didn't. But you are rare. I left my dog in the States.'

'You have a dog now?'

'No. He died. Just a few weeks ago. I wasn't there.'

Was that it? Was that what made him cry? My heart contracts with compassion. No, he wouldn't want it seen. Of course not.

'Tell me about him?'

'He was a Dalmatian. Quite dark. I called him Chester.'

'Not Pongo.'

'No,' Jack smiles. 'The first Dalmatian was Pongo, but you grow out of that!'

'But you couldn't have brought him—not unless the whole family came over. What happened to him?'

'Old age really. But I think he lost interest because I wasn't there. He was always my dog, not Karen's. He was twelve and he wasn't well last time I left but I think he could have pulled round.'

'If you had been there?'

'Yep.' Now he wants to change the subject and drinks his coffee, still looking out over the beach. 'So did your husband leave you for another woman?'

'Yes.'

'Was it an affair? Did you know?'

'Can we stop this Jack? If we go on, I'll cry and I don't want to. Not now.'

His hand is resting on mine. Just briefly. More like a gentle pat than anything else.

'Okay,' he says. 'Drink your coffee. I'll tell you about Barney and me.'

We drive home at about four o'clock, quiet and companionable. I wish we could go on talking; spend the evening together even.

What am I thinking of?

In any case Jack drops me off firmly, so there is no option. 'I think we both have things to do,' he says. (Like what things?).

'I'm going to Madrid tomorrow but come and have supper with me on Friday at my place. About eight?'

I would love to—but paradoxically I am now feeling rather uncomfortable about that. It must show because he laughs. 'Is it my cooking that worries you or being alone in the house with a ferocious man? You can bring Frankly to protect you…'

'A fat lot of use that would be!'

'And if you come to my house, you can leave whenever you want to. It gives you more options.'

That's considerate—and I do feel nervous about this. But I also don't want him to go off to Madrid for four days. Oh good grief! I don't need complications but I am surely creating them.

Jack takes my hand and kisses it just as I am opening the car door.

'*Hasta luego*' (until next time), he says.

I smile at him briefly, not showing the heart-jump of surprise and delight from such an elegant courtesy, and slide as gracefully as I can out of the car.

I know that I am already missing him as I battle with the key in the lock of *Casa Taylor*. I give Frankly the piece of fish he saved for her and got the waiter to wrap in silver foil and, inexplicably, I burst into tears.

This will not do.

A brisk walk is what we need. Come on Frankly, let's go.

Chapter Nine

TODAY WAS NEVER going to be a good day. I have to take the car back but the feeling I had on waking up signified something worse than that. God knows what but sometimes you just know.

On the good side, it does look as if the finances over the house will be sorted out. But not soon enough and I simply cannot afford to keep the car any longer.

It takes all day; two and a half hours driving to the airport and then all the palaver of finding buses to get back. They run pretty regularly and I have had good instructions from Rani and Sylvia who use them all the time. On a good day it might even be fun but today just doesn't feel right—and I am quite panicky about living without a car.

I left Frankly with Katherine—or, more accurately, I left Frankly with Katherine's sofa. They have a deep and meaningful relationship nowadays—and Katherine says she enjoys Frankly's company. One wonders if her husband ignored her and slept all day when he was here. If so, there wouldn't be an awful lot of difference.

Katherine is a sweetheart and says she'll be glad to take me to the shops when she's going but it's not the same. Independence is lost. Suddenly I realise how far from anywhere Los Poops is.

I'm whingeing a bit, I know. It wouldn't have been so bad today if I hadn't missed the shuttle car from the coast up to Los Poops. There is one three times a day for the villagers and, had the bus from Malaga not had that altercation with a lorry, I would have been in plenty of time for the last one. As it is, I now have to walk home up the ten kilometres of road or risk cutting across country. It will be dusk in an hour. Whichever way, it's very seriously uphill and it's going to take a long time.

So I am walking ferociously upwards in as straight a line as I can while the light remains. From here you can't see Los Poops so it's all guesswork.

And I do feel ferocious. All the anger and hatred against Alex and his bloody self-righteous behaviour is seething inside me. I got an email from William the Saint yesterday saying that Alex had told him that he knew I would be better off without him and I should be glad to be set free.

Firstly, it is not Alex's place to tell me that; secondly it is patronising and thirdly, I hate his fucking guts.

I'm growing interested in Buddhism and I rather like the idea of reincarnation and Karma (slowly but surely, I am making my way through that amazing wall of books). It's all a bit odd for a lapsed Catholic—but Buddhism and mystical Judaism are holding my interest a lot and, paradoxically, seem to be making more sense of silly old St. Augustine.

It makes me wonder what I must have done in a past life—or several—to be abandoned twice. First Danny and now Alex. Yes, it's different but both times I end up alone, having to cope with the anger and loss.

However, Danny is closer to me now that Alex has gone. That's quite nice in a funny sort of way. I think more fondly of him than I have for years. I wish I had a photograph of him here.

It's amazing how fast you throw the previous loves away when you have someone new.

Anyway, I like the idea that I am paying off past Karma when Alex is accruing it. He's left three women in his life now and, in retrospect, I am aghast that it never occurred to me that he was almost certain to leave me too. You don't break patterns unless you are what the Buddhists call 'awake.'

Oh God, where's the bloody road gone?

I want a drink.

I want to watch Alex be beaten senseless by someone who loves me.

I want Suzie to dump him. Oh, how I want Suzie to dump him!

This is not helping. I may be moving fast through fury but it isn't exactly comfortable. And the light's getting a bit dim. Next time I cross the road I'd better start following it. There's already been a car going up and I could have got a lift if I had kept to the road. I am amazed that I am not even more furious about this—after all, I could be home now. Perhaps I am at the limit of my fury? Is there a depth or a height that you can reach? I guess so. I remember the depth of the anguish a couple of weeks after Danny died and going right down into it after one gin and tonic too many. Just at the point when I thought I would die, where the pain was shot through with strange silver darts, it stopped getting worse. It seemed to bottom out and from then on there was nowhere to go but up. I remember being quite cross about that at the time—after all, there is a certain self-satisfaction in being righteously miserable beyond all reason. And then, to add insult to injury, bowed over in sorrow and angst I suddenly seemed to see myself from outside—and I began to giggle.

And, damn it, I'm giggling now. Outrageous. Just when I was getting a really good strop going.

There will be another car. And people do tend to give you a lift on this kind of terrain. After all, even I did!

I find the road again and, apart from obvious loops where you don't lose sight of it, I keep to the tarmac. Consigning Alex to a pit of boiling oil, I start to think about my friendship with Jack (now don't start putting any angles on this. It's a friendship, nothing more.)

Yes, I do find him attractive (well, quite) but he is married and he intends to stay that way and, even if I fancied the socks off him there's nothing doing there from my point of view even if there were from his.

After all, that would make me no better than Alex, would it? And even if I didn't already know that it was wrong, that part of it would put me off for a start.

This is a man who may or may not still love his wife in the same way that he used to but who honours her and is willing to make compromises for her. This is a man who had a vasectomy when doctors told his wife she shouldn't have more children (for a moment I am shocked at the casual intimacy of his having told me that). He is not about to leave her and I like him all the more for that.

I think I'll leave that point now because I'm feeling rather jealous of Karen, having such a good and honest man. Not to mention one where rubber, drugs or bodily inserts aren't required during sex. Why couldn't I find one?

Even so, I am cheered. There *are* such honourable men in the world and, whenever it's time, maybe I will find one who's available. Or, even better, he will find me.

With the murdering hatred abated—and the road a little less steep now—I can even enjoy the sunset which is uncurling gently across the sky behind me and to my left and sending soft tendrils of light across my shoulders. First they are just silvery with tinges of grey as the sun hides behind clouds and then it slides below them to roar scarlet heat in all directions across the landscape.

I think I must be about halfway—and in front of me I can see the shepherd and his flock. They are quite a distance ahead and, I would have thought, very late getting home. How ironic that I should be following him up the hill when I gave him a lift only a week or so ago.

Yiannis is standing still, shading his eyes and watching the sunset. Will he see me? Do I want him to?

Yes, he does, and his hand arcs up in greeting. Then, leaving the dogs to drive the sheep along the old, established route, he comes bounding down the hill towards me.

I stand, perplexed. I am not such a friend of his that he would want to do such a thing. I even look behind me to see if there is some other person whom he has seen. But no, it is me. How strange.

'*¡Hola!*' the deeply tanned face is alight with pleasure and he is almost bouncing over the rough bushes that punctuate the dry and barren land between almond trees.

Actually he really is quite handsome, if ridiculously young. And for some, strange reason, he really likes me. This is stupid, of course.

Now he's chatting away at me—oh, he's asking where Frankly is.

'I have come from Malaga on the bus,' I say. 'She is in the village.'

He seems pleased and gestures that I can walk with him and the sheep. Well, they will know the shortcuts so I might as well. And I do love the scent of him. Not to mention enjoying the obvious youthful admiration. Yiannis whistles to the dogs and they halt the line of sheep and goats and stand waiting for us.

Hmm, it must be nice to have a dog that obeys you.

'You are leaving the village?' I say.

'*Si, mañana*'

Tomorrow! Actually I feel a rush of relief. Youthful adoration is one thing but it can easily get out of hand and I don't want any awkwardness.

By now we are walking among the sheep and goats and the dogs are herding them again instead of guarding them. But the sheep know where to go anyway and meander on in their own peaceful, munching way.

Yiannis and I walk companionably talking more with our hands than anything else. The sun is dipping over the horizon now and the colours of the sky are indescribably magnificent. I stop for a moment, wiping sweat from my forehead and enjoying the encroaching coolness of evening.

Yiannis asks me something—I think it is whether I will have a drink with him. He is meeting his friends at the bar as it is his goodbye party. Well, there's no objection to going to the bar—but I'd want a shower first. I explain that I would like to wash and change first and he says '*¿Ocho?*' meaning eight o'clock.

'*Bueno.*' How funny—I have a kind of date!

It is another half hour before we are back in Los Poops and I am so tired. But I am grateful to Yiannis for his company and we smile at each other on parting. '*Hasta luego,*' we say.

Frankly is squeaky and pleased to see me and has that indefinable 'I've been over-fed' look. Katherine coos over her and says she's welcome anytime and what a little rascal she is, isn't she?

'What did she steal?' I say wearily.

'Oh, nothing. She found some chicken in the fridge.'

'*In* the fridge?'

I remember then that Katherine has what Frankly would term A Walk-In Fridge, all too easily accessible to a beagle. Also that I have seen Katherine leave the fridge door open as she pours milk in tea on the other side of the kitchen or makes more than one journey with some of its contents. Frankly will have observed this closely and lurked like the shark she is until Katherine opened the fridge door and left it—and dived for the nearest piece of food.

'Oh Katherine, I'm so sorry,' I say. 'I'll buy you some more.'

'No need,' says Katherine, beaming. 'She's such a sweetheart, I didn't mind.'

Hmm. I must remember not to feed Frankly any other time I ask Katherine to look after her.

We walk home together with the beagle rolling like a barrel with her slightly distended tummy. She isn't interested in a proper walk (which is a relief after all the walking I've done) so we just go straight home.

There isn't really time to go round to *Casa Blanca* even though I would love a bath, so it's into the shower and a quick turnaround. A little make-up and the blue dress—after all, why not? It's all perfectly above board.

I am meeting Yiannis in the bar. Rani and Sylvia are there, too, as well as a German couple who are on holiday here. Yiannis comes up to me as I walk in and shakes my hand (how sweet!). He buys me a gin and tonic and we are surrounded by people of all nationalities chatting to each other. My Spanish is not good enough to catch most of it at the speed it is going but it is all very pleasant and there is a happy joke that I am Yiannis's date for the night. He is beaming and I am making happy faces about it so that everyone is laughing.

I don't usually spend much time in the bar but this evening is different. Dion, who owns it, stands a round for Yiannis as everyone knows he's leaving and, by 10pm, we're all a little merry. It's fun!

By midnight I am more than just a little drunk and it is time to go. I say goodbye to Yiannis and kiss him on both cheeks. Sylvia and Rani wave at me—they are good for another hour or until Dion decides to close tonight and the night closes over everyone else.

Golly, I'm sozzled! How lovely! And I can weave my way home via *Casa Blanca* and have that much-wanted bath.

Yiannis catches up with me just as I open the door of the

house. He is running and he is in the doorway with me before I realise what is happening. He is asking me why I am here as he was looking for me at *Casa Taylor*.

I'm too drunk to mind so I tell him that I am going to have a bath. He has a bottle of wine in his hand and I am not stupid—I know what he is hoping for.

This is out of the question. But before I realise that fully, Jack's face comes up in my mind. Jack Risborough, faithful husband. Jack Risborough, who will never make love to me.

Before I know it, Yiannis and I are in the house together.

This is not wise.

Neither is responding as his mouth meets mine and his arms pull me to him. Neither is allowing him to kiss me again and push against me with what is obviously great enthusiasm.

But, oh God, how wonderful it is to be wanted by a man. And such a youthful, beautiful one too. It would be almost safe—my period is just about to start and surely he won't be desperately infected with anything vile.

Stop it Anna! You can't even consider anything like that. And what if he is?

But I want to, says my body and Yiannis's hand is on my breast making me breathless with the shock of how wonderful that is.

I need a someone to expunge Alex from my body—and Yiannis is leaving tomorrow. What better opportunity could there be?

If I say no, I will regret it. If I say yes, I will be overcome with embarrassment tomorrow.

But I will have had sex.

Madness and alcohol are too much for me. I want this so much. I so want to be fucked—to have pure, mindless man and woman sex. And by God that's what I'm going to get!

I leave him, dozing on the uncovered bed, at about 5am. He squeezes my hand sleepily as I go, understanding why I'm leaving and smiling up at me. He can let himself out and I really must get back before the morning is fully awake and anyone is up who knows me—and before full awareness of my trollopdom hits me.

God, I feel wonderful! I can hardly walk—yes, really! But I feel fabulous. My lips are swollen, my nipples are sore and if I don't have a series of love-bites, I'm a Dutchman!

Oh Alex! You are out of my body! You are gone and, what's more, he was brilliant and loving and caring and he made me feel like a million dollars. He told me I was beautiful in Spanish and proved it to me—four times. FOUR times! And he made you look like an insensitive oik.

And it was great. Just brilliant.

Even more brilliant is that my period is just starting—so I don't even have to worry about that. I think I have suddenly been allotted a guardian angel who is working overtime.

About time too. Thank you whoever or whatever. God, that does feel better.

Frankly is asleep down the bed but she wakes, squeaking, as I clamber in. We have a cuddle and I curl up to savour the glorious feelings of soreness and awareness of having been filled to the hilt and pushed around just enough to feel it and feel mastered but not enough actually to hurt.

I remember a friend who was having an affair telling me she hadn't realised how mundane sex with her husband had got. I hadn't realised how mundane it was with Alex. Soon, he and Suzie will be heading for the same mundanity (is there such a word?). And I've just had the best shagging of my life. Hooray.

Excuse me for all this bragging. But it is a very special occasion.

Of course, when I wake up four hours later I am paralysed with embarrassment. However, I expected that and it hasn't completely vanquished the silly grin on my face as I look in the bathroom window. The damage isn't too bad—just the one conspicuous bite on the side of my neck and I can wear a scarf. Down lower there is plenty of evidence.

'Goodness me!' I say, sounding like a vicar's wife. 'I don't even remember that bit.'

Oh yes, I do…

A cup of tea never tasted so good. Neither did a slice of toast and honey.

Actually, it turned out to be quite a good day in the end…

* * *

With an attractive purple and gold chiffon scarf round my neck and a terrible, delayed hangover, I join the rest of the village in the square at noon to say goodbye to Yiannis. He grins at me and nods as he gets into his uncle's car and they drive away, hooting merrily on the horn. I don't even know him in the daylight and that feels really odd. But I know that over the next few days I will pay for my delight because my body will crave him again. Oh well. It's best as it is.

'Great evening last night,' says Rani, at my shoulder.

'Yes, I enjoyed myself.'

He smiles at me. 'Supper tomorrow night?'

'No thanks. Can't. Having supper with Watlington P. tomorrow.'

'Really? Didn't know you knew him that well.'

'I don't, but he comes from Colorado and I lived there so I think I may even get a picture show.'

Rani laughs and claps me on the back. 'Careful, girl,' he says. 'Rumours start easily enough round here. Just don't let Stella see you go in the door.'

I am amused at the idea of being warned against a rumour considering what I have already been up to. And I am looking forward to seeing Jack again. It's nice to have a cerebral relationship with someone without even thinking about sex.

At least, it is when you've just had some.

Half of me is expecting Jack to cancel or not to turn up. It would seem too much like a good thing to have a great evening with him after such a surprising week. But I think my luck has changed.

About time, too.

Most of Friday is spent catching up on emails and sorting out my non-existent life in England. Good news though, Frankly's blood test is through and she has passed so in she can go home when the Pet Passport scheme starts in March. The test is backdated to the day the blood was taken—the whole process is meant to take six months.

Alex has completely capitulated over the money for the house.

I have to admire that solicitor—he said that rather than hurrying up the divorce, Alex's actions were postponing it. If he released the money I might cite—if not, I would keep him waiting for a minimum of two years. It seems to have worked.

I am intending to ask Jack what to do about a car. Perhaps I could buy a cheap local one from someone just for the next few months?

Of course, I have nothing to wear, having worn the blue dress last time. The bronze-coloured one will have to do; only I know how old it is.

I would like to take a bottle of wine but the only stuff available in the village shop is disgusting so I think I will pick him some flowers instead. He won't appreciate them but he might appreciate the thought, if you see what I mean. There are still roses blooming down by that old ruined house where I first saw him so I take Frankly down there for her late afternoon walk. It must have been a lovely home once.

As we are walking back and I am carrying an armful of pink and yellow roses, Frankly starts to retch. She throws up some kind of sludge but, unusually, does not pick up immediately as she always does when sick. Her eyes look glazed and she is panting. Oh God, what is it?

Poison! Oh God, she's eaten poison—and I don't have a car. Dear God, what shall I do?

She is staggering now. I drop the roses and snatch her up in my arms and now I am running up the path to the village. But she is too heavy and I can't carry her far. I must get help. Can she walk? No. And I can't leave her, I just can't. So I pick her up again and stagger on. God knows how long it takes us to get to the edge of the village. I lay her down in the shade and run as fast as I can up to Jack's house. Please God may he be in!

I am practically knocking the door down—but he is there.

'Anna! What is it?'

'Frankly... poison,' I stammer.

Jack's face goes white. 'Where is she?'

'Down the hill, by the square.'

He is racing away from me now and I lean against the door,

tears beginning to flood down my cheeks. Before I can muster the strength to follow him he is running back up the hill with Frankly limp in his arms.

'Oh God…'

'Has she been sick?'

'Yes.'

'Then there's hope. Hold her while I get the antidote.'

He places my shivering little beagle in my arms and runs into the house. Antidote? There's an antidote? He returns with a bottle of fluid which he practically forces down Frankly's throat. She chokes and is sick all over me. I don't care. Jack tips her head back and forces more into her. She is sick again. More goes down with her resisting now.

'Good sign,' says Jack, ruthlessly making her drink.

This time the fluid stays down.

'Okay,' he says. 'That's all we can do for now. We have to get her to a vet. I'll get the car.'

He leaves me holding the still quivering dog and weeping unashamedly. 'Oh Frankly, don't leave me, please don't leave me.'

Then the BMW is beside us and Jack has sprung out to open the door. Before I have fastened the seat belt we are out of the village and taking the first bend down the hill as fast as is safe.

Frankly is sick again, half over me, half over the car.

'Don't worry about it,' says Jack curtly. 'Cars can be cleaned. It's a good sign.'

God I love him.

'Which vet?' he says.

'I go to Almeria,' I say. 'But it's too far.'

'There's one in Motril,' he says. 'It's only five miles. I know where it is.'

We fly those five miles and are outside a shop with a green cross before I can get myself together. I am watching Frankly anxiously and stroking her. She is rigid and shivering but manages to lick my hand once.

Jack bangs on the door before coming round to my side of the car to lift Frankly out. Someone opens the door saying that the vet's is closed.

'Emergencia!' says Jack. 'Anna, park the car somewhere.'

'But…'

'Do it! I'll take care of her.' And he is gone.

I do park the car. It isn't easy because it's huge and I don't know the town. Part of me is furious but another part recognises that I might not want to be there if Frankly's stomach is being pumped or they are doing things to her that would make everything look worse.

But what if she dies and I'm not there? I should be there… at least I should be there.

Oh God, don't let her die. Please don't let her die.

I am crying again as I stagger back to the vet's. They are, technically, closed but, thank God, the vet obviously lives just above the premises. I bang on the door but have to wait. If they are saving her life in that time, so be it.

Jack lets me in. He looks strained and guides me into the consulting room with a hand on my back. A young woman is stroking Frankly who is lying still on the bench.

No! Frankly! No!

The woman is talking to me gently but I can't hear her. Jack catches me and turns me into his arms.

'It's all right, Anna.'

'No, no!' I am screaming.

'Shut up!' he says. 'You'll wake her! She's alive. It's okay.'

My legs give way for a second and he pulls me up.

'She's under a light anaesthetic,' he says. 'It's to calm the system down. The stomach's clear and she hasn't taken very much in. She'll have to stay overnight but it doesn't look too bad, Anna.'

I am at the bench, touching Frankly and feeling the warmth in her body. The vet is talking to me again, in very heavily accented English. I am so relieved and so exhausted and tear-ridden and I feel like a little girl with a grown-up comforting her.

The vet is kind. I must leave Frankly with her but there is good hope. She was sick soon enough and the medicine Jack gave her probably saved her life. The vet will telephone later this evening and again in the morning to tell us how she is.

'Do we have to leave her?' I say pathetically. 'She'll be lost when she wakes up.'

'She will be in my living room,' says the vet. 'I will keep her with me. Try not to worry.'

I can hardly remember being shepherded out and then I can only just remember where the car is.

'Have a good cry,' says Jack comfortingly, handing me a big, white handkerchief. So I do.

We are back at his house before I remember that I didn't give the vet my telephone number.'

'She's got mine,' says Jack. 'You're coming to supper, remember? You can give her your number then.'

I don't think I could eat a thing.

But slowly, as I sit with a glass of Sancerre and watch Jack doing things with a wok I start to relax a little. This was not how I envisaged the evening—I am still in jeans and trainers and am wearing no make-up.

'I went to pick you some flowers,' I say. 'I didn't have any decent wine. I went down to the ruined house where I first saw you. She must have picked it up there. The poison, I mean.'

'Unlikely,' he says. 'Why would there be poison there? No one wants to kill rats there.'

'But there are people who deliberately poison dogs.'

'Yes, and the hunting season is just starting—but it seems odd to place it there. We may never know, Anna.'

'I don't know how I can let her off the lead again.'

'Oh, we'll find out who's laying poison,' says Jack grimly. 'Don't you worry about that. Just keep her safe for a week or so and it'll be sorted.'

'If she's okay,'

'She'll be okay.'

'We don't know that.'

He touches my shoulder. 'We don't know anything,' he says. 'But the odds are in her favour. Now, I want you to tell me something Anna.'

'Yes?'

'When did you see me down at the ruined house?'

Oh shit.

Well, nothing for it now but to own up.

'When you first saw Frankly. I was there too. But… I hid.'

'Any particular reason?'

'Well, you looked as if you wanted to be alone.'

There is silence for a moment.

'You don't have to tell me anything,' I say. 'I didn't want to intrude then and I don't now.'

'Oh, it's okay.' But he is shaking his head.

The food is ready and he is tipping it out into two white bowls, chicken livers and rice and mushrooms and cream. Delicious.

We don't say anything as we sit down at the little round wooden table in the corner of the beautiful blue and white tiled kitchen. Jack pours me more wine and avoids my gaze.

'Oh for God's sake, Jack!' I say. 'Okay, I saw you crying. It's allowed. Something upset you. It's nothing to be ashamed of. Why is it such a problem?'

'Oh it isn't,' he says, looking down at his food. 'It's just that… well, that was the day that I heard my dog was dead.'

Ah, that's what I thought. Poor man.

I don't need to say anything but I put my hand out to touch his, just as he did for me last week.

'I'm sorry.'

'Yeah.'

I think he wants to say something else so I wait.

'It's just that…'

Say nothing Anna. Say nothing. Just wait. Yes, here it comes.

'It's just that he wasn't that ill. He could have been fine with medication. But he was a bother. Karen had him put down.'

The chicken livers taste like ash in my mouth.

'Without asking you?'

'Without asking me.'

'Oh God, Jack.'

I am round the table and holding him and he is holding me back. It only lasts a second and, by mutual consent we are back in our places and eating our supper before we can even register it.

'This is great,' I say, indicating the food. 'You're a brilliant cook.'

Jack smiles at me. 'Tell me a good story,' he says. 'We could both do with cheering up.'

'Okay,' I rack my brains and remember the story of the buffalo ghost in the Madison Hotel in Unityville. He'll like that.

I start rather hurriedly and he is concentrating too hard but it is a good story and we begin to relax.

The Madison is not a motel—those are up on 19th Street together with McDonalds and Taco Bell—but to be honest it is not a hotel either. It used to be one and it still has a big sign on the top saying that it *is* a hotel so that when the tourists flock into town they get neatly fooled and the staff have to explain for the hundredth time that it is now private apartments.

There are three restaurants on the ground floor of The Madison which adds to the confusion. One is permanently closed; one is a bar with burgers and pasta and the other is a mixture of Thai, Indian and Chinese cooking all thrown together. There are not enough people in Unityville for all three cultures to have their own restaurants and nobody in this wonderful cowboy town really knows the difference. They just think that it is incredibly cultured and add soy sauce to everything.

It seems doubly incongruous to have oriental cuisine here because the lobby is so typically Western with wooden furniture and stuffed animal trophies all over the walls. You walk in and are assaulted with images of dead elk, moose and bear. Once, when they ran out of room on the walls, they started tacking moose and bear skin onto the ceiling but one of them fell on someone during the annual New Year Dance and they sued.

The Madison Hotel is haunted. Not by a '49er' or an old cowpoke or a saloon girl who went to the bad or even a gunfighter who drew just one second too slowly. No, it's far more interesting than that: it is haunted by a buffalo.

Once you have got past the inevitable disappointment that the haunting has nothing to do with a sex scandal or a shoot-out, a buffalo is one of the better kind of ghosts. It is not likely to be vindictive or particularly scary and there can be so much enjoyable speculation about how a buffalo got there in the first place; how it died and why it would bother to become a ghost about it all.

On a particularly dark night you could be forgiven for thinking that you had seen the ghost—and that it actually *was* playing silly buggers with the wall—because the stuffed busts of animals hanging everywhere do include one of a massive buffalo right by the stairs. No one will confirm or deny whether this particular buffalo is the originator of the ghost story but the less imaginative will, of course, claim authoritatively that it is; that there is no ghost and the story was just invented by the over-inebriated imagination of a few local cowboys.

Others say that it's not surprising that the spirit of the buffalo haunts the lobby if half of its physical remains have been stapled to the wall. One wonders at that point whether it is the *other half* of the buffalo which does the haunting or whether it is just the front bit wafting out of its immaculately stuffed remains when it feels particularly bored. However, two things militate against the original theory behind this. The first is that it is definitely a whole buffalo that does the haunting and the second is that it does it almost exclusively in the lift.

In most buildings, fitting a buffalo into a lift would appear to be a pretty tall order and this particular lift is no exception. It is a small lift—a *very* small lift—and it has those old-fashioned hand-pulled metal doors which contract and expand and which would be completely incapable of closing over a buffalo's behind. But the dear departed of this planet are not limited by physical laws and it would appear that the buffalo fits whatever part of its non-anatomy is required into the lift together with the passengers and lets the rest of it ride up and down through the lobby ceiling as required.

'I know the Madison,' says Jack. 'I went there once, but I never saw the ghost.'

'You went to Unityville?'

'Yeah, now and again. When I couldn't avoid it.'

I flip a piece of bread at him and we laugh. There is still a sickness in the bottom of my stomach and a fear that is simmering but I couldn't ask for a better companion.

Now we have finished the meal but there is more wine. The telephone hasn't rung.

'Okay,' says Jack. 'She will ring when she can. It doesn't matter if it's late. Neither of us has to get up and go to work. We have all night if need be. Why don't you start at the beginning and go on to the end?'

'Of what?'

'Of your story. Tell me about Alex. You already feel like death, so this is the perfect time.'

Yes it is.

Chapter Ten

I AM WALKING Frankly among the sagebrush and Indian Paint on the hillside above Unityville, watching for the first slivers of silver sunset that will soon engulf the enormous Rocky Mountain sky. Following the silver will be pink and orange, crimson and vermilion, purple and gold; all the colours spreading, dancing and weaving themselves across the great arc of sky above. The people of Unityville come out of their houses each evening just to watch it, night upon night. Never was anywhere so beautiful to them or to me.

I throw my arms out as I walk, drinking in the spring air and rejoicing that the harshness of winter is through. Even in April there is snow on the ground but only in little pockets here and there on the higher ground. It still falls in the night now and again but people go to work in shorts (even wading through a foot of snowfall) knowing that it will melt in hours and the temperature will be up to 70 degrees by noon.

Alex will be on his way home now, walking back from the campus, and we shall reach the house at roughly the same time with Frankly scampering ahead to greet him with squeaks of joy. This is our afternoon routine and every day I look forward to seeing his smiling face. Alex has been so happy in Colorado; happier than I have ever seen him. And, although I know that my own happiness is just as important, life is always easier if Alex is content.

It is time now to make our way down from Amity Park and walk back along Granville Street to our 1920s wooden home at 626 South Fifth. I call to Frankly, who ignores me on purpose just to make the point, and set off back down the narrow path. She will follow in her own good time; there is never any point in hurrying Frankly. She drives Alex crazy with her bolshieness but it rarely bothers me. Frankly knows on which side her bread is buttered and it is suppertime at the end of this walk. By the time I get to the edge of the road, Frankly will be right by my feet looking as if it were entirely an accident that we should meet just there and it was Nothing At All To Do With Supper.

The upheaval in moving to Colorado, just two years after we married, was huge. Everything that was any good could go with us (a twelve-week trip via the Panama Canal) but there was a lot that had to go and it got to the point that the charity shops in the local High Street put out a red carpet every time they saw my car.

And the car had to go too. And all the bills wound up. Horrifically complicated. Not to mention saying goodbye to friends and family who either thought it would be a great idea to spend holidays in Colorado or who thought that the end of the world had come.

And now, here we are, settling in well and over the difficulties of losing old friends, coping with AT&T and dealing with different shops and supermarkets with new brand names, leading to endless experiments over what bathroom cleaners actually work. This particular afternoon, I am walking back down Granville Street, counting my blessings and dancing a little. We have steak and kidney pie for supper and it is *Ally McBeal* and *Frazier* on TV.

Surprisingly, Alex is already home. I call out a greeting as I walk in through the unlocked door (no one ever locks their doors in Unityville). Frankly clatters past me on the wooden floor and goes to investigate in case Supper has already, magically, appeared in the kitchen. Alex is making tea.

When he turns to face me I can see that his face is like thunder. 'Oh, not another row with the Principal,' I think with an all-too familiar feeling of weariness settling down in my stomach. These have happened on and off for the last couple of months and, though they do not seem all that serious to me, Alex hates them and hours afterwards are filled with discussion of the Principal's stupidity or lack of vision. It never lasts—Alex is mercurial at the best of times and the row is forgotten in twenty-four hours. But it takes its toll on me. Mentally I wave goodbye to *Ally* and resign myself to a tedious evening.

152

'Are you okay?' I ask, reaching up for our customary kiss.

'No.' The answer is curt and the kiss is partially avoided. Alex puts the teapot, cups and milk on a tray. 'Come into the living room,' he says. 'I need to talk to you.'

You know when there's a serious problem. All my senses are tensed and I follow him nervously, ignoring Frankly who is beginning to fuss for her food.

She follows us into the living room and squeaks. Alex shouts at her and she backs out, ears flattened against her head. She has heard that tone of voice before and knows that it is not to be messed with.

I sit on the edge of the sofa and Alex begins.

He has resigned from his job. It is just too much to have to work with an idiot like Brinkley. He is applying for another position and he hopes to hear if he has an interview in the next few days. The current job here will finish at the end of the month.

It does not sink in at first. I assume that the 'other job' is in the same department of the University; but no. 'In Colorado?' I ask nervously, thinking of the complications of moving again.

'No,' says Alex. 'In London.'

You can become very American very quickly in many ways. In a tentative voice I say: 'London, England?'

'Yes,' says Alex. 'I've had it with here. I want to work with genuine academics. The people here don't know what they're talking about.

'In any case, without a job I don't have a visa. We'll have to go home.'

There is silence. I look at Frankly who is sitting watching us from the doorway, still hoping for movement on the Supper Situation. She is nearly ten years old and, even if I could believe that she would survive six months in quarantine, I know that I could not bear to put her through it. Both Alex and I know of dogs that have died in the long six months of separation and life in a sterilised cage.

'But…' I say, stunned. 'What about Frankly?'

Alex takes my hand. 'I know,' he says. 'I'm sorry. We'll have to re-home her. We both know that she would never make it through quarantine and neither of us could put her through that.

'We can take her to the Humane Society tomorrow to give them enough time to find someone nice.'

We sleep apart that night after an evening of bitter recriminations. Could he not transfer to another department? Could he not at least stay on until the end of the college year so that I can work something out about Frankly? Could he not just say that he'd been wrong and stay on?

'For a dog?' says Alex, icily. 'You want me to stay on for the sake of a dog? What is the matter with you, Anna? It's *only* a dog, for God's sake. She won't even miss you after the first few weeks.'

And I am weeping. I know that, in his logical mind, he is right but emotionally he is nowhere. Frankly *would* miss me. And does he not love this furry scrap that clambers all over us and plants wet-nose kisses on our faces?

'You can't love a dog,' says Alex. 'You can only cathect a dog.' Cathexis, he explains, is a one-way thing. As the dog can't love you back it can't be love.

'She does love us,' I say. 'And I love her.'

'More than me?' says Alex. And I am silent. At that moment I wonder if it is true that I might.

'Don't make me choose,' I say wretchedly.

'You shouldn't have to even consider choosing,' says Alex, walking out of the room.

'But what about Colorado?' I ask, following him and changing the subject. 'You love it here. You were so excited to be here! You want to live here!'

'It was you who wanted to live here,' says Alex. 'I didn't mind. But it was you who fell in love with the place. I'll be perfectly happy back in London.'

I am silent. There is nothing that I can say. I know him very well, you see, and there is a side to him that means that Alex is never wrong. If he has changed his mind about something, then he never wanted it in the first place. He did want to come to Colorado but now he wants to go home. That is it.

'How can you make such a huge decision unilaterally,' I ask, eventually. 'Why didn't you talk to me first?' But as the spare room door closes behind him, I know the reason why the question has been unanswered. If Alex had talked to me first, I might have been able to talk him out of this; make him change his mind. All those evenings of discussing Brinkley's faults and problems in the department were not just little things; every time I shored Alex up or told him that it was a storm in a teacup I managed to make him feel better and stronger. But now he doesn't want to risk that. He has made up his mind. And we are going back to England. Without Frankly.

I cannot do it. It is just impossible. But what can I do? In the night I toss and turn, fretting and crying in turn. I do not want to go back to England. I want to stay in Colorado. It was a big enough change to come here—and now I have to go back? And without my little beagle.

It is horrific to realise that I could even think about making that choice. Alex is my husband but Frankly is not *only* a dog; she is *my* dog and my friend and my companion. A dog is for life, not just for Christmas—or for convenience—and I will not let her go.

Suddenly, the memory of the planned Passports for Pets scheme slips into my mind. It is not running yet—and it is only for animals going to Europe—but what if…?

It is three o'clock in the morning; ten o'clock in England. I slip downstairs and call AT&T international enquiries.

'London, England please,' I say. 'The Ministry of Agriculture, Farming and Fisheries.'

It is strange to hear an English voice at the end of the line. 'The Pet Travel Scheme Office please,' I say, with a lump of anxiety in my throat. It seems to take ages but then I am through.'

'Can I help you?'

'Yes please. I want to know whether, if a dog from America goes to Europe and lives there for six months, it would then qualify as a European dog as far as the scheme goes,' I say.

There is silence while the woman is thinking.

'I don't know,' she says. 'I would imagine so. Hold on, I'll check.'

She comes back after what seems to be an age.

'Yes, that's fine,' she says, little knowing that I am crying silently at the end of the phone. 'Although it would have to be seven months to fit the full criteria. The dog has to have a microchip in Europe, then a rabies injection and then wait a month for the blood test. However, the seven months in Europe would count the same as quarantine. Is there anything else I can help you with?'

But I can't answer. I am crying too much and I put down the phone.

For a while, I can do nothing. Then I walk to the back door and go out into the garden barefoot. It is a clear night with the stars glittering in the deep velvet sky. I do not know how I shall do it; how to afford it or where I begin. I shall have to find care for Frankly somewhere in Europe while I go back to England with Alex to work out our new life. But I know that I will bring her home, somehow. I will.

'No,' says Alex. He is eating home-made muesli with a mulish expression on his face. Hostilities had been suspended temporarily while we got ourselves up but now that I have re-opened the subject over the breakfast table, blood is flowing again.

'You don't have to do anything,' I say. 'I'll find somewhere in Europe. France or Spain. We must know someone who has a friend somewhere who can help.

'I'll just take her there and find some care for her and come back to England to you.'

To be honest, my heart sinks at both thoughts. How do you find dog care in a country where you do not even speak the language? And even if I can do it, returning to the Tupperware-box skies of England is so depressing. And London! Everyone loves London except me. I was born and raised in Warwickshire, used to woods and fields and hedges, and even life in Warrington was only twenty minutes from the countryside. To me, London is just big and dirty and crowded. Looking out of the window here, in Unityville, I can see no traffic and no smog. The sky is bright blue—almost echoing in its vastness and beauty—and the only sounds are bird calls or people chatting in the street. No, I am wrong. A car has just gone past. In fact, it has just skidded on some ice and crashed into another car at the junction up the road.

That is surreal.

It happens quite a lot in the winter, when there is ice four inches thick on the roads, despite the snow tyres on our cars. We go out to check that no one is hurt (they are not) and just that little action seems to help us to get a grip on things. I tuck my hand into Alex's arm and he smiles down at me. We are always okay as long as we can touch.

So we hug and all is better and Alex goes off to work and I take Frankly for her morning walk around the houses.

Today is a lovely day, bright and still and here and there a few of the first spring flowers are beginning to peep through the grass. Spring comes late in the Rockies and all the rich folk run away in March, having become tired of waiting for snowdrops, daffodils, tulips and lilacs. Confusingly, all the spring flowers turn up at once at the end of April, making a riot of colours which perplex English senses and make the air redolent with scent.

My mind is reeling. I love this place; truly love it. I have felt such a sense of freedom here and such companionship from the people of the town. When we arrived and all our furniture was making its way across the sea and through the Panama Canal, our brand-new next-door neighbours turned up with all the furniture from their basement. They did not need it, they said; we might as well use it until our own came. Others, from across the road, chipped in over the next week and before we knew it we were more than comfortable when we thought that we would have to camp like squatters for months.

We will have to sell the house and arrange for all the furniture to go back to the UK. And I have to find someone who is willing to care for a dog in Europe. Where do I start? What do I do? Alex's objections are pushed aside in my mind—I simply cannot believe them. When he has sorted himself out, he must see that I cannot leave Frankly behind.

Frankly, of course, knows nothing of this. She is trotting along happily, enjoying the smells of spring and doing what comes naturally in her happy, doggy way.

She should be on a lead, it is mandatory here, but I always go down the back roads between gardens (sorry, yarrrrds) and the lone cop who patrols these streets never looks down there.

Between Seventh and Eight Street is Palmer Park, the entry to a long, narrow ribbon of land which once was a railroad track and which follows the little Diamond River all the way to the edge of town. Frankly perks up as soon as we get there and looks back at me with her We Are Going Further Aren't We? look.

'Yes!' I say and she trots happily onwards. I still wonder whether she understands the difference in smells from the ones that she grew up with. Here, the passers-by are raccoons, chipmunks, gophers, prairie dogs—even the foxes are different. I suppose it is too much to expect her to look surprised at different smells (and anyway, she is used to them by now) but her calm acceptance seems strange to me. I am amazed at how much I still feel the loss of the English robin. But then I shake myself because I am going to see English robins again very soon.

Not that soon. There is a stubbornness inherent in me that will not give up on my plan.

But, in the meantime, we are walking along Diamond Walkway and the Sangre de Christo Mountains are twinkling at us, still snowy here and there, as the sun does not penetrate the creases where the hills were rolled up by God at the dawn of time.

Every day I look at them and wonder at their beauty. At sunset, the light that washes over them is so glorious that I feel my jaw drop and I have to say 'Thank you!' to the force of creation for the opportunity to see something so completely breathtaking.

Halfway down the walkway is the turn-off for Main Street and I am tempted to stop for a coffee. It is too cool for an espresso shake (glorious, thick and stuffed with ice cream and caffeine) but a mocha would be fine and, even though I am not carrying money, I have credit at the *Die Happy Café*. With any luck I will bump into Ella who almost lives in the health centre next door. This is innovatively called *Unityville Health* and is staffed mostly by well-meaning vegans. By well-meaning, I mean that they do not try to convert you more than twice a week and are not actively hostile to anyone with leather shoes.

Ella is not a vegan but she does eat frighteningly healthily—except for Terry's Health Bars which she adores and makes sure

158

that she buys on a daily basis. Ella thinks that they actually *are* health bars but then she does not know Terry very well and, at forty-eight, she is far too decrepit in his eyes to be hit with the full force of his sexual charm.

Terry's Health Bars for Fucking Vegan Assholes just masquerade as being good for you. They are deliberately chock full of sugar and syrup and occasionally, when he can get some, lard. One day someone is going to find him out but, for the moment, all the health freaks in town think that the bars are wonderful. They do taste great but even looking at one will add half an inch around your middle.

Ella is free for a coffee, so we sit down and run the gamut of about seven of her friends stopping off to say hello while we try to chat to each other. Unityville is like this; you cannot go anywhere without having a relationship. Eventually, the stream quietens down and I tell her about leaving and the problem over Frankly. Ella is horrified. Of course, I have to explain the whole UK quarantine system which bodes well to being a nightmare of failed communication to people who, mostly, have never even travelled to a foreign country but, luckily, Ella knows that Hawaii has a similar system.

'Honey,' she says. 'If you need a place to stay while you sort this out, you just come and move in with me.'

That is what Americans are like. Amazing. Most Brits would rather have their spleen pulled out with a spaghetti server than make an offer to someone like that; especially someone with a beagle.

Ella's trailer is very beautiful—like a studio flat. But the thought of Frankly, Ella and me all living in a trailer surrounded by chickens and cattle does not inspire me. I tell her that I am grateful for the offer and secretly send up a prayer that it won't happen.

But, by evening, it is beginning to look as though it might. Alex comes home somewhat stressed but still friendly and we have a cuddle before supper and a glass of wine. Then he starts talking about the move. Alex enjoys change, whereas it takes me half the morning just to get out of bed.

He is talking about booking flights. But what about selling the house? I ask. Or taking some time for a holiday?

'The agent can sell it,' says Alex. 'There are always people looking for premises this side of town.

This is true. We live in an area which is truly lovely; lined with trees and with wide grass verges.

'What about packing everything up?' I ask. 'It took weeks to get everything sorted to bring over here.'

'We'll manage if we start now,' says Alex. He hesitates a moment and then speaks rather swiftly.

'Did you call the Humane Society?'

'No,' I look at my glass of wine.

'Come on Anna!' this is Alex's jollying-along sort of voice. 'There isn't any alternative. You know we can't put her through quarantine. She would simply curl up and die.'

'Why not just have her put down then,' I mutter, rather unfairly and Alex reacts with anger.

'You know perfectly well I wouldn't have a healthy dog put down,' he says. 'For God's sake, Anna, be reasonable! She will have forgotten about us in less than a month. She's only a dog, Anna. We can get another one when we get back if you like.'

I think that was Alex's big mistake. It demonstrates so clearly the sheer gulf that lies between us. With tears starting in my eyes, I stand up, pushing my chair back so clumsily that it falls over, and half-run, half-walk out of the room.

My mother phones later that evening and, from the sanctuary of the bath, I hear Alex telling her the good news that he has decided to leave the university and has applied for a job in London. Yes, that does mean that we are coming home. She is obviously surprised but Alex is convincing and confident. To listen to him you would never have thought that he was the one who wanted to come here in the first place.

A horribly familiar dread sinks on my heart and I am reaching for my towel as Mum's inevitable question follows.

'We're re-homing her,' says Alex. 'Yes, I know. It's very sad but we've both agreed that quarantine isn't an option and there really isn't any sensible alternative.'

Cold with fury I run from the bathroom across the hallway to the kitchen where the phone is. Alex sees me and holds his hand up to stop me, his face stern as though I were one of his students.

'Well, Anna *is* very upset about it,' he says. 'But I'm sure she'll realise that it's all for the best.'

I want to snatch the phone out of his hand but, like a wimp, I am waiting until he will deign to give it to me. Suddenly I feel very defeated and small and deeply, bitterly resentful.

'Here she is,' says Alex. 'Just out of the bath to talk to you.' And he hands the telephone over to me with what I, maybe unfairly, interpret to be a warning look and walks out of the kitchen.

'Mum?'

'Oh Anna,' says my mother. 'Are you all right?'

'No,' I say, torn between a sob and a terrible calm. 'No, I'm not,' and I begin to cry in earnest.

She is loving and comforting and supportive but, even so, the only thing I remember about that conversation is my mother (*my* mother) saying, 'You mustn't let Frankly come between you and your husband,' and some part of myself closing off in disbelief.

We are taking Frankly down to the Humane Society this morning. I think that the telephone call from my Mother knocked the stuffing out of me and now Alex has managed to talk me into letting them see her. That way, he says, they can at least let us know if there is anyone on their address book who is looking for a beagle.

The women at the Humane Society are very kind but I can see that they despise us for wanting to leave Frankly behind. They are very surface-friendly but they say that it is always difficult to re-home an elderly dog, especially in somewhere as small as Unityville. I want to mutter that Frankly is not elderly but technically, of course, she is.

Alex is cheery and matter-of-fact and I'm sure that their dislike is more for me than for him. They can see that he does not care but that I do and that I am letting this happen against my will. I feel sick.

'Why don't you put her through quarantine?' the women ask.

'Because we both know people whose dogs have died in quarantine,' I say.

'That's very rare,' says one of the women.

I know it is but it still happens.

The women are wise enough to say no more because I am on the verge of tears as it is.

Alex wants Frankly to stay at the kennels so that she will be available for anyone looking for a dog to see immediately but I will not let them keep her. That earns me one of Alex's hard looks and those usually make me quake. But I could not have borne it. Should the perfect owner be waiting, then they must come to our home to see her and to meet me.

All through this, Frankly potters around the Society's reception area sniffing for food until she is completely satisfied that there is absolutely nothing to eat at all and then she begins giving my hand 'Why Are We Here? I'm Bored. When Can We Go?' nudges. She reluctantly allows the women to stroke her and, when she realises that they do have biscuits after all, she becomes all supplication and sweetness, wrinkling her furry brow endearingly and pawing at them with her 'I'm Not Loved And I'm Not Fed,' act. They know perfectly well that she is loved and fed and that is what makes it worse.

We drive home in silence. I know Alex is searingly angry with me; some of the things that he has said over these last few days will probably stay with me until my dying day. He says that my attitude to the dog feels as though I am being unfaithful to him (where does that come from? After all, it's *only* a dog) and that he cannot force me to re-home her because I would always feel resentful towards him if he did.

So, now the people of Colorado are being given the chance to run to claim a wonderful middle-aged beagle. Without my mother to support me, I don't know what else to do. Maybe I am just buying time or maybe it is a step to a deeper surrender into marriage. But maybe too, it is time to grow up? And yet, I thought that I was grown up and independent. I do earn from my writing; not as much as I used to earlier on in our marriage but I am not destitute nor stupid. But I feel stupid. I cannot understand how this husband, whom I love, can be so blind to what I want and need. Is this new or has it been creeping in over the last few years without my noticing it? That is scary, because I do not know.

In the afternoon, when Alex goes back to work, I telephone my brother. Odd that; we do not have the closest of relationships and there is no reason why Richard should support me when Alex and my mother do not. But he does.

'Some things are immutable in a marriage,' he says. 'Grace and I know what is immutable in ours. I need my space in some areas and she needs her space in others. It took a while to work it out but we did it and that's what makes our marriage strong.

'For Alex, it now appears immutable that he wants to leave Colorado and live in London. For you, it is immutable that you will not leave Frankly.'

'But we went down to the Humane Society today,' I said. 'And I have allowed them to take her details in case someone does want her. So I haven't been very immutable.'

I don't think that statement makes any sense linguistically, let alone grammatically, but Richard ponders what I meant to say.

'No, you haven't,' he says (and I think how kind it is of him not to correct my grammar, as Alex would have done). 'But I think that it's time that you started to be. If the "right" person does come along for Frankly and you give way on this, then Alex is right: you will resent him, no matter how good a home she might get.

'Even worse, you will find it hard to forgive yourself and you will always wonder why you were not as strong as you wanted to be. And, in that case, you will stop being you and it's you that Alex loves. At least, I hope it is.'

So do I.

'If I were you,' says Richard. 'I'd take Alex out for supper and talk it over in a neutral space. It's always easier to talk away from home if there's a problem.

'Be enthusiastic about leaving Colorado because I expect that your reluctance to go is half the problem. Try and say positive things about London—there are some! And think about some things that you can suggest that you can do together in England so that you can say that you are looking forward to going home together. Then he can see that you genuinely want to be with him and that this is just a little hiccup rather than something that is threatening the marriage. Then, and only then, make it very clear that you are taking Frankly to Europe and that you will pay for it yourself as well as doing all the organising to get her home and that you will take as little time about it as possible so that you can come home to him as soon as you can.'

We talk a little more and he also reminds me that he has a friend who lives in northern France. 'Tell Alex that I am pretty certain that Carlos will take Frankly for the six months,' he says. 'I don't know if he will, but I will ask—and you need to have that certainty to tell Alex. It makes the whole situation easier if half of it is dealt with already. We can deal with the rest of it later.'

How did I get to have such a wise brother? How come I never noticed before?

Alex is amenable to going out for supper and, as there is very little choice in Unityville we end up at The Madison where the buffalo ghost hangs out.

Tonight, I remind Alex of the ghost story and we start off well having a bit of a laugh and extending our good humour over the mixture of hardened hunters and gun-carrying Republicans and the politically-correct Californians who spar in Unityville all the time.

Over soup and steak we talk of England and where in London we want to live and what to do if Alex's new hoped-for job does not transpire. It would appear that it should do so—the wheels are in motion and, all being well, they will need Alex there for the next term which means moving pretty fast.

We have an open ticket to return to the UK, thank God. It was expensive but it did, at least, mean that the return dates can be altered. We were planning to go back for a break at the end of May but now Alex is wanting to leave in two weeks' time.

I have done some research today on how I could get Frankly out of here (to where is tomorrow's problem) and I know that it is going to take longer than a fortnight so, effectively, I am going to have to say that I want to stay behind. Tentatively, I raise the subject, waiting until we have had most of a bottle of wine and have been talking for long enough about the attractions of life "back home."

I point out again that the house has to be sold and that we will get a better price if it is still furnished and being lived in. Empty homes lose value immediately, I say. Also, we will need to sell the car, which can take time. So why don't I stay behind for a month or so to pack up, supervise the sales and sort out the situation with Frankly?

'That makes it easier for you not to have to stay with your parents—you could go and bunk at your mate Jim's if it's just you. And you know that you can get on with things much better without your Mum hanging over your shoulder all the time,' I say, perfectly truthfully as Alex has a real problem with his mother.

'And you won't have to rush out looking for somewhere to live either. You can take your time and find us somewhere that you really like.'

'But you'd want to choose our new home,' says Alex, surprised. He has always deferred to my taste as we both know that his is pretty well non-existent. But maybe it is time for that to change.

'I don't know London so you would know better where we would be comfortable. You can do it perfectly well,' I say, bravely because the thought of moving into somewhere sight unseen is very scary.

Alex is coming round to the idea. If it is just him, he can squeeze into Jim's flat and they can spend evenings laughing, watching football, instead of the two of us having to live his parents' restricted life, sleeping on their sofa bed and having to listen to and cope with all their (very natural) anxieties.

'And there's Frankly,' I say, carefully. 'The Humane Society may not find her a home at all and if they do, they may need longer than two weeks. If they don't find one, I can take her to Richard's friend Carlos in France. He's already got a dog and Richard says there wouldn't be a problem. All it would mean would be my spending a few days in France on the way back—and you could come out to meet me there and have a bit of a break. Wouldn't that be lovely?'

And it works. Oh dear God, it works! Alex is still reluctant to leave Colorado without me but I think he is convinced. Perhaps, like me, he is just tired of the conflict and wants to find the easiest route. Perhaps he has had time to consider that I have the right to some say in the future of the dog that was mine before we even met.

The financial considerations *are* important; we did invest quite a lot of money in our lovely home but I think, on balance, that Richard was right: it was the enthusiasm for England which has swung it. Alex does not feel unloved any more because he knows that I do want to go home with him and rebuild a life in England and Frankly is just a side issue.

Or is she? 'I think you should leave Frankly on the Humane Society list even so,' says Alex, before bed. 'If the perfect home comes up, you should take it. It's a lot less bother for both of us.'

Over my dead body, says my soul while my mouth behaves nicely and says, 'Okay.'

Even so, by the end of the evening, all is pretty much well again and Alex and I are back in the same bed and loving each other. If I had known what an asset my brother would turn out to be, I would never have superglued his Beatles albums together when I was ten after he pretended to be a ghost. I must apologise for that sometime.

The next two weeks are pretty frantic and I am frightened—I cannot deny it. I am now totally responsible for selling the house and car so I have to deal with all these strange American "realtors" on my own instead of with Alex's habitual manner of being in charge beside me. He has changed from the man who loved America to the man who cannot wait to get back home. He is also looking forward to some time on his own, he says.

The realtors seem to take personal umbrage that we are leaving so soon. 'You're as bad as Californians,' says one, who obviously does not want my business. 'One winter and they are running back home with their tails between their legs.'

'We've been here more than three years and I love the winters here,' I say, defensively. 'It's just my husband's job. He has to go back to England.' And, as I think back to the months of snow and the one great icicle that hung, each winter, from our guttering outside the bedroom, growing inch by inch every day until it was as thick as Alex's thigh, I know that I am speaking the truth. I do love the winter. It is beautiful with houses dripping in fairy lights way past Christmas; mornings so cold that my eyelashes become covered with crystal ice and Frankly has to dance on the pavements so that her paws do not freeze. I love the open log fires and the hot tubs in the snow and the reality behind all the snow-covered Christmas cards I had in England where half an inch of sludge was the most you could hope for.

'So, do you want to sell your house or not?' says the realtor.

'Yes, I do, but not with you,' I say and walk out. Not a good idea in a town as small as this where word spreads so swiftly but, even so, by the end of the day I have the house listed at three firms and people are already ringing up to view.

One couple is keen. A young man and his wife who live in Buena Vista and who have two young children. It would be a good house for kids—an upstairs area where they could have a play room as well as bedrooms—and an enclosed "yard". They are keen on Frankly too. 'She comes with the house, if you want her,' says Alex and I hold my breath while they stroke her knowing that Alex means it but they have just taken it to be a joke.

'We're serious,' says Alex. 'We can't take her back to England.'

The man looks at his wife. He is tempted but she is made of sterner stuff. 'No,' she says. 'No, thank you but we don't want a dog.'

I try hard not to show my relief and shed a few tears quietly in the bath later that evening.

Worse, it turns out that Richard's friend Carlos is moving to Turkey (a fact which I conceal from Alex) so I will have to look a little further for someone to care for Frankly in Europe. Who do I know who might have friends in France, Germany, the Netherlands or Spain? I even ring the Passports for Pets campaigners in London for help and they put me onto two women in France who would like to help but do not know if they can. It is an impasse.

Finally the day arrives when Alex is due to leave. Neither of us sleeps very well and he wants to make love this morning because he was too busy with the packing and saying goodbye to neighbours and people he worked with last night. In typical American style his colleagues turned up on the doorstep with presents and wine. Hopelessly impractical (one of the presents is a glass flower vase!) but very kind.

So, he is holding me in his arms and kissing me and I don't want to say no because we both know that it will be some time before we meet again but it does not feel right; it feels forced and as if we are doing it because there is a lack of sex ahead of us. If you are not in the mood, you are not in the mood and I'm seriously not in the mood. But I can often get myself into the mood if I try and I would like to *want* to make love—so I make an effort and probably over-compensate. It works for Alex but not for me—in fact it is awful and afterwards I find myself crying.

It does not help and Alex is both irritated and upset. Of course, we are now in a hurry too so everything is fraught. I was going to drive him to the airport but we are late and Alex is the faster driver so it is unspoken but understood that he will now drive. It is a good hour and a half to the airport and usually we would take Frankly but instinct tells me not to put her into the car. Alex and I will need this time alone without her to distract us.

Alex does not even say goodbye to her as we leave the house. There is a fussy little beagle hassling to come with us but he just closes the door and turns away. He used to love her: I am sure he did. They used to play together and I have a dozen pictures of her curled up on his lap. Maybe it is not that: I am too sensitive. Maybe he feels more deeply about leaving Unityville than he has let on. Surely no one could feel as little as he has appeared to do this last fortnight?

Halfway through the drive, as the skyscrapers of Denver are just coming into sight, Alex puts his hand out onto my knee. 'I'm sorry about this morning,' he says. 'I wanted it to be right.'

'So did I. I'm sorry too.' And we smile at each other. He stops the car for a moment and we kiss. 'I suppose I do love you,' says Alex. That is the kind of thing he does say and I've learnt not to take any notice of it.

'I love you, Alex.' And I do. I do love him, for all his idiosyncrasies; for all his changeability and for all his mood swings and occasional lack of kindness. I married him because I loved him and I will always love him, whatever.

I look long and hard at this beloved face with its first signs of growing older; the grey hairs so prominent in the deep brown at his temples, the crinkle lines around his brown eyes and I commit it even deeper to memory than it already is. There is a smile in those eyes and a vision and a belief in the good in the future and I want to hold this man so tightly and say that I don't want him to go.

So, I am crying as I drive away from the airport and start the long journey back to Unityville alone. I stayed until Alex went through to the departure lounges and we hugged and kissed again but airports are funny things. The one who is leaving is half gone by the time you get there and there is no point in hanging around. But now I am entering a different reality—living and coping alone. How long for? I don't know. A month? Two? It is all very unreal.

I spend a fruitless half hour trying to find a radio station which plays anything except country music and slip in a cassette of favourites instead. They flood the car with memories and beauty as we rise back up the road into the mountains and the glory that is Colorado surrounds me again.

The first thing I do when I get back home (apart from greeting a very vocal and pathetic beagle, of course) is telephone the Humane Society and tell them to take Frankly off their list. They are slightly snotty with me because of the paperwork they have done and they hint very strongly that I should make a large voluntary donation but I do not care. She is my dog; she is not going to anyone else; I am taking her home.

That night, I go through my address book with a fine-tooth comb. There, deep in the recesses of the scrawled-over pages, is the name Ben Taylor, the friend of my father's with a holiday home in Spain.

Ten minutes later, I know that I am going to Los Poops.

Later that night, in the bath, I search my mind for the long-forgotten prayers of my childhood to give thanks for this miracle (for miracle it is). My Godmother once told me that if you were doing God's will, everything fell into place and the path before you was smooth. At the time I had thought it pretty sanctimonious (or I would have if I had known what the word meant) but now I can see what she means.

'You're coming home,' I say to Frankly who has pattered into the bathroom to see if she can get away with one of her favourite pastimes—licking my wet arm or leg as it hangs over the side of the bath. 'You're going to be a Spanish beagle and then you are coming back to England.

'It's really going to happen! Frankly, we're going home.'

Whatever, says the beagle, standing on her hind legs and resting her head on the side of the bath. Home Is With You.

'And with you,' I say, stroking the soft golden-brown head and smoothing the wrinkled brow as she starts to lick my hand and arm.

Chapter Eleven

EVERY EVENING, I tell Alex all about my day by e-mail. I know that I can entertain him with my writing and, with seven hours' time difference between us, there is no possibility of talking by telephone in the evenings. By the time that I have settled down with a glass of wine and a beagle on my lap he is in bed, so this is as good a way of talking as there is. Alex is an economical writer, not prone to endearments by e-mail, but at least we are in touch every day and I love to write.

Tonight, there is the usual one in from him and he is concerned that the house in Unityville has not yet sold.

'I think that we should set a deadline,' he writes. 'One more month and then you should come home whether or not the house has sold. You will have done all you can in that time.

'I have found a nice little flat in Highgate which I can rent for a year but I need to make a quick decision. Second floor in a block with a communal garden. No pets.'

No pets. Just like that. But I have told Alex about Ben Taylor and Spain and that I now know that Frankly can be home in less than a year.

My heart sinks.

'Can you take the flat for six months or ask for a six-month break clause?' I write after telling the story of my day. 'Frankly will be back in February or March and we will need a home for her too.

'In any case, I do not want to live in London without my own personal piece of garden, so I would not want a second floor flat without its own little bit of ground even if we didn't have a dog. Please can you look again?'

Carefully, I add: 'I think that it is an excellent idea to set a deadline—I suggest six weeks, to give the house a bit more of a chance and I'll make sure I leave in the middle of July or thereabouts. I am so looking forward to seeing you again and having a hug (and a lot more!). I do miss you very much. Lots and lots of love, Anna XXX.'

Dear God, it surely is not too much to ask him to find another flat? But in my heart I know that war has been declared yet again. Alex wants me home under his conditions and, no matter how I manoeuvre, it always seems to come back to that. I am stuck between a rock and a hard place. Actually I am stuck between a rock and a soft, warm, furry and loving place—but thinking like that is not going to help the situation one bit.

I can't sleep for worry so, probably stupidly, I am on the telephone to Alex at 5am (11am where he is). I get through on his mobile at the second attempt. He has just been to close the deal on the flat.

'But I asked you not to.'

'Anna, it is not easy to get a flat in London. You told me that I got to choose so I have. This one is fine. It's very nice.'

'But Frankly…'

'Anna, give up on this. Re-home the dog. Take her back to the Humane Society, sell the house and come back to England.'

'Alex, you aren't listening to me.'

'And you aren't listening to me. You are putting a dog ahead of your husband.'

'I'm not! I'm coming home. I just want to sort her out first. And I don't want to live in a flat without a garden. Surely there must be others?'

'I've taken the lease, Anna. That's final. Now when are you coming home?'

'I don't know,' I say weakly. I want to say 'Never' but I do not dare. I cannot believe this is happening to me.

'I'll talk to you later,' says Alex. 'I'm going to meet my new work colleagues and I'll be on the tube in a moment. Try not to fuss, Anna. You know that you have to see sense. Goodbye.'

I go back to bed, shaking a little. I look out of the open curtains and up into the deep black velvet of night with the diamond stars, so clear and bright, and wish that I could have all the things I want. The answer is clear and cool and simple. What I want is love, as do we all. And there is love enough here, in Colorado, for anyone.

A week later the house is sold—so that is one good thing. But I did not like the people who want to buy it and I feel stupidly resentful that they are going to live in the place where I wanted to stay forever. They want some of the furniture, too, so that is helpful in that there will not be so much to take back to England. We cannot cram much into a flat after all.

I should be pleased. Alex is. But I am living a lie with Alex right now because I do not mention Frankly at all and neither does he. It seems as though she is gone already or, maybe, even dead. I do not mention Spain either. I just don't know what to do.

We have talked on the telephone about three times this week and, of course, there are all the emails. The tenor of his writing shows just how quickly he is adapting back to England and Colorado seems very far away to him now. When I write about some American idiosyncrasy or kindness he is laughing *at* the people and not with them: he has christened them "Golden Retrievers," all full of bounce and enthusiasm but no brains whatsoever.

When did Alex get this arrogant and why did I not notice?

I feel depressed when I wake this particular morning. Ella is staying after her face-lift and I am glad that she is having a lie-in. Ella is not impressed with Alex and I feel such a wimp when she gets onto the subject. Frankly seems a bit stodgy and unenthusiastic today, too, but I insist that we go out for a walk and I try as hard as I can to look at the beauty of the day. The back streets are quiet and peaceful and there are flocks of red-headed finches in the seed-encrusted lilac trees. I go down to the *Die Happy Café* to have a latte and to think.

Gilbert brings me my drink and looks at me quizzically. 'Something wrong, darling?' he asks and the word "Darling" is enough to start me off into tears again. Alex has not called me 'darling' since he left Colorado. He is not the Alex that I married any more and I do not know where he went.

Gilbert sits down beside me and listens to my tale of woe.

'Well, you have two options,' he says. 'Either you go home now and save your marriage or you stay here for longer.'

'Go home now?' I am amazed at the thought.

'Just for a week or two,' says Gilbert. 'If you have the money.'

'I don't.' It is £400 for a flight to the UK and I cannot spare that. Or can I? Maybe I don't want to.

'Well I can't stay here indefinitely,' I say. 'I don't have a visa so I can't work.'

'You could work here,' says Gilbert. 'I'm going to need a manager in a couple of weeks—I'm off on a course and I can't trust Terry.'

Too right, I think, looking at the Fucking Asshole Vegan Health Bars being enjoyed to the last crumb by the girls with Rastafarian hairdos on the next table. They've probably never touched a meat product before in their life and those bars are loaded with lard or I'm a teapot.

'I don't know that I'd want to work with Terry either,' I say cautiously. 'He's not the easiest of men.'

'Oh, you just ignore him,' says Gilbert. 'Really, you do. If he gets seriously out of order, Martine just clouts him.'

'Oh.' This is not exactly encouraging but Gilbert continues with great enthusiasm. 'You know Martine don't you? She's just great. She does martial arts and she drops Terry like an elk pumped full of lead with one hand if he gets obnoxious.'

'Yes, I do know Martine,' I say faintly. She's the waitress with the leopard skin hairdo...

'Thank you. I'll think about it.'

I do not seriously think that I will. I certainly will not fly back to England, either, even for a brief trip. It would do no good even if I wanted to. I do know Alex well enough to know that he is immovable when he is in a mood and he is certainly in a mood lately. The new flat is not even available until the beginning of next month and it is no use in my expecting to stay with him at Jim's. Besides, I am crawling with anger at the moment and what if he managed to stop me from coming back to Colorado now that the house is sold? That would certainly sort out the Frankly problem. My blood runs cold at the thought.

Anyway, there is Ella.

'Do think about it,' says Gilbert. 'But let me know as soon as you can. I'll pay you in cash so it doesn't have to be official.'

Suddenly I am tempted. Whatever happens I will not be leaving Unityville for another five weeks and I need money for all Frankly's jabs and certificates, not to mention the cost of her flight. I know already that the Spanish authorities require Frankly not to travel for a full month after the extra rabies jab that she has to have—so what have I got to lose? If things are as bad as I suspect they are with Alex then I'll be grateful enough to have something to fill my time.

'I am interested,' I say. 'I'll let you know by the end of the week.'

And I walk Frankly home pensively. It seems almost as if there are two or three alternate lives opening up pathways before me. Perhaps I shall take all three in different dimensions. 'Please God,' I say suddenly. 'Let me take the one which keeps me both Alex and Frankly.' But something within me that I don't want to acknowledge is saying that that is a dimension that is already closed.

The next morning I ring British Airways to ask about suitable dates for transporting Frankly to Spain and it appears that it can be done with the greatest of ease on the day that I had already planned to leave Denver. She has to be transited through Heathrow (and so, for that matter, do I) and fly with a different carrier to Malaga but there is a good connection and space for an animal on the flight that I have decided to book. It is in six weeks' time, not five, and I know that it is time to make that commitment. With Ella smiling at me, I say 'Yes' to the operator and give him my credit card details.

The enormity of it hits me once I have put the phone down. I really am going to Spain with my dog. I do not speak Spanish and I know absolutely no one out there. Ben has told me that there are English-speaking people in the village but I do not even know where it is, let alone how to get there from the airport! What is more, the flight arrives at 9pm so it will be dark. Obviously I will have to hire a car—and that is yet more money to lay out.

So, I will work at the *Die Happy Café* whether or not it is legal. Ella is happy to stay on here for as long as I want her to and the house sale completion date can wait on our convenience, so I will not even be leaving Frankly alone all day.

Poor Ella. She skulks around all morning and takes as many painkillers as she can get away with, together with arnica and a lot more Bach Flower Rescue Remedy than I can really spare. I'm going to need some myself over the next few weeks, so I email a friend in England and ask her to send me a couple of bottles.

Ruth replies almost by return. What is happening? She has seen Alex and he has been most peculiar with her. Am I all right?

I have not kept in touch with people in England these last few weeks but maybe now I have to start communicating. And I should phone my mother, too, and tell her what I am planning to do. I have noticeably avoided calling her recently and when we have spoken it has only been generalities. It is time I stood up and was counted.

But first, Frankly and I go down to the café and I wave at Gilbert through the windows and wait for him to come out to me.

'Have you thought it over?' He is obviously keen enough.

'Yes. How much can you pay me and when do I start?'

The wages are minimal but they are still income and I won't be paying tax on them. I can start today if I want but I put it off until tomorrow as a reflex. And I remember that I have forgotten to ask Gilbert how the review went.

He looks around him cautiously.

'Wonderful,' he whispers. 'There were Queens from all over the state and some came from as far as Montana!'

'Montana? I would have thought any guy in a frock would have been lynched in Montana.'

'Oh, it's very liberal in places,' says Gilbert. 'A lot of Californians live there, you know. It's Wyoming that's the real problem'.

Ah yes. And Gilbert is off with a series of outrageous stories which would have a redneck reaching for his rifle.

Frankly sits down and 'huk-huks' with boredom, then creates a diversion by licking her backside on the pavement. Gilbert watches her with fascination for a moment and Frankly senses an audience. Stop It, This Is Private, she says indignantly, giving him a baleful look before continuing her ablutions.

Gilbert kisses me on the cheek. 'I must go; there's a delivery arriving. I'll see you tomorrow at ten.'

'Okay.' Oh my God, what have I let myself in for?

Walking Frankly home, I am aware that this is a last day of freedom. How many years is it since I had a "proper job"? With some vanity I look down at my hands; the skin has been roughened by a year in Colorado—I should wear gloves more. But what will washing up and café life do for them? Still, I can calculate my possible wages and they are enough to buy Frankly's fare to Spain. 'All this for a beagle!' I say to her but Frankly is more interested in whether there is any food left at the end of the scent of chicken wings she can detect in the gutter.

The crate that she came here in is currently in the hallway of the house, covered in white linen and pretending to be a table. I lift the cloth and check that it is still in full working order with bolts that lock and the grille firmly attached. Frankly is curious and assumes that if I want to get into the crate there must be something interesting in there for her. So, we are both trying to squeeze into it simultaneously and get stuck. I am breathless with laughter by the time we have extracted ourselves and Frankly is standing on my stomach with her front paws, licking my face.

This morning I am delighted to see that I have two letters from England. One is a cheque from my mum! How wonderful! Bless her! The second looks like Alex's handwriting. That is very odd.

I open it and it is as if I am watching myself from a distance. I am standing up in the hallway and I am screaming. 'No, No, NO! Dear God *please no!*'

A part of me looks down on this slightly dishevelled woman in her dressing gown and bare feet reading her fate in the cold, hard print of a typewritten page.

> *Dear Anna,*
> *I guess there is no easy way to say that I have decided*

that I want to end our marriage. It has come home to me since I have been back in England that you and I really have nothing left in common. There are just too many points of mutual incomprehension.

It seemed like a sign when you emailed me that the exchange of contracts on the house had taken place that we were now free to go our separate ways. We can divide the money equally between us and each start our new life.

I ask your forgiveness for any pain that this may cause you and I hope that you can see that it is entirely for the best for you as well as for me.

I hope that we can achieve this parting with dignity and I want you to know that I shall always look back with affection on the happy times that we spent together.

The letter goes on—but it is all about finances and bank accounts being changed and closed. I cannot read it. I cannot think. I cannot live.

I am on the floor, curled up in a foetal position and sobbing helplessly, hopelessly and seemingly without end. What am I going to do? Where am I going to go? How am I going to live?

Frankly comes to me after a few minutes. She has been standing, watching, from the bedroom and she is afraid. She has seen and felt something like this before—when she was a puppy and I was grieving for Danny—so she knows that something is seriously wrong.

Usually she would paw at me for attention to distract me from tears but this time she lies down, leaning her strong, warm body against me and resting her head on my arm. I hold her, half-sobbing, half-retching with the fear and the pain and she starts to lick my hands as if I were her puppy.

It's All Right, she is saying. I'm Here. We Are Together. Home Is With Me.

There is silence. I am sitting in Jack Risborough's kitchen in Los Poops. My wine glass is empty and the horrible irony of the situation is hanging unspoken in the air between us.

'He would have left you anyway,' says Jack. 'Even without Frankly.'

'Yes.'

'It was just an excuse to put you in the wrong.'

'Yes.'

'He was looking for a way out even before he left the job. And when he met the other woman, she gave him the impetus to do it. There was another woman, wasn't there? Men generally don't leave without another woman to go to.'

'Stop it Jack. I don't think I can take it right now… And if I lose Frankly…'

As I speak, the phone shrills out and I jump. Jack walks across the kitchen and picks it up.

'¿*Hola?*' He listens. '*Si, gracias*—I'll pass you over to her.'

I catch the receiver and the female vet's soft, accented voice tells me that Frankly has recovered consciousness; her temperature has returned to normal and she has drunk a little milk.

'Does that mean she's going to live?'

'Yes, I think so,' says the vet. 'I'll keep an eye on her overnight but she's out of danger now. You can come and fetch her in the morning.'

'Thank you. Oh, thank you.'

I put the phone down,

'She's going to be okay,' I say.

'Yes.'

I am in his arms, hugging and crying and he is stroking my head.

'It's over now Anna. All of it. You are free and you can be happy again.'

We pull apart, both aware that it is important to do so in case something else might happen.

'Coffee?'

'Please.'

I go to the loo and have a little cry while he is making strong, aromatic coffee. Thank you God. Thank you. Thank you. Frankly is going to be okay. Thank you.

Jack and I drink our coffee in silence. I have told him so much and I feel rather naked now.

'Did anything funny happen after Alex left?' he says, surprisingly.

'What?'

'Sometimes something happens which is ironic and kinda breaks up the bad energy. It can help to remember that.'

I ponder. 'Well there were the phone calls with the parents. Those were surreal.'

'Tell me about the phone calls.'

Ella has a lot to say about the letter, as you might expect. 'Cowardly bastard' is about the least offensive term she uses. Anyway, later on, when we have talked ourselves into silence, she runs me a bath and puts lavish amounts of my rose oil into the water. God knows how long I lie there, dry-eyed and hopeless, mixing Alex and Danny in my mind until I think I must be going mad.

The telephone rings and Ella answers it.

'Hold on a minute please,' she says, having explained that I am in the bath.

'It's your mother,' she says. 'Do you want me to tell her?'

'Yes. Please.' That, too, is a parallel. I remember friends breaking the news of Danny's death for me as I sat, listening to my fate, in the terracotta-coloured living room of my old home.

Fascinated, I hear Ella's voice from the kitchen.

'No, she can't come at the moment,' she says. 'But she has asked me to tell you something. I'm afraid she has had bad news this morning. Alex has left her. He wrote her a letter from England which she received this morning saying that the marriage is over. And, if I may say so, it is a despicable letter written by a coward.'

There is silence. What will Mum be saying?

'Well I'm afraid it's true,' says Ella. 'I appreciate your shock and I'm sure that Anna would like to talk to you very much when she's a little more recovered. She only found out an hour ago.'

There is silence while she listens again. And then she continues speaking as only Ella could.

'I don't know why you're sticking up for him,' she says. 'The man has behaved like an asshole. I've got the letter in my hand and it is cold, heartless and as arrogant as you can get.'

180

A wrong note is sounding here. Mum would never stick up for Alex in the way Ella is implying. A horrible suspicion settles on me. I don't think that this is my mother calling at all.

'Oh my God,' I say to myself, closing my eyes and sinking down below the water level so I cannot hear any more.

But then, I cannot resist…

'Oh I see,' Ella is saying. 'Well Mrs Marks, I still stand by what I said. Your son has behaved like a coward and he has abandoned his wife in a foreign country with no warning whatsoever. You should be ashamed of him.'

Wow. I could never have said that. And I think it needed saying.

Later, I ring my own mother. She is glad to hear from me, but Julianne has come round so she can't talk just now. Could I ring her tomorrow?

'Yes,' I say feebly and put the phone down.

'Brilliant,' says Jack. 'Your mother-in-law gets some home truths about her son… and you're trying to tell your mother that your husband has left you and she's too busy having tea with a friend. Just great. That's exactly the way it goes when there's a crisis.'

'Yeah.' I am smiling.

'Now tell me something good about Alex and Frankly,' he says.

'What?'

'Back to the good times. I know it's hard to think of them but tell me something about Frankly and Alex being happy together.'

I think for a minute. 'Well there was the oven,' I say, doubtfully.

'Tell me about the oven.'

Alex had never had a dog, so he didn't get many of the doggy things. He certainly didn't go for the idea of putting a bowl down on the floor for a dog to lick. No matter how much I told him it could be sterilised with boiling water.

But then, there were the sausages.

We had grilled sausages for supper—cooked on foil which broke.

So, now it is the following morning and Alex is preparing to have his customary slice of toast. Except the grill is disgusting and greasy. I stand there thinking 'Oops!' because Alex is never at his best until after breakfast. But Alex is looking at Frankly and Frankly is looking up at Alex with all the lust of a beagle who can smell sausage fat. And I can see how his mind is working:

'Up to ten minutes of scraping and scrubbing to get this pan clean—or two minutes down on the floor and a kettle of boiling water,' he is thinking. There is a moment's hesitation, and his eyes meet Frankly's. He is lost.

The grill pan goes down on the floor and Frankly's tongue begins its eager and thorough work.

Alex got his toast on a sparklingly clean grill pan and Frankly was in bliss. It is what you call a 'win-win situation.'

After that, Alex was converted. He was even known, when the oven top got particularly disgusting, to take the burners off and lift Frankly up to clear away the burnt bits and grease. However, he did overstep himself with the Hungarian Goulash.

It was sick over the side of the Le Creuset and made a terrible mess in the oven.

'No problem,' says Alex, cheerfully, opening the oven door and reaching out to grab Frankly.

A short but violent altercation follows. Frankly is outraged. I'm Not Going In There! I Know An Oven When I See One! she is bellowing while Alex lurches all over the floor. Eventually, she has dived through his legs and is hiding under a cushion on the sofa.

I am laughing out loud as I finish. And so is Jack.

'If I were you, I'd keep hold of the ridiculousness,' he says. 'I read a book once where they advised women to imagine their ex-lover in a tutu and ballet shoes. They said it helped.'

Yes, Alex would look especially stupid in a tutu and, knowing him, he'd wear socks with the ballet shoes.

I do feel better.

It is time to go. Jack will pick me up to take me down to the vet's in the morning and I am deeply grateful. I would imagine that Los Poops is one of the safest human environments in the modern world but, even so, he insists on walking me back to Casa Taylor. We talk about the stars and walk a couple of feet apart but we are companionable. In fact I would rather like to tell him about Yiannis—but I don't think his male ego could take it.

We hug goodnight and I close the door on him. The house is horribly empty without a little beagle presence. Frankly's rug is on the floor by the window seat and her metal food and drinking bowls are on the kitchen floor. For a second I imagine what it would have been like to come home to them with Frankly gone.

But it is all okay. A shower, I think, and bed. But even so, I miss her warm and solid presence on my feet.

In the morning, Jack telephones to arrange a time to pick me up and we are back at the vet's at opening time—ten o'clock. Frankly is in the consulting room behind a closed door but she can hear my voice and is squeaking and sniffing under the door as we introduce ourselves to the receptionist.

The vet comes out, smiling, with Frankly on a lead and she comes over to me pushing her head against my legs and whining, as she does when she feels upset or confused.

'It's all right, darling,' I say, going down on my knees and stroking her. 'It's all over.'

'She's still a bit delicate,' says the vet. 'Just give her liquids for twenty-four hours. Chicken stock would be best.'

'Sod That,' says Frankly looking up at me with brown eyes wide and appealing. 'I Need Food And Lots Of It.'

Fortunately, the vet can't speak Frankly's language.

Then there is the bill to pay. It is not exactly cheap and I feel as if I go white when I see it. Jack has his back tactfully turned and is stroking Frankly. I am glad because otherwise he might offer to pay and I couldn't bear to be so beholden. Luckily they take credit cards.

Frankly sits on my lap on the way home, pawing at me. Her eyes are a little dopey but she is fine. I am just so glad to feel her solid warmth again.

Of course, within two hours she has stolen some bread, demanded attention and then ignored me when I gave in, made a nest in my bed and been as utterly obnoxious as only she knows how.

Chapter Twelve

THE STORM WAKES me in the night. It is extraordinary. I've heard of rain like stair rods but I never really believed it. The sound on the plastic skylight overhead is deafening and there are leaks springing everywhere. As for the thunder and lightning—well, I would be barking too if I were a beagle. It's really scary.

She follows me, nose to heel, as I rearrange all Ben's plants and a couple of saucepans to catch the water that is, fortunately, only dripping from the ceiling.

I reassure her and stroke her and we have a cup of hot chocolate together in bed which is calming for both of us but mostly for Frankly who, sensibly, has her head under the duvet.

The milk is fresh but very strong—it is goat's milk and unpasteurised —but I am getting used to it and even starting to like it. The milk and cheese are sold by Adela, a gruff and impossibly ancient crone who lives down by the sheep pen in what appears to be a haze of flies. She is either the grandmother or the great-grandmother of most of the shepherd family and has milked her goats for more years than the village can remember.

Sylvia took me to meet her so that I could order my mug of goat's milk per day. I don't have to collect it daily but I do have to provide a bottle for it to be poured into through a funnel and, if I don't collect, my daily share is added to the bottle until it is full. It costs all of twenty pence a pint and it is rich and creamy. I was almost sick when I tried it the first time, warm and frothing and fresh from the teat. Milk should be cold and inoffensive, said my stomach, not like this.

But I persevered and the taste has grown on me. The cheeses, on the other hand, were utterly scrumptious from day one. Adela does soft whey cheeses once a week and has an unending supply of hard, maturing cheeses in the back room of her tiny house. She speaks no English at all and her own dialect is almost unintelligible so we go through an arm-waving mime each time we meet. She loves people to try out her cheeses before they buy. I don't know if she fancies herself as a master cheese maker but it seems that she has a new recipe every time I go down.

Collecting milk and buying cheese are two entirely different rituals. With the milk it's a brief greeting, a hand held out for money and your own personal bottle handed to you. And woe betide you if you haven't bought another identical, spotlessly clean bottle to replace it for the next helping; then Adela grumbles and mumbles through her toothless gums and waves you off with clucks like an anguished hen. A dirty bottle would be a worse crime than no bottle at all. There is no compromise with a borrowed bottle of Adela's—oh no! You go without milk full stop and that is sufficient enough punishment to make sure no one makes that mistake more than once.

However, the cheese ritual is as complicated, ornate and integral to life as the Japanese Tea Ceremony. Always there is the offer of a cup of home-brewed herbal tea and, if you don't like that, some of the coarse local wine. You sit and wait for the brew, looking around at the sparse wooden furniture in the whitewashed kitchen-living room and the faded but lovingly mended patchwork quilt over the settee. The pictures on the wall are of the standard of the 1970s *Green Woman* or the *Crying Boy* and there are carefully cleaned glasswork animals and plaster ornaments of the kind I won at funfairs when I was a child.

Adela has plastic flowers on the windowsill that bear no resemblance to anything that ever lived and on the floor lies an ancient, frayed and faded rug in browns and reds with grey fringes at either end.

First you must sip your drink and exchange the time of day. This is done between Adela and me with exactly the same words each time which is helpful because I am getting the hang of it now. I use what Spanish I have and Adela speaks a brand of Los Poopian which is almost totally incomprehensible. I do sometimes wonder if the conversation actually is going in the way I imagine. I *think* that we ask kindly after each other's health and then nod wisely at the answer. Then Adela says something about the weather (I worked that out from the wave of her hand in the general direction of the window and the different expressions according to what the sun appeared to be doing at that point). I reply that it is lovely weather and better than it is in England, whereupon she asks me a question about England in comparison with Los Poops. Something along the lines of 'do you have such beautiful flowers?' The answer is always 'No.' Whatever we may have in England, it is vital that it is not as nice as it would be in Los Poops. I did attempt to disagree with her once on the subject of Buckingham Palace being more attractive than *The Bay House* where Stella and David live. This was not a good idea. After a brief argument which I lost on the simple grounds that I didn't know what we were arguing about, Adela went conveniently deaf and wandered off into the back room. She came back with a particularly hard and tasteless cheese and I had no option but to take that or nothing.

So, now, I always say that Los Poops is better, prettier or nicer than anywhere in Britain or America. I cannot, obviously, say that it is bigger but when that difficult question comes, the acceptable answer is 'No, not bigger—but a much better place to live.' I also point out the lack of crime (conveniently forgetting the conspiracy to murder Aldo and the dog poisoners) and the kindness of the people.

Once this ritual is successfully completed, Adela proffers a big green, pottery plate on which is arranged a selection of slivers of cheese. After these have been admired with the correct enthusiasm, one of them may be tried with suitable reverence. Words are not required but lip-smacking and wide-eyed appreciation are to be encouraged. Two more pieces may then be taken with impunity but then one or more of the three already tasted must be selected. The ritual never varies. Try more than three and you are presumptuous; try fewer than three and you are not playing the game.

Once the cheese has been decided upon, Adela re-fills both glasses of tea or wine and disappears into the back room to cut or select your cheese, according to its size, wrap it carefully in waxed paper and tie it with red string with a loop to act as a handle.

Only then does the sordid matter of money come up and she prefers you simply to place the correct amount on the table. It's better for you to know the amount—or at least the approximate sum—because Adela really doesn't do change and it isn't a good idea to try and make her work it out.

And the rain still falls. At least it will wash away the last remnants of the poison hidden in the hills. I know Jack made enquiries about who had put poison out and where it might be. It was all done with care along the grapevine so that no one got blamed for anything and now, at least, I know which areas to avoid. The poisoning only happens at the start of the hunting season—to stop stray dogs from taking the game—and there are usually plenty of stray dogs around. According to the ex-pats, the Spaniards think nothing of throwing a dog out of the car when they are sick of it and the ones that have some kind of heart know to do it near a village where there are foreigners because then the dog might get adopted or fed. I used to feed some of them myself but it is not a good idea, even though it breaks your heart to seem so cruel. If you are kind, a queue will form outside your house every day and if you're not quick enough with the distribution you can even get a nasty bite. My conscience is salved by the fact that Katherine always feeds them.

But that little problem has gone because over the last week, all the strays have vanished. They weren't lucky enough to be forced to take an antidote and rushed in a BMW to the nearest vet.

For the privately-owned dogs which are left there is, of course, the regular problem of poison put down for rats but that's generally in barns and places where they wouldn't be walked anyway. And, although I hope and pray it will never be needed I now have a bottle of antidote in the bathroom.

If this rain goes on, it will ruin the Fiesta. We have all been looking forward to that for weeks. Most Fiestas are inextricably linked to The Virgin Mary and, if he's lucky, Jesus. However, he rarely does get lucky as he's considered very much an also-ran around here. However, Los Poops and Larita, the village a mile even further up the hill, are different. Oh yes, they have the requisite Virgin Mary festivals but The Fiesta with Capital Letters is the biggie. It's the time when Los Poops' very own special Saint Perpetua is taken down from her plinth in the church and, complete with a couple of bony digits from her alleged left hand which are encased in glass by the altar, paraded up the hill to Larita. Why? Because Larita has her twin-saint Sergio in its own church. The two apparently converted the hill people from their heresy and sins at the time of Ferdinand and Isabella. Probably not that hard to convert people when the Spanish Inquisition was breathing down your neck but they probably saved quite a few lives. Sylvia had already told me that Los Poops was a town of *conversos*—Jewish people who converted to the Catholic faith centuries ago.

Saints Perpetua and Sergio, who were monk and nun working in the same order, are united in the church in Larita one day every year and left overnight to pray together for our sins. Rani, probably quite rightly, thinks it's just an old pagan mating ritual. He says that you only have to look at the Virgin Mary Festivals to see that they are modelled on nature goddess fertility festivals from before the dawn of time and the original Perpetua and Sergio were probably also two nature gods way before Christianity hit these shores. They just got transmuted and hooked on a convenient monk and nun so that everyone could continue having fun and getting drunk at the same old festival.

'It's actually harvest festival,' Rani says (repeatedly) if asked. 'The consummation of a new marriage which will bear fruit in the spring so that the natural cycle continues. Very pagan; very mystical. Sod all to do with Christianity.'

But, for all that, St. Perpetua is much revered as she stands, po-faced and suspiciously pink, looking disdainfully over her little church as if it never quite comes up to her expectations. I have been in the church several times now—though not for services— and it is a peaceful place where there are always fresh flowers or leaves on the altar and never a spot of dust anywhere. I go there sometimes just to be quiet and think. That sounds a bit odd in a village in the middle of the mountains but there's an atmosphere there that I like and, as I'm now getting fairly well-read on such matters, thanks to Ben's extensive library, it's interesting to look at Rani's theory and link it in to what I'm reading.

Perpetua has her own little side chapel with votive candles and, even though her festival is the Los Poopians' favourite, it's the Virgin who gets most of the attention for the rest of the year. I think Perpetua's just a bit bored with her life. I'm all for monogamy but perhaps sex once a year with the same guy for four hundred years would lack something of what it takes to make a relationship shine.

Rani and Sylvia told me that one year Perpetua went missing and she was found three days later, all chipped paint and on her back halfway up the hill with vines twined all around her. Rumour has it she had a silly grin on her face and her legs were akimbo but that was just a slander set about by the ungodly. Nobody ever found who did it or why. Rani thinks it was the god, Pan. If so, he never had the decency to call her afterwards or take her out again which is probably why she looks so pissed off.

The fiesta starts tomorrow and, once Pet and Serge are spiritually at it in the church on the hill, all hell will let loose down here with mule racing, dancing and *muchas* alcohol. I'm rather looking forward to it.

If it stops raining, that is.

It rained like this at festival time when I was working at the *Die Happy Café*. Curled up here, safe and warm in my tiny little home, with a peacefully sleeping beagle and the steady thrum-thrum of rain on (and through) the roof, I slip back in time…

The event was called *The Taste of Unityville*; an evening where all the restaurants and towns put tables and chairs out on the street and served set menus to the crowd of people who had pre-booked. All the cafés served food to passers-by who had come for the street musicians and for the general atmosphere.

Gilbert, of course, was out of town and it was only my second week of work at the *Die Happy Café*.

The Taste of Unityville was the major event of the culinary calendar. Great. Gilbert said it was really important and that without the takings from the festival evening he wouldn't be able to pay the wages at the end of next week. So *now* he's gone away?

The *Die Happy Café* was doing wraps, organic juices, cakes, brownies and pretzels. I'd never made a wrap in my life and we didn't have a juicer for the organic juices. Life has such jolly surprises in store for us when we plan ahead. 'If you want to make God laugh, tell him your plans,' says the Jewish proverb.

But there was Ella by my side. Her face had healed enough now for her to be able to cover most of the damage with make-up and she knew how to make a wrap. On the day itself, while Martine and the rest of the staff got on with the everyday jobs, I annexed the newest hireling, a cuddly teddy bear of a boy, also called Terry so known as TK for clarification, and he was an angel, preparing everything I could possibly need and putting it out so that as long as one person steamed the wraps I had the minimum work to do in filling them.

Terry, of course, hadn't turned up for work. However, there was a paragraph in the *Unity Times* about someone being arrested, drunk, for climbing the Federal Building and shouting insults at passers-by so we were not expecting Terry in again until one of his ex-wives arrived to post bail.

Ella steamed the wraps and I filled them and we got a good rhythm going and talked confidently of the pleasure we would get in selling every one.

'You know, TK,' I said meditatively. 'Gilbert and I were talking about you last week and one of us thinks that you're incredibly cute.'

TK stopped and thought with his bristly bear's head on one side.

'Which one?' he said, suspiciously.

'Yes, it's tough,' I say. 'Because I'm not going to tell you. So it's either a circular guy in shorts with plucked eyebrows and shaved legs or a woman who's seriously old enough to be your mother. Be afraid, TK. Be very afraid.'

TK just laughed.

So, the wraps were nearly done; but the preparation of the table outside was not and there was a list of health department regulations as long as my arm which didn't even appear to be written in English.

However, TK knew the score. TK was willing to help. Just as

everyone else sloped off to start having fun (the dancing should be starting in an hour) he stood firm and volunteered to continue helping.

I considered recommending him for a sainthood. The dialogue went something like this:

TK: 'Have you got more than one ice box?'

Me: 'No.'

TK: 'I'll find something.'

And he did.

TK: 'Have you got containers for all the wraps?'

Me: 'No.'

TK: 'I'll find something.'

And he did.

TK: 'Have you got enough containers for all the drinks?'

Me: 'No.'

TK: 'I'll find something.'

And he did.

He worked so hard and did it all so well that the health inspector, when she came, had nothing to say but 'well done.' (Thank God Terry was in the local jail). Then she went and stood in the walk-in fridge for fifteen minutes. Ostensibly this was to check that the temperature in there was correct; but it couldn't be. There was a thermometer in the fridge that showed the temperature. All health inspectors are mad.

I went in to fetch something and she was just standing there, deep in thought. Maybe she was meditating? I apologised because opening the door would make the temperature go up and she sighed a little and said it just meant another couple of minutes.

I meant to check at the end of the evening whether she was still there… but I forgot.

So, everything was ready. Ten minutes to go. The rain clouds that had been gathering steadily were obviously an illusion; it never had rained for *The Taste of Unityville* and it never will.

And then the skies opened. Floods—and I mean *floods*—of water descended. TK raced out to cover the table and all the prepared goods with polythene (where did he find *that?* I certainly didn't have any). The water started running down the road in rivulets and then it covered the street entirely so that you couldn't even see the kerb.

In the midst of the huge disappointment and irritation I went out to see what was happening to the restaurants who were planning to serve food in the street. It was chaos. Barbecue fires were out and smoking; tables and chairs were being washed away by the water; people were cowering under show awnings or simply running away.

It took the organiser twenty minutes to get down this end of Main Street to tell us that the event was cancelled. Yes, we had noticed.

I wondered whether to tell the Health Inspector that she could come out of the fridge but decided not.

But, as we have mentioned before, Ella is a Scorpio. The words "let's give up and go home" do not exist in her vocabulary.

'Open the café!' she shouted and, sure enough, as we opened the doors and floated the portable sign outside, twelve soaking wet and disreputable people staggered in.

'Brew tea', said Ella.

'Not coffee?' I asked, perplexed.

'No, tea. Tea doesn't spoil the appetite,' said Ella, wisely. She welcomed all the people, took down the chairs which had been stacked on the tables when we closed and we served them tea and brownies. And then wraps and pretzels as they were joined by twenty other refugees from the cold.

Frank Sinatra warbled happily through the speakers, the customers began to steam and to giggle and TK and Ella carried all the food and drinks from outside back into the cafe.

The rain stopped.

'Can you cope?' Ella asked TK.

'Sure,' he said.

I looked puzzled.

'Come on,' said Ella. 'We're going to take a table down into the centre of town and sell wraps.'

'Who to?' I asked.

'People will come now,' said Ella. 'And all the restaurants are shut.'

So, we hurried down the pavement and watched the water subsiding slowly as we picked an over-turned table out of the gutter and set it up two blocks into town. Then we took it in turns to carry the food and drinks down the road and, within seconds, we were selling.

I couldn't believe it but, of course, Coloradans are used to far worse weather than this. In the distance great streaks of lightning slashed the sky and there were still drops falling here and there but the people of Unityville were reappearing in waterproofs. And they were hungry!

We sold and sold and sold. Both of us were frozen solid because we were dressed only in flimsy tee-shirts (the temperature was eighty-five degrees until the rain fell. Now it was perhaps fifty degrees). Ella was anxious that some of her make-up had run to reveal the Yogi Bear circle of pink around her mouth. Actually it had a bit but I couldn't spare her. 'You look fine' I said. 'Don't worry.'

But she did. After all, she was an actress and what she called "the moment of utmost humiliation" arrived. Someone important who saw her in a play a few weeks ago and whom she wanted to impress. He came up and bought a pretzel and looked at her curiously.

'Didn't I see you in *A Streetcar Named Desire*?' he asked and she had to admit he did. Poor Ella. Her hair was bedraggled and wet; her face in the gloaming was somewhat strange with different colours showing through; her whole upper torso was mottled with cold and goose-bumps.

But she did not run away; she faced it with laughter and told the truth. That she had had jaw surgery and followed it up with a face lift; that she was bloody cold but that I was her friend and helped her and now she was only too delighted to help me. I could see in the man's face that although he didn't admire her features any more, he did admire her strength and spirit—and I told her so when he had gone.

Nevertheless, she insisted on going to make some repairs back at the cafe and, for half an hour, it was just me on the sodden streets, selling wraps and pretzels and brownies. It was fun and I danced to keep warm and shouted like a fishwife street-seller: 'The last chocolate on Main Street! Don't make me eat it all myself!'

After two hours the rush was over. We were not sold out but we had done very well and earned more in the evening than the cafe did all day. TK was back in the café and we all cleared up together.

Frankly was ecstatic when I got home, half-dead with fatigue. She had been left for far too long and she needed a walk. The rain had started again and it was still incredibly damp. In the distance I could hear the sound of the street musicians still playing and I had a strange contentment deep inside. We did the impossible that night and, although I could not have done it, I had found friends who could—and you can't really ask for more than that.

Suddenly, the telephone rings and I am jerked back into reality. What the…? It is four o'clock in the morning.

It is Jack.

'I saw your light was on. Are you okay?'

'Yes thanks. It's a bit un-nerving though.'

'Yeah. A real blaster. Your roof holding up okay?'

'Some leaks but nothing more serious. I've got enough buckets and plants.'

'And Frankly?'

'She's asleep now. She tried out-barking the thunder but didn't quite make it.'

'This could last a while.'

'But what about the fiesta?'

'Yeah, it's a problem. I guess they'll go ahead unless it's just impossible —and then they'll just put it off for a day.'

'Poor St. Pet and St. Serge. They must be gagging for it.'

'What?'

'The two saints… the ones that have it off together in the church in Larita one night a year.'

Jack chuckles. 'I'd heard that they prayed together for tolerance and peace.'

'Ah. Oops. My mistake then.'

'Hmmm. Sounds like you might be projecting.'

'I beg your pardon!'

'No, I beg yours. I shouldn't have said that. It's just that you had a love bite on your neck as big as Rhode Island.'

I am speechless with embarrassment.

'Anna?'

'Jack, you are unforgivable. You have no tact at all.'

'None,' he agrees amiably. 'Hey, Anna, I was glad for you. If anyone deserves a good time, you do.'

Now why does that make me furious?

'It was a one-off,' I say grudgingly. 'No one from the village and no repeat.'

'Oh. Shame.'

'Jack, just leave it, will you?'

'Okay, okay. No offence intended. But it was one helluva bite.'

'Shut up!'

'Okay.'

Silence.

'You mad at me?'

'Yes.'

'Oh well. You won't dance with me at the fiesta then?'

My heart leaps.

'Everyone dances at the fiesta, don't they?'

'Sure, but I'd like you to dance with me.'

'There'll be a rumour.'

'There always is.'

'Okay.'

'Great.'

Silence.

'Goodnight then, Anna. Give Frankly a pat from me.'

'Goodnight, Jack.'

And I am warm and comfortable curled up in the duvet with my snoring and stinky little beagle. The fiesta will go ahead even if it's a whole day late. And I am going to dance with Jack.

Chapter Thirteen

THE RAIN STOPPED. The day dawned bright and steaming as the water rose in clouds to meet the morning sun. Fiesta!

The lights that the villagers strung across the houses have turned the white walls pink and Los Poops is alive with music and fumes of alcohol. The saints are up in their connubial church being either chaste or chased, whichever they happen to go for. And it is a fun day.

The mule race comes first. Seventeen mules are entered. Seventeen! Some of them came down from the other villages and it is quite a sight to see them all gathered in the village square, the products of their excitement (or rather, their excrement) steaming gently in the pale, recovering sunlight and attracting their own special class of fly.

Each mule is decked out in crêpe paper streamers and their riders arrayed in old and shiny culottes with clean white shirts and religious icons pinned to every available part of their anatomy.

The village policeman is trying to line them up for the race and the signal to start them off is to be him firing his pistol.

'Doesn't that scare them?' I ask Rani, thinking I'm glad I've left a sulky beagle back at the house.

'Oh yes,' he says with a grin. 'It's a proper stampede. Legs going in all different directions and mules up in the air with fright. Someone always falls off and at least three people say it's a false start. The fiesta wouldn't be the same without it!'

The mules are supposed to race up to the top of the hill where their riders have to take a ribbon from a young girl, who is meant to be a virgin, and then race back down to the village square again.

This year, for sure, she is a virgin. It's Bianca and she's six. One year, says Rani, there was a bit of a problem because in the time it took the mules to get up the hill, the virgin had just stopped being

196

a virgin courtesy of the son of the local butcher—and hadn't come out from behind the trees in time to hold the ribbons out. So there were about twenty hot and sweating mules milling about with twenty hot and furious men shouting and a rather hot and sticky girl eventually appearing rather sheepishly with a pile of very bedraggled ribbons.

'No one was awarded the prize that year,' says Sylvia. 'The race was ruled invalid because the ribbons had been sullied.'

'What happened to the girl?'

'I think she moved away fairly quickly. She had a rather hasty wedding and is spending the rest of her life in a butcher's shop. Probably not quite what she had hoped for.'

'Ah, well, if you play with fertility Devas you'll get the expected result,' says Rani.

'Divas?' I have images of large fat women singing.

'Earth spirits. The beings that live in and around nature. Have you ever read the *Narnia* stories?'

'Oh yes,'

'Remember the naiads and dryads? The tree spirits?'

'Well, yes.'

'That kind of thing. They can be very powerful in a place where there isn't too much civilisation to block them. A few glasses of alcohol or a fiesta and everyone round here is at it like rabbits.'

'Everyone?' I have a sudden flashback of myself and Yiannis.

'Yes, just take care of yourself or you'll find an ageing Spaniard making up to you with a toothless grin! Surprised it hasn't happened already with you being on your own.'

'Oh God!'

'Come on, come on!' Stella has appeared beside us, all brisk and busy in a pseudo-Spanish outfit with a bodice and white blouse. 'Are you going to place your bets? You're running out of time!'

'Bets?'

'Of course. You must pick your mule and place a bet. Of course I don't usually approve of gambling but this is such a village tradition that it's important to play along. It helps bring the community together. Very important.'

She leads the way, head up and striding around the mule dung to where the priest has a trestle table next to the church. He is doing a blinding trade with cloakroom tickets marked with the names of the mule owners and chalking up the odds in brown on the outside of the church wall.

I put my hundred pesetas on the Sad Mule With The Crinkly Eyelids which I have to point out because I don't know his owner's name. I choose him simply because I have to choose someone fast and I don't have any idea of the form.

'Is there a favourite?' I ask David who, as usual, is standing, half-invisible, just far enough away from Stella for you to be able to talk to him without her hearing.

'Not this year,' he says. 'The mule that won four years in a row has left town. The men arranged for his owner to receive an offer he couldn't refuse so he sold the beast. There's a lot at stake on this race. The winner gets a free drink every night for a year.'

'For a year! Wow!'

Now the mules are gathering in a very ragged line in the square.

'Back off,' says David warningly. 'Anything could happen.'

We gather at the other end, together with a gaggle of villagers who are talking excitedly. But, of course, there is a delay while the policeman insists on a proper line-up and the riders thump the mules and the mules take no notice. This goes on until there is muttering and grumbling among the rest of the villagers because good drinking time is being wasted and eventually the policeman gets as impatient as the rest of us, shrugs his shoulders, raises his pistol and fires without warning.

All hell breaks loose.

Mules go in all directions: left, right, down, up, prone and supine. They tread on people, kick and bite, fall over and go round in circles. Women scream, men swear, dogs bark and mules bray. Three riders, bucked into the air, crash into each other about two feet above their respective mounts and, I swear, one of them lands again on the wrong beast while the others tumble down to the cobbles.

And then, just as suddenly as it started, the furore is over and there is a stream (or should it be a steam?) of mules lumbering crazily up the road to the top of the village as their riders thump their sides and wave their arms around in the air.

I am helpless with laughter and can barely take a sugar cake from the tray being handed round by a small girl in a bright yellow polka-dot flamenco costume. All the children are in fancy dress for the occasion, although Batman and a character from *Star Wars* over by the Municipal building look a little odd in a tiny Spanish town.

'It's disgraceful,' fumes Stella nibbling at a cake. 'Someone is really going to get hurt one day. They should organise things better.'

Everyone has their own opinion which now needs to be aired as bumps and bruises are rubbed and the piles of dung swept off the cobbles by the ever-present army of elderly women dressed in black. The fearsome debates only stop when Rani shouts out and points up the hill where the stream of mules is just visible proceeding at a vague kind of lope.

'Paco is in front!'

'No, it's Domingo!'

'Paco!'

'Domingo!'

'Who did you bet on?' says a quiet American voice in my ear.

I turn swiftly. I didn't think he was there and I had tried not to miss him.

'The Sad Mule With Crinkly Eyelids,' I say. 'I don't know who his owner is.'

'Which one?' Jack is smiling down into my eyes and my stomach is doing funny things which I don't want to acknowledge.

'I can't describe him any better than that.'

'Not one of the ones over there, by any chance?'

Oh good grief. Has my mule been a non-starter? But no, the three mules left standing in the square as their former riders rub their bruises and accept a consolation drink are all too dark-coloured.

'No. He made it out of the starting gate.'

Jack smiles. 'It's fun, isn't it?'

'Oh yes!'

'Come and have a drink.'

But my nod of assent is unnecessary for the drinks are coming to us. Tray after tray of local wine now being served by the girls of the village. It is all free and it is all very, very alcoholic.

Next on the agenda is the setting up of the finishing line for the winning mule. A long rope is stretched across the square at what would be about breast height for a mule. Rani explains that the coloured streamers flowing from it were added after the winning mule one year didn't see it and was tripped up at the final moment, catapulting his rider over his head and giving him concussion. The second mule then trod on the first one, putting it on the injury list for two months and that caused a vendetta between two families which only ended when the village policeman banged the two main protagonist's heads together in the bar one night. They then united in their outrage at him and arranged for mule dung to be smeared inside his bed on a Saturday night when he was liable to come home rather late and under the influence and didn't notice until it was too late.

The owner of the winning mule gets an old silver trophy as well as free drinks for a year. I sneak a look at it and discover that it was once awarded to someone called Johansson for long service in the civil engineering industry.

'*¿Es bueno, si?*' It is Sanchia, the only woman in the village who couldn't possibly be a murderer.

'*¡Es muy bueno!*' I smile at her, happy that I am beginning to be accepted as a part of Los Poops. We chat for a moment in alleged Spanish and I can understand a good fifty per cent of what she is saying and make an educated guess at the rest. Sanchia gestures towards Jack who is talking to Stella and David. I don't understand exactly what she is saying but the implication is clear. 'Is he your man?' she is asking.

'No,' I shrug and look regretful. 'He is already married.'

'Poof!' says Sanchia, dismissively, and goes on to explain in graphic and incomprehensible detail about making hay while the sun shines. A man needs a woman, she says—and we are both alone. I smile and shake my head.

Shouts from up the hill alert us to the approach of the mules and the crowd falls back to the edges of the square while two sturdy lads hold up the rope for the finishing line. I had expected an explosion of galloping mules clattering at speed into the square but the two that appear, covered with sweat and being thumped rhythmically by their riders, are only trotting, albeit with bulging eyes and tongues hanging out as if they were about to explode. As they approach the winning line, one of them breaks into a distinct canter and the crowd raises a cheer.

Then, suddenly, from the ranks of people, a golden blur appears, barking furiously, and Tigger bounces onto the leading mule.

It goes berserk. It's bad enough to be thumped up a hill and then down again when most of what you do is stand under an olive tree and doze all day without being bounced on by an overgrown hearthrug. The mule stops dead, turns on a sixpence and, astonishingly neatly, kicks Tigger with both rear hooves, knocking him flying. The rider falls off, right into the path of the second mule which grinds to a halt. The Sad Mule With Crinkly Eyelids ambles round the corner with his rider flailing arms and legs like a dervish… and crosses the finishing line at a relaxed trot.

Well.

You can imagine!

Nothing better could possibly have happened. The fiesta is a bona-fide success simply because everyone has something to argue about. Who actually should have won that race?

Tigger is fine, by the way, if a little bruised and surprised. Stella, of course, is threatening to sue and glaring at anyone who dares to suggest that it was Tigger's own fault—or, more likely, hers.

David has vanished into thin air.

I collect 15,000 pesetas which comes as a very pleasant surprise, especially when I work out that it's nearly £60. Sixty whole pounds for a single bet on a mule! Hastily I stick about a fiver into the universal donations box which is there to pay for all the free drink (and get a cheer for my pains) and then pocket the rest joyfully. The house and the money from America are being sorted out but cash in hand is always better than promises in the bank and my credit cards are nearly up to the hilt.

Next on the agenda—although interspersed with more argument—is the children's fancy dress competition and then it's lunch: ham rolls and local fruit provided gratis with home-made lemonade and yet more wine for those who aren't already plastered. Or, perhaps, for those who already are.

Stella has taken Tigger home to bathe his wounds so David turns up cheerfully. I don't know quite how he survives but he is quite jolly as we ex-pats sit together in the sunshine eating and drinking and loving this funny little village.

Jack is less American than I expected him to be. He doesn't dominate the conversation and he actually listens to people. I watch him as he sits quietly next to Katherine, listening to her talking about her husband. There is a peace about him which is warming.

David is sitting next to me.

'You won't like me for saying this,' he says. 'But people are beginning to notice.'

I look at him and he nods at Jack and then back at me.'

'I know,' I say. 'Sanchia said something earlier. I told her that there's nothing going on—and there isn't.'

'I believe you,' said David, and he is telling the truth. 'The trouble is that gossip runs ahead of itself. And it is obvious that you two like each other. I don't suppose there's anything you can do if a rumour is going to start. I just thought you should be warned.'

'Thanks.' But I am angry. Not with David, so much, but with everyone who sees it their duty to gossip and jump to conclusions. But are they so very wrong? If Jack were single, would I not be with him now? And wouldn't I jump to exactly the same conclusions if I saw someone else behaving the way we are?

"The way we are" means catching eyes and smiling, a hand under my elbow to guide me when we go into the bar and a conspicuous not standing and talking to each other. Yes, I would see those as signs of an affair.

Now Stella is back, busily telling everyone how Tigger is where a more tactful woman would realise that there are at least two people who want to kill her and shut up. The owner of the Sad Mule With Crinkly Eyelids is Pedro, a diminutive, gnarled man who looks as if he's in his sixties but who is probably only my age. He sits, somewhat bemused, in the bar being alternatively fêted and ostracised by those who think he had a fair win and those who think he didn't.

The fun and frivolity continue for another couple of hours and then there's a natural lull while everyone gathers their energies for the evening marathon.

I am avoiding Jack slightly and he either understands or hasn't noticed which irritates me slightly. The ex-Pats are going back to *La Posada* for tea—apart from Stella and me who both have dogs to feed and walk. I take an apple from the still-abundant pile of food on a trestle table in the square and go and find my hero, the mule. He is back in his stable, sweating a little and rubbing his leg with his nose; not acting like the superstar he is.

Tentatively, I make clicking noises and hold a piece of the apple out on a flat hand. The mule ignores me.

I call again and it flickers its ears warily and goes back to the safer option of continuing to ignore me.

'Oh come on!'

I'm not even speaking his language so that isn't going to work. Defeated, I toss a piece of apple as near to his nose as I can, causing him to back off, snorting with surprise. Then the long, prehensile nose quivers as the scent works its way through the dung and flies and the mule turns slightly to lip the piece of fruit. It is found to be acceptable and is crunched up. The mule's eyes are closed with concentration and, I think, enjoyment.

However, the seemingly natural follow-on of turning towards me to look for more apple where that came from, simply doesn't wash. The mule just hangs its head and goes back into ignoring mode. Or maybe it's even sleep.

I throw the rest of the apple and go to feed Frankly and take her out for a walk. She is squeakily happy to see me and I feel a rat for planning to leave her for the rest of the day. Stella had offered to have her with Tigger—so it's probably my fault that poor, pathetic Tigger couldn't be left on his own—but I thought Frankly would prefer the Callousness Of Solitary Confinement to spending any time whatsoever with Tigger.

I know I would.

As I walk Frankly down below the town, I can hear the church bell ringing over the hills just as it has for hundreds of years. Time stands still; it could be any century; the landscape would look just the same. The last of the lavender is drying on the stalk and I can rub my fingers on it as I pass. I love this place, just as I loved Colorado. I don't want to go back to England.

I will have to, of course. I have to earn a living and, although I am managing to sell some short stories and articles, I am not making enough to live on even with no rent to pay. I am responsible for the utility bills here—and my food—both of which cost very little but I can't stay my whole life in a tiny Spanish village.

And I think I am falling in love... with someone totally, hopelessly unavailable and completely inappropriate but who loves Frankly the way that I do. Utterly, utterly stupid. I suppose I was bound to hit the rebound at some point and at least it takes my mind off Alex.

Alex. Already it seems so long ago.

My brother and his family want to come out and stay at Christmas—and possibly my mother too. I have very mixed feelings about that. Of course I would love to see them, but Los Poops "belongs" to me (how silly!) and I don't want outsiders to criticise it.

My thoughts whirl on; and I am taking no notice whatsoever of the pathway or of Frankly. Time can stand still in any country and I might just as well be walking on an ugly London pavement.

The sound of shouting raises me from the reverie. Some celebration has boiled over in the village and it sounds like some kind of fight has broken out.

Frankly is sniffing nearby so I clip her lead on and head back to the house.

Grumbling, she follows me and I am lost in a dream again, only to be pulled up short. Stella is sitting on the cobbles in the courtyard by my front door, crying.

'Stella! What's wrong?'

'They killed Tigger.'

'What!'

'Tigger,' she says, weeping copiously. 'He was poisoned. Someone threw some poisoned meat in through the window.'

'And he's dead? Not just ill?'

Now I am on my knees beside her and cradling her in my arms. Poor stupid, arrogant Stella. That should not have happened to her—or to silly bouncing Tigger.

'He was already stiff when I got home,' says Stella. She is shaking.

'Where's David.'

'He's gone to find the people who did it.'

I am silent. I suspect that David will succeed and, in his own quiet way, make his opinion felt. But that won't help Tigger now.

Oh, poor Tigger. And poor Stella.

Frankly is uninterested and potters around the courtyard at the end of the lead, bored. But I am sitting with Stella and rocking her like a baby as she cries.

I would have thought she would have been angry. She is such a bossy boots and so fierce, normally, but all the stuffing has been knocked out of her. It is me who is angry. Those bastards! They nearly got Frankly and now they have killed Tigger. You just can't do that!

But obviously they can. And people lost money on the mule race and it was Tigger who changed the result, simply because he wasn't restrained—or trained—properly.

But it isn't fair; it isn't fair.

And Stella loved Tigger like I love Frankly and her heart is broken. Never again will she go home to the ecstatic welcome; never again get irritated over the hair on her clothes and the floor; never have that warmth and living joy to hug.

Thank you God that it wasn't Frankly. Thank you so, so much for Jack Risborough and his antidote. Oh why wasn't Tigger found in time to save him too?

'Come in and have a drink.' I have some gin in the house and it might help.

Or tea—the great panacea? Would Stella prefer tea?

She nods and lets me pull her up and lead her in to the house with Frankly trotting in briskly as if nothing were wrong and asking for her evening rawhide chew. I give it to her as I put the kettle on, acutely aware that the house is a mess. Stella has turned her nose up at it more than once and, even now, dusts down the chair before sitting on it.

I make tea silently and serve it and listen to the story of how she went home at six o'clock having left Tigger for only a couple of hours. She and David opened the door and walked in without a care in the world and there was the stiff carcass of what had been a vibrant and loving dog, lying on the kitchen floor. There were still some pieces of meat on the floor which Tigger hadn't had time to eat—and, even to the casual observer, it was obvious they were dusted with rat poison.

This whole village reeks with poison, I thought, all my love for it vanishing in this latest atrocity.

I get Stella to tell me all about Tigger and where he came from and stories about his life and she drinks her tea and appears a little comforted. She even tells me about the two previous dogs, also poisoned but not deliberately—they just found poison on the hillside in the hunting season like Frankly did.

'But Tigger was special,' she is saying. 'You know there's always one dog that is simply the most special one.'

I know. And it takes months to get over the loss of a dog, even if Stella dares to get another one. And how can she trust any of the villagers again? It could have been one of a hundred people.

I am tactfully silent as Stella enumerates Tigger's virtues. They were rather outnumbered by his enthusiasm but he was not a bad dog, just a bouncy one with no discipline. I look across at where Frankly has settled herself on the rug by the French windows and my heart contracts again with gratitude that she is safe.

'I knew you'd understand,' Stella is saying. 'You're the only other Brit with a dog. You know what they mean to us.'

And I do. In fact I find myself telling her the whole of Frankly's and my story. I shall probably regret it but there is a link between dog-lovers and it might take her mind off her loss.

David arrives silently half an hour later and knocks gently on the door—which is open.

Stella gets up and runs to him and he holds her tightly. It is good to see such moments of marital solidarity especially in a couple who seem so mismatched.

'Steady, old girl,' he says, as if she were a horse.

I put my fingers into a 'T' sign with a query in my face and he nods so I put the kettle on again, half listening as he talks to his wife with affection.

He has asked around the village and found that Jacob and Jose-Luis had both threatened to poison Tigger—but they did not answer the door when he knocked and no one has seen them in the village this afternoon. There are several messages of condolence from both Brits and Spaniards alike, even people who loathed Stella and her dog. Even so, this is a time for solidarity and no one likes to think of the ruthless killing of a harmless if stupid beast.

As I leave Stella and David to talk together and retire behind the pillar that separates living area from kitchen it hits me like a mallet. Frankly could have been there too—and she would have eaten that meat. If I had succumbed to Stella's entreaties to leave the dogs together my dog would be dead too.

Or maybe Tigger would be alive because he wouldn't have been down in the square.

How can I go on living here with all this going on? But where else could I go?

We drink tea. I was going to leave them alone but David pulls a chair out for me and we sit in the companionable way of our tribe when tragedy has struck. It was only a dog. That's what Alex would have said. But it's not what Jack would say.

Only a dog.

Only a heart of strength and loyalty; only a spirit of mischievousness and instant forgiveness. Only a dog.

We talk of dogs and childhood; of deaths both natural and, sometimes, through the gentler hands of a vet. We speak of years of love, irritation and laughter and I remember the poem my mother kept in her file of special cards and letters. I learnt it by heart for school and nearly everyone cried.

'Do you want to hear it?' I ask doubtfully.

'Oh yes.'

'You'll cry more.'

'Well maybe this is just a time for crying,' says Stella sensibly.

So I recite the poem from *Honorary Dog* by Dora Wright:

Take what you want, says God
And pay for it. I've paid.
I've paid in money, effort, comfort, time,
In broken flowers, in crumpled mud-stained clothes,
In trampled carpets, sleepless nights, in rage,
And in that bitter moment at the end,
When on the table, circled in arms of love,
With gentle, grateful eyes, she glides at last
Into her endless sleep.

I've paid. What have I taken
Worth all this price of ruined chairs, ripped books,
Chewed shoes and soon-forgotten crime on crime?
I've taken lives that centred all on me.
I've taken joy and laughter for my tears,
With dividends of friends and hopes and fears,
I've taken love and walked as one bewitched,
Safe through life's snares, while I gave thought
To lustrous eyes, to brilliant coats, to forms
That spring and leap and run—enchanted beings
Taking my spirit with them as they fly.
And when the reckoning's made on my last day
Of all my foolish work and lack of thrift,
Whether in debt or credit it will stay—
I'll not have bought, for no price buys a gift.

Stella doesn't weep; she sighs.

'Yes, that's it,' she nods. 'You do understand.'

And across the miles of discomfort that have sat between us is a sisterhood. We smile. It's a rather watery smile but a smile nonetheless.

Stella and David are leaving now, going home together rather than going to the bar. I can't blame them. I say I will walk back with them as far as the square although I'm really not sure if I feel like joining in with any of the festivities. But I want to see Jack and that's where he will be. Frankly is outraged at being left behind again but I shut her in extra firmly, making sure that all the windows are closed as well. It's quite a cool evening and she'll be fine.

The music is loud—a local band playing a mixture of traditional and modern tunes in a very Los Poopian way on the terrace behind the bar—and there are coloured lanterns across the streets casting pink and yellow lights everywhere. The bar is crammed to overflowing with people and some are dancing already. There are dozens of strangers here. I suppose they are friends and relatives of the Los Poopians; or maybe there's a kind of rent-a-mob for fiestas in the Alpujarras?

One last hug for Stella who is still white-faced but bearing up like the trouper she is. They plan to bury Tigger's body out in the fields tonight, somewhere nice and shady where he will rest in comfort, Stella says. Probably next to Steel and Compo, their other dogs.

'Will you have another dog?' I ask tentatively. I don't know if I could have another dog here if Frankly were poisoned; but Stella is made of sterner stuff.

'Oh yes,' she says. And, by way of explanation: 'I don't want to leave here and I don't want to live without a dog. So I have to risk it. Not yet though. Certainly not yet.'

'The villagers aren't bad people,' says David. 'The other dogs were poisoned by hunters—they just laid the stuff around everywhere in those days. It doesn't happen so much now. But a deliberate poisoning is another thing.

'That will be called to account.'

Yes, it will.

I wish them luck and say goodnight and stand, thinking, in the shadow of the bar for a moment. I don't feel very festive but, equally, I don't want just to go home. I can't see Jack in the melée through the open door.

Come on Anna! But no, I can't. Not yet. I go and sit on the wall overlooking the rubbish tip and the trees and swing my feet like a little girl. The square is not empty and it looks from all the preparations that the party will spill out here at some point. I can see the terrace, jutting out over the hillside and the band is doing a sterling job. It's made up from four middle-aged men who look as if they're related; three of them with tendrils of hair, once scraped across balding pates, now flying in the breeze. The fiddler is the star with the two guitarists coming in a close second. The clarinet player is shorter than the others but is leaping around frantically like a slightly lost whirling dervish emitting squeaks and wails which add surprisingly un-discordant harmonies to the others.

Ah, there is movement. The band is beginning to work its way through the people, who fall back obediently. They are inside the bar itself now and I suspect will emerge on the street like four middle-aged pied pipers.

And the plaza is suddenly filled with laughter, colour and movement. The people swing into dancing as soon as their feet touch the cobbles. Wizened old men and ladies sway in what would be a mockery of Flamenco if it weren't so touching; the younger ones either adapt on ballroom or dance disco. The kids just go wild.

Jack is there, dancing with Sylvia and my heart jumps before I can stop it.

I'm aware of some part of me watching critically—a man needs to be able to dance! He has rhythm and he is matching his steps to hers. They look as if they are having a great time.

'Dance, Anna?' says Rani to my left.

'Yes,' I jump down. 'Thanks.'

It is very good to dance—and Rani is an excellent dancer. How long has it been? My body remembers… all those teenage and early-twenties discos and parties when people still did dance in England. I wonder if they do now or whether I just stopped being invited to those kinds of parties? Everything feels like it is loosening up although I'm pleased now that I only have flat sandals to wear. Heels would be murder on the cobbles.

But as I do dance with Rani something inside me begins to worry a little. After all, he is single and I don't want him to get the wrong message. I think a lot of people could get wrong messages (or even temporarily correct messages) on a night like this. The air is crackling with sexual tension.

Or is that just me? Good grief, do I actually fancy Rani?

The answer to that comes in a sudden shiver down the spine as Jack cuts in and, with a cheerful nod to Rani, catches my hands and whirls me off to join something that looks rather like a conga. A train of people are circling the square with their hands on each other's hips. Jack's hands are on mine and they feel wonderful; strong and masculine. I dance with renewed vigour until I catch Sanchia's eye sparkling at me and realise what it must look like to everybody here.

Oh to hell with it! I take a deep, deep breath of the spicy night air, put one hand up to pull the tie-back from my hair so I can let it fall loose and give myself up to St. Perpetua—or the earth goddess; tonight is special and tonight will be remembered.

It is such fun! We are all drunk and we are all dancing and everyone is kissing everyone else. Jack is kissing Sylvia and even Stella who has bravely come down for the festival's conclusion. Not passionate kisses but the kind that would be thought a bit off in a Washington social element. He kisses me too, just in passing; just friendly enough and so much a part of the dance that it isn't special in any way—and he squeezes my hand. And suddenly I feel free to enjoy myself just knowing that he is there. I can choose who kisses me and who doesn't and let caution go to the winds when I want to. Everyone else is. And I know that Jack understands. He isn't going to compromise me here.

Actually, Rani isn't a bad kisser at all.

The last ritual of the evening is the walk up the hill to Larita to fetch St. Perpetua and bring her back down to her lonely church where the Virgin can look at her with renewed grief at her licentiousness—or, perhaps, discuss the finer points of deep prayer with a soulmate.

The villagers who can still walk trail up the hill with lanterns looking like a scene from *Fantasia*. I'm not planning to go with them but, suddenly, there is a hand on my shoulder. 'Shall we follow them?' says Jack.

'Yes.'

And suddenly I am breathless.

We walk behind the others, silently, not touching all the way up the hill. It's enough. I can feel his masculinity and his strength and all around me are the soft scents of night. Any breath that I might have left from the climb will be needed for the hymns as St. Perpetua is welcomed back into the fold. She has her own hand-held carriage, resting on the shoulders of four of the villagers and surrounded with candles. The priest goes ahead to meet the villagers of Larita and both Serge and Pet are brought out to a great cheer and a swelling of voices in song. Nobody here can sing particularly well—the voices are cracked and atonal—but it's beautiful in the deep dark of night with the stars soaring above us in the great arc of the Milky Way.

The saints bid each other farewell; Serge goes back into his church and Pet is placed reverently on her perch, the candles are lit and she is raised to shoulder height, her shadow dancing uncertainly on the trees and walls of the edge of the village.

Then it is back down the hill with most of Larita following us because there will be one almighty booze-up once Pet is safely back home.

'That was fun,' I say.

'Wasn't it?'

We are walking back together as comfortable as old friends and before I know it Jack's arm is around my waist and I love it. I love it. I love it. Oh, to lean against him and respond. But I mustn't. He turns slightly towards me and says something inconsequential about one of the villagers and I lift myself up on my toes and kiss him on the mouth. Just a brief moment, nothing more. It is a strong mouth. Masculine.

Oh fuck, oh shit, oh God.

We walk on down the hill, invisible to everyone else in the darkness. Nothing is said. I am aghast at what I have done. He has been so circumspect, so sensible, so married. And so have I. I am an idiot. I have blown it. I am drunk.

We are back at the top of *Calle La Era* now. I pull away.

'I can make it safely from here,' I say.

'No you can't,' he says. 'You're drunk.'

212

The arm tightens around me and we walk down the perpendicular hill together, saying nothing. At the doorway I pull my arm away to fumble for my keys. I am about to stammer something breathtakingly inarticulate when his hand comes up to my face, encircling my cheek and ear, and I am lifted to him so that he can kiss me briefly. The kind of kiss which is over before you realise the intimacy of it but which carries an echo through my body that I cannot yet catch.

So we stand there, saying nothing, his head bent to mine and our foreheads touching. I have one hand on his arm above the elbow and I know that if he moves away something inside me will break.

Then the kiss. The real, heartfelt kiss in its completeness which pulls me up onto tiptoe into his arms and makes my knees go weak and makes tears form in my eyes.

It lasts forever. And then is over. And Frankly is scratching on the door and squeaking.

'I love you, Anna,' says Jack.

'Yes.'

'And you love me.'

'Yes.'

He smiles. 'You know I have to go.'

'Yes.'

'Goodnight.'

'Goodnight.'

And he is gone; slipped into the darkness and, blindly, I am stabbing the key in the door. There are tears in my eyes and I have no idea if they are happiness or grief.

Chapter Fourteen

'I THINK WE need to talk.'

We all know that phrase. It means 'we have a problem.' Sometimes it means 'it's over.' If it has never really begun, it generally means that it never will.

I know that. He knows that.

For us it means, 'This stops now.'

It would be all too easy to take this further; to fall into bed together and have a passionate affair—but we don't want to.

No, it's not that we don't want to. It's that we won't.

I know this sounds odd and archaic as the twentieth century turns into the twenty-first but look at it this way:

If Jack leaves Karen for me then he is no better than Alex. It would mean that I was betraying Karen as Suzie betrayed me. It would mean that nothing meant anything and that marriage was not a sacred commitment.

'A what?!' you may say. 'You've just kissed him. He just ratted on his wife in quite a big enough way for her to hit the roof. What's sacred about that.'

Well, it was sacred. That's the point. It was a one-time moment of sanctuary. It shouldn't have happened although it was always on the cards that it would.

But that's it.

Yeah, yeah, you say. What a load of holier-than-thou shit. (At least, I can hear Ella saying it). Okay, what we did was wrong, even if it feels so right. How many pop songs are there on that theme? Yes it was wrong. So we won't do it again.

I won't be an adulteress. I won't be "the other woman." I won't break up a marriage.

I had mine broken up and I didn't like it. Therefore I won't do it myself.

If you think I'm sounding too precious here, it's not that I'm a prude. To be honest, I've done it before—a very long time ago. And if you don't learn from your mistakes, you're never going to get very far.

Many years ago I fell in love with a married man and he with me and we became lovers. For two years. During that time I hoped and prayed that he would leave her for me, but he never did.

Actually, I am very glad about that now.

I am also glad that, (as far as I know) she never knew.

I did it because I was young and irresponsible and stupid and desperately in love. And I got hurt a lot.

So, in a way, I got my comeuppance when Alex left me for Suzie. I got a bit more than I'd handed out but the lesson has been learnt. I am never going to hand out that kind of pain to any other woman.

I'm sorry, Karen, for what happened. But I never meant to hurt you and, hopefully, you will never know.

He won't leave you. He made a mistake and that is it.

No matter that it would be heaven. No matter that it would be the coming together of two halves of the same soul. No matter.

What if it did go on and he didn't leave you? What kind of a fool would I be then? And he wouldn't leave you. And I wouldn't want him to.

Even if your marriage stinks, Karen, how could I trust a man who left you—someone with whom he had shared so many intimate years? If he left you for me, he would leave again. And again.

Hercule Poirot used to say that murder gets easier every time. So does leaving wives or husbands. Simple logic. Also, I now know that any man who left a good woman for me wouldn't deserve my respect.

So when Jack rings up and says 'We have to talk,' I am ready to talk. But I really don't have to say very much because we are of one mind, Jack and I. We agree totally. He won't leave Karen and he won't continue with us. I wouldn't let him anyway.

So, he comes round and we talk. We don't use the "L-word" again because that's too dangerous but we know by look and touch of the hand that we are lovers on another level even if last night never happened.

And so we have to part. And that means that he has to leave Los Poops. At least until Frankly and I return to England. Which is only three months away now.

Oh God it hurts.

In books, in movies, in fairy tales, he would turn back as he leaves and we would run into each other's arms and miraculously everything would work out fine.

Except that this is real life and it doesn't happen.

He does kiss me again as he goes. We do need to make that acknowledgement of each other. And it is a wonderful kiss… the kind that melts your heart from within and runs silver through your bones so that you are beautiful without question. It is so wonderful that it is enough for nearly twenty-four hours.

It will have to be enough for a lot longer than that because he is leaving today.

Resolutely, I get on with the day. I don't even listen out for the sound of the BMW, so I don't hear it. I take Frankly for supper with Stella and John and Frankly sits on Stella's lap and loves her while we talk dogs. When we get back, I go to sleep quite easily.

And I wake in the morning with a hole in my heart so large that the memory of Alex is nothing within it.

It's a different pain though. It's a clean pain. I never understood before that a pain could be clean—or even, in a funny kind of way, good.

There are no regrets; there is a longing that won't be fulfilled and there is grief but nothing to remember as bad. Nothing at all.

And, there is a BMW.

This comes as a bit of a shock. But when the post arrives next day, it has a note from Jack. Of course my heart leaps and sinks. It's the kind of note that could be read by anyone; which is *meant* to be read by anyone.

> *Anna,*
> *I have left the BMW behind as I have left for the*
> *States and I won't be needing it. I know you don't have a*

car so please feel free to use it. It has fully comprehensive insurance and I have added your name to it. Don't worry, I've had it cleaned!

I'd be grateful if you'd keep an eye out for the house. The key is under the second plant pot to the right of the front door.

I hope to be back next summer so I won't see you before you and Frankly head for England. You've got my email address—let me know how you get on.

With best wishes,

Watlington P. Risborough (Jack)

PS. It's fine with me if you want to drive Frankly back to the UK in the car. I can arrange to have it picked up in London—or you could drive it back for a holiday in the summer and take a flight home. Whatever you want. J.

Do you know, I had almost forgotten what a stupid name he has.

But I am crying now. He has lent me his BMW! I can do what I like with it. I can even drive Frankly home. What luxury! How wonderful.

But I miss him so much. I will miss him for the rest of my life.

Chapter Fifteen

DEAR ANNA,

Happy holidays to you! Colorado is beautiful—under about three feet of snow where we are and all the holiday lights on the houses twinkling like a thousand points of light. I can't imagine what it's like to have a Christmas without snow!

Of course it's icy-cold and, yes, my eyelashes ice up when I go out in the morning. I bet Frankly's glad not to have her paws freezing on the pavement.

Poor thing! I remember her trying to work out why it was so uncomfortable to walk—and you trying to get her to wear doggy boots. She wasn't having any of that, was she? But she soon learnt that once the sun had come out it was fine to walk and I loved seeing her bouncing in the snow and sneezing. She really loved it.

So glad your family are coming out to visit you for New Year's. Your brother sounds like a really good guy and the kids will have a great time in Los Poops. It isn't long now before you can go home, is it? Or do you still not want to go?

Oh Honey, my heart sank when you wrote about how much you still miss Jack. Yes, I know you've got the car and access to his house... and you've had the experience of an honourable man in your life... but you don't need any more pain and I can sense it all around you. Apart from anything else, what the hell do the rest of the village think about your using the car and going in and out of his house at all hours? There'll be talk, darling. There always is. And they won't think either of you has been honourable at all.

Anna, I do understand. Really I do. I wasn't going to say anything but I can feel you still hurting. To have someone in your life who loves you but won't leave a loyal wife for you is proof that such men do exist; and gives you hope that you might find one. But be honest, it's not someone else you want to find; you hope something will happen in the States, you hope that Jack's wife will leave him and he'll come racing back to you all innocent and betrayed and you'll walk off into the sunset together.

Honey, I'm sorry. It just won't happen. Karen Risborough is completely wedded to the lifestyle that her husband can give her. Her children are grown and she is a feature of the Washington social scene. All the charity balls; the receptions; the coffee mornings. She ain't letting go of that.

And she wouldn't jump from one man to another either. Good God! She'd have to go back to all that messy sex stuff for a start. I bet that's all down to the regular 'we must do it once a fortnight because we're happily married' routine.

So, she's had a face lift. No, it isn't because she wants to attract some other guy. It's because it's the thing to do and she wants to look younger. In that world it's not about love; it's about social position and the quality of your teeth.

And he's wedded to it too. He's a consultant in the corporate world. He doesn't need to work for a living even if he does disappear off to Madrid every now and then just to look important. He does all the charity dos as well. He loves the social scene. And that link between him and his wife is huge.

Just suppose his marriage does break up and he comes back to Los Poops for you. You have to go into that world (where his wife is) and live that kind of life. It isn't you. You would hate it. And he would still swan off to Spain and places like that and leave you alone in the States.

Oh Anna, I'm sorry to lecture you like this but you're on your own. There won't be a white knight on a horse to rescue you. Yes, there may be a good man around but not a distant American. Whoever he is, he'll find you back in the UK when you're good and over Alex. I know it's tough— but it's the real world, honey.

Have a date with that guy Rani. How many more times

has he got to ask you out? If it's really cool with his house-mate (though that is one weird set-up!) go for it! You never know, he might be the one and your feelings for Jack are just stopping that happening.

Hope you'll still talk to me after this! Do enjoy your Christmas, darling.

Let me have your phone number and I'll give you a call. AT&T rates are dead cheap for Spain—because hardly anyone on their lines ever calls there!

Much love,

Ella.

PS Have you heard about Terry? If Gilbert's not told you, let me know and I'll fill you in with the scandal.

Dearest Anna,

Happy Holidays Darling! Hope you get some festive spirit in Spain. I know you guys eat turkey for Christmas but can you get one over there? It sounds seriously primitive to me. Chickens with heads and feet on—Yuk!

Hope Frankly's fine and stinky. Bet she's alpha bitch of the village now.

You wanted to know about Terry—Oh my dear! What a disaster! He got two years. 18 months for the assault and six months for aiming a punch at the judge on the way out of the courtroom. So now I don't have a chef. Maxine's doing what she can but she doesn't have the touch. Mind you, at least it looks edible nowadays, even if it doesn't taste that good.

You could have the job, honey, if you wanted. I could pay you cash and after five years you could come clean and get naturalisation. Truly—that's what the immigrants do… lie low for long enough and you're an honorary American.

Anyway, life goes on boringly here. Dane never emailed or called. I wrote him telling him how I felt but it was obviously the wrong thing to do. I guess I scared him off. But why shouldn't a Coloradan homo be wanting a real relationship? Cyber-sex was great but I guess when he saw me he couldn't take the whole package.

But you don't want to hear about that.

Hunting season's in full force. You can't go down Main Street without seeing a truck go past with hooves sticking up over the sides. My neighbour got an elk and has been cutting it up and freezing it. He gave me some steaks which is great and almost makes up for the smell of carcass everywhere! He cures the skin as well and his whole house is just covered in pelts.

Maxine's had her nipples pierced. She's been walking around all hunched forwards to stop her teeshirt rubbing on the sore bits. Looks like someone stuck a pineapple up her ass—I thought of having it done myself but not now I've seen what she's going through. I might have my ears done though—what do you think?

Keep your head up Darling—the exile must be going to end soon and then you'll be back in the glitz and glamour of London. I suppose you are going to London?

Lots of love,
Gilbert.

Dear Anna,

Just a note to say hi and to wish you and Frankly happy holidays. I think you mentioned that your brother and his family were coming out. Tell them they're welcome to use the house; they'll be more comfortable there than at La Posada. *I know you'll take care of it.*

I kinda miss Los Poops and would love to be there looking at the stars and doing nothing all evening. Or in Colorado doing the same. The holiday scene here in Washington is frantic; we are out every night and it won't calm down until after New Year's. I hope we'll get to Denver for some skiing at the end of January.

Do let me know how you are. When are you taking Frankly back to England?

Best wishes,
Jack.

Dear Anna,

Three days to go! We are really looking forward to seeing you. Thanks for the directions. I expect we'll be in Los Poops at about 10.30pm. Thanks too for the offer of your friend's house but Grace would rather be somewhere where she doesn't have to cook so we have confirmed the booking at La Posada. *Mum will be staying with you as arranged before.*

Will you meet us at La Posada? *The lady there says she'll have tea and sandwiches waiting which is very kind. Is it walking distance to your house from there or should I drop Mum off before we get to* La Posada?

I hardly know how we'll get everything on the aeroplane, let alone in the hire car. Mum seems to have bought you enough food to keep you going until this time next year. You will be the size of a house if you eat all the chocolate she's bringing! I had to stop her trying to pack a frozen turkey. She said it would defrost nicely on the journey. I ask you! Grace says to ask you what the weather's like. Should she bring mackintoshes and gumboots for the kids?

Glad things sorted themselves out about the house. I think you're very wise to wait until you are ready before divorcing. It gives time for things to settle down and by the time you are ready, you and Alex may be able to talk quite easily about things. And perhaps you'll be with someone nice and be happy again. I do hope so. You haven't had a lot of luck.

We are looking forward to seeing you.
Love,
Richard.

The Spanish do Christmas well and very prettily. Every window of every shop down in Motril and Almeria and all the seaside villages has a crèche so there must be more than a thousand holy families within half a day's journey of here. Some have just the three necessary figures—and others have huge scenes of life in Judaea with the shepherds on one side and the wise men approaching from another. The models are all shapes and sizes and there are whole craftsmen's shops where you can buy them all year round. Some are garish and, to be honest, if you met most of the angels in a dark alley after midnight you'd be running for your life but the general effect is nearly always charming.

The baby Jesus gets popped into the manger at midnight on Christmas Eve so that Mary gets to have a nice Christmas day instead of wasting it in labour. She's still pretty stiff and sore and hasn't had anything like enough breakfast by the look on her face in most of the statues and, with the size of the baby Jesus who's going to turn up in the church up the hill here, that pop-eyed look of astonishment that Joseph has will be well-founded too. 'How could a baby that size come out of my wife and leave her in one piece?' he's wondering while Mary's just boss-eyed with relief that the whole thing's safely over.

I've seen the baby Jesus. Top secret that, because he's brand new this year. The last one got chewed by some mice that got into the church store cupboard and lost half his head and all of his halo.

I saw him courtesy of Frankly's and my new friend Bianca, who lives just down the hill and whose family's roof terrace is just below ours. It was Frankly who met Bianca first, by hanging her head and front paws over the edge of the roof terrace. Bianca had a biscuit and Frankly could smell it and therefore friendship was always on the cards.

I was hanging out some washing and laughing to myself at how I would have harried Frankly away from the edge only a few months ago. Now I know I can trust her and she spends half her time on the roof watching what's going on around her. It's funny how children and animals can talk to each other. Almost like Frankly and me…

Hello! says Frankly, hanging over the edge.

'*Hola perro*,' says the little girl looking up at the wrinkled furry face which is regarding her (or, rather, her biscuit) with deep attention. Frankly gives the faintest of squeaks and wags her tail. Bianca can't see the tail but she can see the rest of the little dog wagging. She and Frankly understand each other immediately. Bianca looks at the biscuit and at Frankly, considers deeply whether she would have the most pleasure in eating the biscuit or watching Frankly eat it. The conclusion does not take long— Frankly puts her head on one side and squeaks oh-so-slightly. Immediately, Bianca holds the biscuit up, smiling.

Frankly, bless her, is the gentlest of dogs when it comes to children. She takes the biscuit politely and neatly and backs away so she can eat it on the roof terrace.

'¿Perro?' calls Bianca, saddened that she won't see the perro eat. And Frankly, having finished, puts her head back over the edge.

There is no more biscuit but there is a friendly little hand that can just reach far enough to stroke ears and a soft voice cooing and that is better than nothing. A friendship is forged—and I am permitted to have a part in it too.

Every day from then on, Bianca appears on the roof after school with a biscuit and Frankly insists on being there to greet her. Pretty soon she has explained to Bianca that it's a lot of hard work to get me to let her out so that she can get up onto the roof and that it would be better if Bianca brought the biscuit round. Or, even better, three or four biscuits.

I am now cutting back on Frankly's supper. Her arse is expanding.

So, Bianca comes round after school now. She says, somewhat shyly that she prefers it here because her two brothers are so… well, male. At least I think that's what she said. But I get the gist of it.

This has been going on for a couple of weeks and, somewhat to my surprise, I've been invited round for supper. It was Frankly who was invited really, because Bianca's totally in love with her now, but you take what you can get when it's a small village like this, you've finished all the readable books and there isn't a TV. Actually, it's quite a compliment. The invitation is written on a little card in Spanish and brought round gravely just before Bianca's bedtime. With an extra biscuit. Tomorrow night, if it would be convenient.

It Would Be Convenient, Frankly tells her when the last crumb has gone. Thank You Very Much.

Bianca doesn't have a mother. She has told me before that

Mama died when she was born. She says it again as she comes to fetch me for supper (supposing that, as a foreigner, I won't know my way around the village). I think she is just trying to make sure that I don't look for her Mama when I go into the house.

'Are you still sad?' I ask.

'*Si.*'

'Did you ever know your Mama?'

'No.'

So why is she so sad?

Maybe she simply wishes that she had a Mum like all the other girls. That would be entirely reasonable.

I stop and crouch down, put my hands on her shoulders and touch her hair and the deep brown eyes look up into mine with almost as much entreaty as Frankly at her most winning. Who, less circumspect than me, bodges Bianca on the arm to get her attention and then flaps her ears to break up the conversation and get on with the journey. There May Be Food At The End Of It.

Bianca laughs. I think she just needs a puppy.

Bianca lives with her Dad, her Grandma and two brothers and, momentary grief forgotten, she is terribly excited that she is bringing a new friend home. And that the new friend has a nice owner too.

I am greeted very politely by Isabella, who is a rather square, heavily lined woman who has lost three children but keeps her faith in the Lord. She looks fairly formidable but when it comes to her granddaughter her face softens. Bianca introduces Frankly to her and Frankly, who is being obnoxiously cute, offers a paw to shake. Isabella shakes it solemnly and greets her in Spanish while I try not to vomit. Ritual sniffing of the house then ensues— by Frankly, not me—while Bianca dances behind her excitedly. When it is established that no food is immediately available, Frankly and Bianca slip away to the far end of the rug-covered sofa for some girl-talk and cuddling and I am left to make small-talk with a virtual stranger. Isabella was one of the women who used to whisper about me in the shop. Damn decent of her, really, to invite a suspected murderer round. Come to think of it, her fearsome attitude towards her son-in-law and grandsons when they come in ten anguishingly awkward minutes later would put her high on my list of suspects. Isabella gives men short shrift.

The two teenage boys and I greet each other warily and I try to forget that I've seen them throwing stones at cats and then Paco offers his work-stained, solid hand for me to shake.

A torrent of abuse is heaped on his head. 'You wash your hands before you shake a lady's hand! Get into the bathroom you filthy beast! Have you no respect? And take off your shoes while you're about it!'

Paco slopes off, sheepishly, and I smile nervously as Isabella launches into a tirade against men in general and sons-in-law in particular. I can't get all of it by any means but something along the lines of Bianca's mother's death being entirely to do with his base lust seems to be at the core of it.

This is really more information than I wanted to know but I nod wisely, wishing that I could be playing burrowing under the blanket with Frankly and Bianca. That looks like a lot of fun from here.

Supper is a little sparse in the way of conversation but it is an excellent pork stew; tender and succulent and cooked with home-grown vegetables. I tell Bianca that Frankly mustn't be fed from the table; but that would not be allowed anyway. Frankly lies down at Bianca's feet and is patient. She knows about Secret Food Later and this is obviously one of those nights.

Bianca's grandma is the one who keeps the figurines for the church's Christmas crib. My stilted conversation manages to ask about them and, after supper, I am given the great honour of seeing the holy family. They are individually wrapped in cloth and kept at the back of a cupboard. So many figures! Probably thirty or more—a real pageant including the innkeeper and his wife and so many animals that Mary must have had a real difficulty in choosing which manger.

Bianca isn't allowed to touch them but, of course, she plays with them in secret while her grandma's out. She knows exactly which is the baby Jesus and which are Mary and Joseph and the angel because she whispers their names in my ear as Grandma reaches for them. The angel is Archangel Raphael, she says. I never knew that. I thought it would be Gabriel.

I expect Grandma knows that Bianca plays with the models—the key players don't seem to be quite as well wrapped as the others—but she pretends she doesn't and the game extends to Bianca being allowed to kiss the baby Jesus as long as Grandma holds him safely.

I've never been a mother but I do know that if you want a child to look at something all you have to do is tell it that it's forbidden. I wonder about God sometimes and the Garden of Eden and I have a theory that he meant Eve to have the apple all along. Let's face it, Adam and Eve were the ultimate kids and being told something was forbidden was a complete guarantee that they'd do it sometime along the line.

If God were their Dad, he'd know that. Even I know that. So I think the serpent and all that was just a set-up. If it hadn't happened, then Adam and Eve would have spent eternity in paradise; nothing would ever have happened and they'd be bored, bored, bored. Probably would have ended up pulling the wings off flies and treading on frogs. The devil finds work for idle hands and, at least when they got kicked out, they ended up being busy.

After the brightly-painted figurines have been duly admired and re-wrapped I take my leave, so speaking my fifth or sixth words to Paco, who is rigid with embarrassment, and winkle Frankly out of Bianca's loving embrace.

'*Mañana*,' she says lovingly, kissing Frankly's head. 'More biscuits *mañana*.'

I have to put this dog on a diet.

We walk home briskly—at least I do, for there's a frost in the air.

Why Are You Going So Fast? Frankly is furious about being on her lead and not allowed to dally.

'Because I'm cold.'

Why Don't You Have Fur Then?

'Design fault.'

Oh.

'Actually, Frankly, you wouldn't like it if I had fur.'

Why?

'I might be as cute as you.'

Don't Be Stupid. You Haven't The Ears.

* * *

Christmas is coming and Frankly is getting fat. I have had to have a word with Bianca and limit her to one of Frankly's own dog biscuits per day. This did not go down well with Frankly or Bianca and I think that, if it weren't for the Even Greater Cruelty of staying away and depriving Frankly of the one, pathetic biscuit, we would have lost our little visitor completely.

But little girls forgive very easily, especially at Christmas time when Auntie Anna can take you for a day out to Almeria in her big fast car and you can see all the dozens of Nativity scenes in the shops and walk by the sea with Frankly and then have a doughnut in a café.

It is December 23rd when I realise that Bianca has become very quiet. She is obviously upset about something—but she won't tell me what it is. I don't want to ask too much but the big brown eyes are genuinely troubled and she is not giving the correct amount of attention to the making of a chocolate roulade for Christmas lunch at *La Posada*.

Frankly, on the other hand, is devout in her worship of cooking, especially cooking involving cream.

I'm not sure how much I should ask—and even the gentlest of promptings causes Bianca to shy away—so I have no alternative but to give her the cream beaters and suggest that she tells Frankly instead. This turns out to be a stroke of genius. While I am behind the pillar in the kitchen and obviously cannot hear a thing, Bianca tells a beagle which is deeply immersed in licking cream beaters, and therefore appears to be concentrating, that the Baby Jesus's head has fallen off.

Somehow I doubt that. I suspect that the baby Jesus's head got broken while Bianca was playing with him. Fortunately Frankly doesn't jump to that kind of conclusion so Bianca doesn't have to explain.

It seems that she has been praying for a miracle ever since his head fell off but nothing has happened yet.

So, I have a choice here. I can tell Bianca that I have overheard, drive her straight into Motril and buy a replacement for the baby—or I can let her continue to believe in miracles.

The former course of action would, obviously, be the right one and I am just about to speak when Bianca says firmly that she *knows* there will be a miracle and that God has lots of time left.

Okay. One very, very last vestige of niceness hits me. And I need fresh cow's milk anyway for the bread sauce.

Chapter Sixteen

CHRISTMAS MORNING IS one of those glorious pale-light and sparkling midwinter days that makes you glad to be alive. I'd been dreading Christmas alone but one of the great things about living in a religious community is that there is plenty to do on Christmas day—as long as you don't mind involving the baby Jesus in it. I think that's reasonable, even if I've learnt from Ben's amazing library exactly how tenuous the whole Christmas day link is to that miraculous baby born in Bethlehem so many years ago.

However, the first (alleged) pleasure of the day comes horribly early. It is Midnight Mass. Usually I wouldn't even consider going but I want to see Bianca's face when the completely whole baby Jesus is revealed in all his glory. And I have earned that pleasure. God, what a palaver it all turned out to be trying to be an angel. I seriously cannot recommend it and, to be honest, I don't know how the real ones put up with all the flak.

I told Rani and Sylvia of my little deception in not letting Bianca know that I had overheard her and shooting off to Motril to find a new baby as soon as she'd gone. They were doubtful but I wasn't going to listen to their doubts even though I couldn't find a suitable Jesus in Motril and had to drive two hours to Almeria instead. There were moments on that drive—even with a BMW—where I did wonder if I had done the right thing but I suppressed them sternly. Frankly was pissed off with me but what's new there?

The baby Jesus cost £20. Twenty pounds! Dammit. I know my house money's come through now but *£20* for a gross pink plaster child masquerading self-satisfiedly as a holy baby? Still, I gritted my teeth and bought it—and damn-well nearly dropped it when I tripped over the kerb on the way back to the car.

Now, of course, I have to find Isabella, tell her what had happened and make her promise not to punish Bianca. That isn't easy without fluent Spanish but, thank God, I don't put my first plan into operation and wait until after Bianca has gone to sleep and Isabella is on her way to the cupboard at 11pm. Isabella's shrieks when she understands what has happened are enough to burst an eardrum at 6pm while Bianca is proudly taking Frankly for a walk. After dark and at the last minute it would have sounded as if Dracula had joined forces with the Grinch and eaten the real, living baby Jesus whole.

'You don't understand, you don't understand!' cries Isabella in hysterics. 'It is the anointed baby that is broken! Blessed by the priest with holy water! This *thing* is not anointed!'

Oh God. Dear Father in Heaven, save me from religion.

So, now we have to take the baby up to the priest and get it blessed. And, for good measure we take the old one too so it can be reverently laid to rest or whatever it is you do with broken bits of Divinity. I don't ask.

The priest, who has the sense of humour and lightness of being of a Russian skyscraper, is pompously of the opinion that Bianca should be punished for desecrating the Holy Child. I play 'the little girl was expecting a miracle' card only to meet a complete stone wall. Apparently God doesn't reward naughty little girls with miracles. He sends them to hell for their irreverence.

Not surprising He's not that popular nowadays, then.

Even with Rani who, having foreseen this, turns up just in time to bail out my rapidly failing Spanish, cannot convince the priest to relent. He is on a roll, as they say. Fire and brimstone everywhere. Isabella is in hysterics again and I am consigning the baby Jesus and all his ilk into the darkest bowels of hell.

God I wish Jack were here.

Then, inspiration strikes.

'Bianca didn't break it; I did,' I say. 'Rani. Please tell them it was me.'

Reluctantly, he does—explaining quite dexterously that they have simply misunderstood my bad Spanish. Then, of course, all hell breaks loose at me instead.

Well, I'm already a murderess; to be a blasphemous unbeliever—and a careless one at that—is all grist to the mill. Fortunately, now blame is correctly apportioned, Bianca is going to be let off. Obviously, she must have been tempted by my evil spirit to allow me to go to the cupboard while her Grandma was out (and when would that have been, pray?) but Satan is notoriously wily.

Somehow I don't think I'll be going to Isabella's for supper again.

Anyway, Rani smooths things over sufficiently for the new Baby Jesus to be correctly blessed, anointed and handed over to the priest in case the vile demoness get her hideous hands on it again in the last vital hours before the blessed day.

I crawl away. If Rani says *anything* about interfering or trying to be a do-gooder, I shall hit him. I know perfectly well what I did wrong: I forgot I was out of nice. Damn. Won't do that again.

Instead, Rani gives me a hug and laughs, which is almost as irritating. 'Now you've got to handle the little girl's reaction to the miracle,' he says.

What on earth does he mean by that?

At Midnight Mass, I find out.

Basically, Bianca expected a different sort of miracle. A superior miracle—the type that real angels can do rather than women listening behind pillars.

Firstly, she thought the *real* Baby Jesus would turn up so another plaster cast is a hideous disappointment. My mind drifts back to the *Peanuts* cartoons and Linus's belief in The Great Pumpkin. Children are very literal. But I couldn't have foreseen that.

However, Bianca is a very religious little girl, so if that miracle is not to be vouchsafed her, then she understands that it is because she was naughty and played with the baby when she wasn't allowed to. But did God have to make the new baby so *very* ugly?

Any decent self-respecting angel wouldn't hang around in order to see the fruits of their labours. They have a lot more sense. I should never have gone to the service anyway; I swear the priest glowered at me especially.

As I stand aghast by the crib, Bianca criticises the baby's hair—which is too curly—and the way he is lying with his feet in the air.

He's also too small. And he is ugly. Well, I agree with the last bit but too small? The Virgin Mary must be pathetically grateful that this year, at least, he's less than fifty percent of her body weight.

I suppose it all gives me an interesting insight into the whole concept of unconditional love. After the third time that Bianca has said how much she doesn't like the expression on the face of the new Jesus and wondered why God sent such an ugly one, I could swat her.

Oh forget it. It's Christmas. It's 1.30 in the morning and Frankly is curled up under the covers of my bed steaming quietly. She loves me unconditionally and doesn't care if I've made a total prat of myself. And I've got a bottle of Spanish brandy. I'm going to have a very large drink.

Christmas lunch is at *La Posada*. It's a tradition for the ex-pats and this year I am helping Katherine to cook it so the morning passes pleasantly enough. Memories of last year with Alex are there—and they hurt like hell—but this is so different that they can't ruin everything.

It's a morning to be tactful. After all, I have been a professional chef and I do know how to cook a turkey with all the trimmings. But when I arrive this morning with the bread sauce—made with fresh full cream milk from Motril with a whole onion spiked with cloves seethed in it until the whole house was redolent with the spice—Katherine isn't at all sure why it should be preferable to the packet mix she's been using for years. And when my Christmas pudding turns out to be homemade and my chocolate roulade is light-as-air because it's made entirely without flour she does have a little trouble with her Christmas spirit. I suppose it was a bit tactless as, until now, she has been queen of the cooking in Los Poops.

With behaviour equal to saintliness I don't criticise any of her cooking methods or suggest any improvements. Luckily, I do want to get rid of any remaining niceness that might have crept up on me over the last few months—and I tell you, the cupboard is well and truly bare by the time everyone else arrives full of bonhomie and sherry.

There are seventeen of us for lunch in all, including a couple of

Spanish 'honorary ex-pats,' Cosimo and Elise, who live up the hill in Larita and Franz, who is a German artist who is an old friend of Stella's and David's and various friends and locals who don't have anything better to do.

Frankly is the only dog and Stella strokes her sadly while no one else is looking. Stella and I exchange glances and her grief touches such a chord in me that I have to put my hand to my mouth to stop an involuntary sound of pain. I *will not* think of Alex who will be celebrating with Suzie while I am lost in a Spanish village with no future. Or that I have to go "home" to England and start again from scratch in a country that I no longer love.

I mustn't think that. I must just live for the moment and be grateful for the love and laughter that surround me now.

Alcohol. That's the ticket right now. Definitely.

Lunch is a success—and it's fun, too. Stella has crackers from Harrods (by Internet mail order) and they are brilliant. The turkey is fine and the bread sauce is tried with some trepidation and then ladled joyfully onto plates. The Christmas pudding, roulade and Katherine's trifle are all swallowed up to the last morsel and we all watch the Queen's speech by satellite and agree that she really is looking her age.

Rani fancies me. There isn't any doubt about that now. Sylvia seems to think it's funny but I'm not so sure. There is a falseness about the way she draws my attention to Rani's kindnesses to me. And he is embarrassed about it. But he still has a look in his eyes when he looks at me which is perturbing. He's nice. He's very nice. And he isn't ugly. But…

But.

Katherine has noticed too. She has this sweet way of thinking that everything will turn out perfectly. For a moment, when I have had quite a lot too much to drink and I'm tired—and Frankly has been just that little bit too demanding and greedy and obnoxious—I lose it slightly in the kitchen and a few tears are shed.

'It's not Alex,' I say when Katherine puts her arm around me sympathetically. 'I've coped with that all day.'

'Now is it someone else you're pining for,' says Katherine, with the slight Irish lilt that sometimes breaks through her gentle voice.

'Yes.'

'It's a shame. You went well together.'

'Oh Katherine, don't! He's married. He's in America. It was just a fantasy. It could never have happened. And it's just the rebound. You know… I was bound to fall for someone impossible. It's what happens.'

'You have the right to be happy,' she says. 'Maybe it could happen. Marriages break, you know that.'

'Don't. I mustn't have that hope. It doesn't help.'

'No. I understand. Well, maybe in a while you could like Rani. Time does heal, even if it seems to take forever.'

'I don't have forever. I have to go back to England in two months. I don't have a home here.'

'You could buy one. We'd be glad to have you stay.'

I hug her, on impulse. So kind! Everyone is so kind. Even Stella is almost human nowadays.

I suppose I could buy a cottage here. But much as I love this village, it isn't a forever place for me. I would slowly die out here on my own. And Rani? No. Not Rani. Not for me.

'Hold faith then,' says Katherine, touching my face with one finger. 'Something will happen. Miracles do happen.'

'What, like the baby Jesus?' That's common knowledge now and we have all had a good laugh about it.

'Never you mind,' says Katherine. 'Anyway, you've got your family coming out later in the week. That's going to keep you busy!'

Oh yes, that will keep me busy all right.

> *Anna,*
>
> *Just a note to wish you Happy Holidays. Give my regards to all the folks in Los Poops. Colorado is down to minus 30 degrees at night. The skiing is great. Glad to hear that the car is being useful. Do use the house whenever you want—I know how you Brits love your baths! And give Frankly a pat from me.*
>
> *Regards,*
> *Jack*

Nothing. Nothing there but friendship. I am mad. Ella is right. I have to look ahead to England.

All is well. Jack and I did the right thing.

But, this Christmas night, as Frankly and I walk back home, both slightly the worse for wear (from too much food in her case and too much drink in mine) I look up at the stars which glisten above. A half-forgotten song comes into my mind, sung by Françoise Hardy:

> 'All over the sky, there is the same warm glow… here, under that star, I'm wanting you to know… wherever you are, that I still love you so.'

It's too early for bed but I have taken care to make sure that I am halfway through a very good book because Christmas night was always likely to be a potential problem. So, I curl up with Frankly by the open fire listening to a cassette of Christmas music sent by Mum from England. Light from the fire and from the candles in Ben's seven-branched menorah send shadows dancing around the walls and Charlotte Church's beautiful voice soars throughout the little house. A wonderful peace has settled on me from somewhere and I find that I do not need to read. Instead I am singing along to the timeless Christmas songs of hope and joy. I have not sung for a very long time. I have loved and lost twice in this last year, not to mention losing a country and a home but perhaps there *is* a Christmas angel because an unexpected sense of happiness pervades my every thought. I can even look forward to a mythical "next year" when I shall have my own home again and all this will be memory.

Frankly leans back against me as I stroke her and we are soon involved in a full-scale beagle-love-in. I don't know which of us enjoys these more; I stroke and scratch and embrace and she rubs her head against me and licks whatever parts of me she can reach. We talk to each other and she paws my face and nudges me, our eyes smiling at each other. I have my face close to her head and the soft, warm smell of beagle mingles with the scent of wood smoke and candles. Sometimes you know when a memory is being created and I know that this scene will stay with me forever. Maybe it's because of love. I love Frankly and I love Jack and the greatest need of any human being is to have someone to love.

I can feel Jack sitting behind me now, as if I were leaning on him instead of the cushions. He is teasing me and flicking Frankly's ear with one hand. In another life we are together in a Colorado ranch house past the stage of first love but settled and strong. Carefully I blank out the parts of my mind which are trying to cut in and revoke the fantasy. This is a time of magic and I can believe it if I want to. This is my Christmas.

Maybe just once in every lifetime there is a moment when everything, *everything* works. A moment when two people make one prayer together and you genuinely wouldn't mind if it were your last moment on earth because what you create in that moment is the culmination of all beauty, love and joy. If you have already experienced it, you will know what I mean.

If Yiannis expunged Alex from my body, then Jack had the power to expunge him from my soul because no matter how much I may want to hold onto the habit of hurting and being "hard done-by" I can't. After Jack, Alex is nothing.

Frankly has settled to doze on my lap now as I lean back on the cushions against the wall. She is curled up in my arms as if she were a tiny puppy instead of a venerable and fractious old lady with a large, solid, lardy arse. I don't mind this "canine paralysis" and I hold her tightly, closing my eyes and rocking gently in time to *The Little Drummer Boy*.

In a novel, Frankly and I would now spend the entire night curled up together in front of the fire. But this is real life and I'm going to get cramp if I stay in this position too long.

Come on Frankly, wake up, it's time for bed.

Three days later, two worlds collide as Richard, Grace, Deborah, Janet and my Mum step out of the people carrier in the main square.

It's wonderful to see them again—the last time was at Dad's funeral so it wasn't the best of times. But they don't fit! Los Poops looks shabby and poor as they stand in the square and look around with tourists' eyes.

And Frankly doesn't recognise them. I am surprised but there is no friendly wagging of the tail and she has no interest barring the normal and necessary checking of luggage for any signs of food.

Richard and his family check into *La Posada* and Mum, Frankly and I go home.

I have cleared one of the rooms downstairs and aired it enough to make it habitable and one of Ben's electric fan heaters has made it warm enough to be welcoming. But it still looks poor and shabby in my eyes now—and Mum cannot hide her surprise at the primitive conditions in which I live.

'But Anna, there isn't even a bath!'

'No, Mum, I wrote to you about that! I bath at Jack Risborough's house once a week. It's fine.'

'Jack who?'

'The American who has a house here. I take care of it while he's back home.'

'Oh yes.' She is plainly uninterested. And why would she be? She doesn't know I love him. Instead, she is examining the kitchen.

'How on earth do you cope? It's *tiny*!'

'There's just me, Mum.'

'And Frankly doesn't remember me. It's so sad.'

'She's just a bit confused Mum.'

'You've still got an American accent.'

'Would you like some tea, Mum?'

Tea, that panacea that aids all things. Over tea we get back into a better groove. Mum has brought me some lovely things— McVitie's ginger nuts and Thorntons' chocolate. For Frankly there's her favourite kibble and that won't be a problem because, even if she's forgotten that it's meant to be her favourite, it's still food and will be leapt upon as if she did remember it.

We catch up on life in England; she isn't really interested in my life and why should she be? She doesn't know any of the people in it. She has seen Alex and Suzie in the High Street but doesn't talk to them. Alex is going bald, she says.

I am cooking supper for everyone and I have a pork casserole with lentils in the oven, cooking deliciously slowly. And it's a lovely evening even if it is almost unbearably strange to see my family here. The children (who are eight and ten) are quite excited by the village and the mules and sheep they have seen so far. But I know they will be bored within twenty-four hours. They've brought their little computer games with them and, even before we adults are drinking coffee they are 'plik plikking' away by the fire.

'There aren't any comfy chairs!' complains Grace. She is right; there aren't. I've got used to cushions by the fire.

Richard is very brotherish and protective. He is already looking out jobs for me and is telling me about websites I can register with. He wonders where I am going to settle—I will be coming back to the north won't I? Or do I think all the best work is in London now?

'I haven't thought.' It's not true. I've thought for hours but the only conclusion I've come to is that I don't want to go back.

'Well you must, Anna! It's only two months before you and Frankly will be coming home.'

Home.

'I still feel that Colorado is home,' I say, stupidly and feel about six as Richard, Grace and my mum explain to me that it isn't; that I'll soon adapt back and soon I won't even miss the States. 'Let alone this place,' seems to hang in the air unspoken.

'Last time I was in England, I was horrified by all the dirt and the litter,' I say, foolishly. 'I'm used to clean air now and small-town life.'

Small-town life? Who can possibly want small town life? Nobody with any sense, obviously.

I wish Mum were staying at *La Posada*. And, I think, so does she; she obviously finds the basement really uncomfortable. I wish I could pack them off and shut the door and cry. But instead, there's the washing up and more family news and then bed. And tomorrow we're going to Granada because there really isn't much to do around here.

We have a very pleasant time and Richard and I have a good talk while the others are in a gift shop. He wants to know if I would rather go somewhere else than Manchester because Alex and Suzie are there. And he is reassuring about how quickly I will find work and adapt back to life in England.

'It's in your blood, Anna,' he says. 'And I know it will hurt to start with. It's bound to. You've had a hell of a time with moving and Frankly and all that. We're proud of you and how you've coped. And I can see the temptation of Los Poops. It's a place to hide and recuperate. But it's not a forever place, Anna.'

I know he's right and I can say so. 'But I still feel lost, Richard. Like I don't have a home.'

'Well, we all expected you to be settled and happy in a nice home, maybe with children of your own and a steady job—and I expect you did too,' says Richard. 'It's what seems right at our age. For you to start again, now, is bound to be difficult. But a lot of people have to do it. And you're still young enough to find someone else and be happy—not that you have to find someone to be happy,' he adds hastily, aware of the political incorrectness of implying that a woman needs a man to be content.

'I still believe in fairy tales,' I say, apropos of nothing.

'So do I!' says my brother with a smile. 'The kids don't, of course. Not any more.'

When they finally go, Frankly and I celebrate with a long, long walk over the hills. Nobody wanted to walk as far as we are used to doing now and it was fairly frustrating for both of us. But I think the visit was fairly frustrating for everybody. Nobody said so and we all persuaded ourselves that we had a good time but I don't fit in my family any more. And I don't want to.

But even so, the village is changed for me, once they have been. The end of my visit is now in sight; and it *is* just a visit. I have given Rani no encouragement and I am not going to buy a house and talk is now turning towards Frankly's and my journey home. Will we drive? Will we fly? Will we take the train? I must book it all soon. Slowly but surely I can feel separation slipping between myself and the others who have committed to their lives here. It's seven weeks away; six, five and four—and the almond trees are coming into bloom.

How utterly beautiful they are! I had no idea how glorious the hills would be in their bridal dresses of white and palest pink blossom and walking in the falling petals is like being caressed by a soft-scented snowstorm. But they are the beginning of the end. And I don't want this to end—but neither do I want it to continue. I feel completely lost.

It's a lovely bright early spring day and Frankly and I have been walking high on the hillside above the village. It's by way of a celebration because I've actually applied for a job over the Internet. It's for a sous-chef at a restaurant in Southport and I don't have a clue if I want it or not and I seriously doubt that they would want me. But it's a start, I suppose. But, having done it, I feel free. Now I don't want to think about anything but the beauty of the day. We walk down the hillside behind the church just as a Fiat Punto hire car sweeps up the road and into the square. It is driven by someone very confident—a woman wearing a headscarf and actually making it look suave. I am interested. Village life does that to you!

The woman gets out of the car and stands looking around her. She is definitely looking for someone. And I am standing stock-still with shock as Frankly begins to bounce and squeak. She races ahead of me yelping Look Mum! It's My Friend! I Remember Her! And Ella crouches down, holding her arms out, a great smile splitting her beautiful face.

Chapter Seventeen

'ELLA! ELLA! *ELLA!*'

We are hugging tightly and I have tears in my eyes from joy. Ella! My best of friends! What are you doing here?

'I got a vacation,' she says with that slow wonderful, glorious grin that spreads from ear to ear and makes Julia Roberts look mealy-mouthed and plain.

'But you didn't tell me you were coming!'

'It was kinda sudden.'

'But you didn't even call for directions!'

'Well, I found it all the same. And I've bought some food and some wine so you don't even have to worry about provisions,' she says. 'I guess I can stay at *La Posada*—if you don't have room.'

'I have room! It's a bit scruffy but I have room!'

'Okay. Well, lets go to your place,' she says laughing. 'I've just driven two hours and I'm dying for a drink. Even more, I really need to go to the john!'

Walking through the village with Ella is so different from being with the family. I must have described it better or something. I am bouncing like a child and Frankly is trotting ahead proudly with her head and tail high as if to say Look, Everyone, Here's My Friend.

'There's the Sad Mule With Crinkly Eyelids in his stable… there's Stella's and David's house… that's the view across to Morocco… there's the Siamese with the aquamarine eyes and some of his latest progeny… there's Big Brown… there's my road… there's the house…'

And Ella loves it just as I do. Even if she picks her way over the cobbles and round the sheep dung in her brand-new canvas sneakers and looks frighteningly elegant in a navy and white linen trouser suit, she is just happy to be here. She has two immaculate

242

Louis Vuitton leather cases and a shoulder bag and she should be in Cannes—but somehow she doesn't look out of place.

We meet Rani and George at the top of *Calle La Era* and their jaws drop visibly at this vision of loveliness. Ella's face lift makes her look about twenty-five and the new nose (the improved dimensions of which I had forgotten) is not just nice; it is a delight.

I introduce everyone and we are invited to drinks, both men almost falling over themselves to get the offer in first. Ella has that effect on men; I had forgotten.

'Well thanks but tonight Anna and I have a lot to catch up on,' she says. 'We'll just take a rain check and see you guys around tomorrow.'

I think they'll be queuing outside the door with their tongues hanging out.

I have real coffee and Ella has Oreos and after she has freshened up and looked all around the house (and taken the obligatory sip of the disgusting sherry from the barrel downstairs with a chuckle which sounds like starlight on a river) we sit down to talk.

One reason that she doesn't look like she's been dragged through a hedge backwards is because she arrived in Malaga yesterday and stayed there overnight.

I'm still perplexed as to why she didn't call me and let me know.

'Like you weren't going to be here?' she says, laughing.

'Well, just so I could prepare. And to give me some time to anticipate and be excited.'

'Oh Anna, I'm sorry. But it really was a last minute thing.'

'But the last I knew, you were still thinking of going back to California because there's not enough work in Denver.'

'Well, I got a job.'

'A job?'

'Yeah, teaching drama.'

'Oh, that's great! Is it?' Suddenly I don't know. Ella is an actress, not a teacher.

'Yeah, it's great! I can still act.'

'But if you've just got a job, how can you take a vacation?'

'I don't start until I get back.'

'Okay.'

But I am still confused. There is some mystery here and I can't put my finger on it. But it is wonderful to have Ella here. And she has brought photographs of Unityville—of Gilbert and the café and all the girls. They were obviously posed specially and some of them are fairly outrageous. It tugs at my heart to see them.

'I haven't heard from Gilbert in a couple of months. Did he get a new chef?'

'No, he tried someone but they didn't fit.'

'I'm not surprised. It would take someone pretty special to work with Gilbert.'

'Like you,' says Ella.

'Yeah, right.'

'You should think about it, Anna.'

'I can't, Ella! You know that… but Ella?'

'Yes.'

'Why are you here? Really? I mean it's not like it's not great… but… why? I mean, you didn't even have a passport when I was in Colorado. And now… I don't understand. You'd have told me!'

And then Ella smiles at me in a very strange way and reaches into her handbag. She pulls out a passport. A European passport.

'I've brought your passport back,' she says simply.

'My passport?' I don't understand. My passport is in the safe at *La Posada.*

I feel as if I am watching myself from a distance as I reach out to take the little maroon booklet. My hand is shaking. It *is* my passport. I look up at Ella, deeply disturbed.

'Look inside it,' she says with a smile.

Inside it? I know my passport. I look at the picture of me— seven years ago now and a happy wife then—and the stamps of all the countries that Alex and I visited together. But hold on a minute… there is a new stamp. With my mind disbelieving what my eyes are seeing, I see an American visa with my photograph on it right on the very last page. A visa. An American B-visa which allows me to work as a freelance in America for the next ten years.

'I think you'd better tell me what's going on,' I say. And it is not only my hands which are shaking now.

244

* * *

It was Jack. Of course it was Jack. He went to Unityville and walked into the *Die Happy Café* one snowy Tuesday afternoon when Gilbert was sitting at one of the tables with the world's largest caramel latte, fretting over his accounts.

He sat down and introduced himself as a friend of mine and asked Gilbert if he needed a chef. Then he got Gilbert to agree to promote the café as "Unityville's English Tea Café" and sign a form saying that he needed an English chef to work there. And that he happened to know the actual one. Then Jack asked him how to find Ella.

'I knew who he was as soon as he got out of his car,' she said. 'I was clearing snow from the trailer steps as he drove in. I've seen his picture in the *Denver Post*—you know I have; I told you. And he just walked up to me and introduced himself.

'We went for a coffee and played this "How much do you know? No, how much do *you* know?" kinda game for about half an hour and then he just said he was going to get you a visa.'

She halts because I am holding my hand up to stop her. I can't handle this.

'Anna, just listen,' she says, gently. 'It's all right. You don't have to do anything. He said he just wanted to give you the choice. He didn't believe that you wanted to go back to England and he wanted you to be able to come back to Unityville if you wanted to. Only if you wanted to.

'Anna, he's got the money and the influence. He knows the US Ambassador to England. Of course he does! It didn't give him any problem at all to get you a visa.

'There's no pressure, Anna. None at all. He's not leaving Karen for you; this is the action of a friend, not a lover. You just have the choice now. That's all.'

I can feel my heart beating inside my chest. I can see myself sitting at the table, my hand still in the air. If I weren't so paralysed I would think the expression on my face was ludicrous.

'But how did he get my passport? And why didn't he tell me? Why didn't anyone tell me?'

'You don't tell people if you're giving them a present,' says Ella.

'And I think he knows that you are just as likely to be furious with him for this as you are to be pleased.'

Too true. I am furious. But I am also aghast and lost for words. I have no idea what to think.

'How did he get my passport,' I say doggedly.

'He got someone called Katherine to send it to him by registered post,' says Ella.

'So Katherine knows.' That does make me angry. It's just bloody interference. And then I remember *why* she interferes and I feel a pricking of tears behind my eyes.

'Anna,' says Ella, putting her beautiful creamy hand on my roughened, brown one. 'You can be as mad as you like. You can throw me out because I agreed with him that it was a good thing to do. It's your choice. But we did it out of love for you. All of us. We did it because you deserve a break. Because you're a good friend. Because we wanted to do what we could to make you happy.'

Why am I crying? I am so sick of crying. It has been a whole year of crying. I don't even know if I'm happy or sad.

'I can't go back, Ella. I love him. It would be hell.'

'He'll be in Washington, Anna.'

'But he comes to Colorado. I'd see him. I'd see *her.*'

'Well, you don't have to go back. You can go on to England. It's your choice. You don't even have to decide now.'

But I know. There's no need to make any decision. I can angst about it and justify it for days and weeks ahead. I can fret about Jack and worry about living in Unityville alone. I can hear the protests of my family and I can be as furious as I like at this gross interference in my life. But Frankly and I are going home.

What a wonderful time Ella and I have for the next two weeks! I have done all the tourist bits with the family but I can do them again. It's fun. And I have a heart that is so much lighter that I don't even feel like the same person any more. We go further afield than is comfortable for families and, with Frankly in the back of the BMW, we visit the beautiful walled town of Cordoba and go shopping in Malaga. We walk Frankly over the mountains and we

FOR THE LOVE OF DOG

have wonderful dinner parties with all the people I know and love in the village. And they are all so happy for me. Even Rani.

I email Jack.

Thank you, I write. Nothing else. It's not wise to try to get into any conversations. I may be going home but this line must not be pursued.

But he is still the most irritating man on the planet.

The return email reads:

> *Dear Anna,*
> *So glad you're pleased. If you do decide to return to the States please let me know so I can arrange a First Class flight for you to Denver. And don't jump down my throat. I'm thinking of Frankly. First class, she can fly in the cabin with you. I think she's getting a bit old to go in the hold on a long-haul flight again.*
> *Best wishes,*
> *Jack.*

Odious, odious, *odious* man!

It's 11pm and it's cold outside. Frankly is curled up beside me on the rug by the fire, dozing peacefully. A late falling of snow deadens all sound from the outside but we are warm and snug. The fire in the grate is blazing, throwing flickering shadows up the white walls; the logs spitting a little and adding to the dancing lights from the candles. Ella has gone home now but I am very content to be alone with my beautiful beagle. I stroke the soft, tawny fur on her head and she stirs in her sleep, whiffling slightly. She is probably chasing something in her own little world. I notice that there is more white around her kohl-ringed eyes than there used to be but that makes them all the more beautiful to me.

I am happy. Very happy. Nothing to do tonight but read or think and go to bed.

I gently disentangle myself from Frankly and she sighs before settling again just a little closer to the fire than she is allowed to be.

'*You* are incorrigible,' I tell her and she opens one eye. I would swear she is winking at me.

Outside the window I can't see anything but the great, soft flakes of white whirling round in spirals. Frankly should go out but I haven't the heart to make her. Instead I pick up the newspaper lying by the grate and wander into the kitchen to boil the kettle for a hot water bottle.

What a year it has been. But I have no regrets.

'Bed, Frankly!' I call.

She will come when she's ready.

While the kettle is boiling, I take one last look at *The Denver Post* which Ella left behind. It is open at the "hatched, matched and dispatched" page with its picture of an elegant fair-haired woman looking radiant on the arm of a distinguished-looking man.

I haven't heard from Jack once in the twelve months that I've been back in Unityville but there has been quite enough to keep me busy and happy here. What was formerly the *Die Happy Café* and is now the *English Tea House* is a success now with its British theme and wonderful cakes and pastries, even if I do say so myself—and Gilbert has taken me on as a partner. We even had enough cash spare to redecorate three months ago and the walls are covered with pictures of England. The café is even being regarded as a tourist attraction. Ella is doing well too—both with her teaching and acting. She even has a screen test next month. Gilbert is still pursuing true love on the Internet and it is still running away from him.

My friends in Los Poops write regularly and Rani and Sylvia are even talking of coming to stay. That will be fun. Bianca writes too—to Frankly rather than to me—but already, I am not finding it as easy to translate her letters. Frankly never read them anyway. They don't contain any biscuits.

It seems so long ago. All of it.

One day, maybe I'll look up as the café door opens and see his beloved face again. And maybe I won't.

But I cannot resist looking again at the paper and read that Karen Risborough, of Denver and Washington high society, is now Karen Forsyth after a quickie divorce from her husband of twenty-three years and her new marriage to a Connecticut congressman.

One day. Maybe. When his heart is healed. He truly loved Karen and it will take him some time. I do know a little bit about these things.

And it doesn't matter because I am happy already. I have everything I need. If he comes, it will just be one more strand in the glory of life.

If.

When.

As I sit on the edge of the bed, brushing my hair, there is a thud as a beagle hurls itself onto the counterpane behind me.

Shove Up Mum, she says, settling down right in the middle of the bed.

I could have given in; I could have let her go but I followed my heart and I am so grateful that I did. Life is made up from all the little choices we make and every choice has its consequence. I chose love and love chose me in return.

Behind me, on the bedside table is the letter from my mother telling me that Alex has married Suzie—and that he is definitely going bald.

Do I care? No. Hand on healed heart. In fact the thought of my mother's kind and anxious concern makes me burst into laughter and cuddle my beautiful beagle.

Frankly, my dear, I don't give a damn.

Also by Maggy Whitehouse...

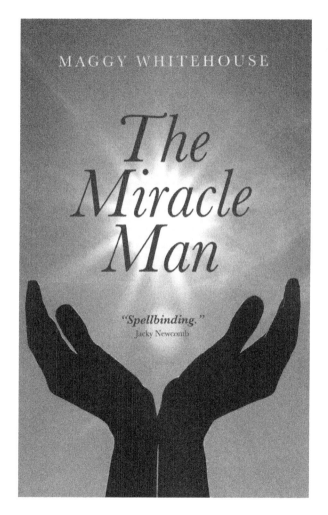

Read on to find out more...

CHAPTER ONE

Gemma Goldstone died when her Aston Martin V8 Vantage crashed over the Hoover Dam.

News like that spreads around the world within minutes; the headlines harsh and filled with excitement.
'Glamour Queen Of Talent Dies In Horror Crash'
'Final Curtain For The Lady With The Midas Touch'
'Crisis As Multi-Million-Dollar *Miracle Mile* Show Threatened.'
Etc., etc.
And that was just what happened but, despite the Hoover Dam tourists' blurred cell phone images, uploaded to the Internet within the hour, the news that it was Gemma who had been killed could not be confirmed immediately. No matter how frantic or voracious the media might be, the police were not releasing the victim's name until next-of-kin were informed.
Next-of-kin was Gemma's husband, Josh. But he was not at any of the celebrity couple's homes in Los Angeles, Las Vegas, London or the South of France, nor at the offices in London, Vegas or New York. Nobody knew where he was and nobody—to start with at least—noticed whether or not there might have been a passenger in the royal blue Aston Martin.
People often didn't notice Josh. Despite his wife's worldwide celebrity, her charity foundations and associates, nobody knew what he did; if he did anything. He certainly didn't have a PA or secretary and there were no children to know where their Dad might be at this time of crisis.
Gemma's entourage never took much notice of the husband; he was the quiet accessory who accompanied their Matriarch everywhere. He had to be tolerated because she operated better when he was around and he was the only one who could deal with her occasional tantrums, which could shake the building with their violence. He had to be present for every public or TV

253

appearance as her support and her Muse; without him, she was uncomfortable and prickly. Exactly what he did with himself at other times—apart from getting slightly in the way of course— nobody knew. Wasn't he some kind of a landscape designer or something? Some years ago, some bright spark had called him 'the Gardener', which about summed up his status, and the turnover within Gemstone Inc was so high that very few of them nowadays realized that actually was his surname. Everyone called him 'Mr. Goldstone' and if he ever bothered to contradict, no one took any notice.

Gemma was a legend; an icon, loved worldwide—and rightly so because she was a ball of golden energy, talent and, unexpectedly, kindness. She was the opposite of a jinx; self-esteem bred in the air around her. Not that she would suffer fools gladly (and those tantrums were legendary). Gemma Goldstone was exceptional and she expected her staff to be the same. She would always say that she needed the talent to be better off-screen than ever it was on-screen. In fact, efficiency was the bare minimum required to work for Gemma. If you put a foot wrong there would always be dozens of production wannabes begging to take your place.

But if you were lucky enough to get in with Gemma on the ground floor, paid your dues and kept your nostrils clean, you were guaranteed to go far.

That was, it seemed, everyone except Josh. He didn't even have style, despite the couple's money and superstar status. His shoes were slightly scuffed, his shirts always seemed crumpled on his lanky body and he looked as though he wore clothes from Walmart. And, my dear—his fingernails! People in Gemma's world noticed that kind of thing. Josh obviously had never seen a manicurist in his life, even though Gemma travelled with her very own team of beauticians. And *per-leez* don't mention the colour of his teeth! What was going on with that? Appropriate flouncing would indicate a group opinion of a man who had access to everything but chose not to use any of the tools provided.

Gemma, on the other hand, was exquisite on every level. A touch of Botox, of course, and a little liposuction. And, of course, breast enhancement. But nothing else was needed yet—she was only thirty-six and at the peak of her physical attractiveness. Not beautiful, exactly, but pixie-faced and arresting with just the right way of looking up at you through her eyelashes.

What this megastar didn't have in physical stature, she had in buckets-full of magnetism and simmering fire. She was a media phenomenon; a power-ball of energy, sometimes even travelling back and forth across the Atlantic every single week when both the Las Vegas-based *Miracle Mile* and her own X-rated, mega-successful late-night British chat show were in production.

Right now it was holiday time, twelve weeks before the re-start of auditioning and just time to begin cutting back on the personal appearances, the book signings and the charity galas, and to begin thinking about gearing up again. Time to hone the diet, check out a startling new hair colour and style, and pull focus before beginning a new season of spotting the extraordinary performers that her show always found, to the continuing amazement of the whole of the Western World. *The Miracle Mile* had been Gemma's idea and it remained Gemma's, not only because she owned the brand and was majority shareholder of the global entertainment franchise that ran it but also because of her style and wit and her ability to choose co-judges who complemented her perfectly. Gemma could scent the very aura of talent in the smallest mouse and she could make even the rejected candidates laugh with her precise and profound assessment of exactly why they were useless.

In the end, it was one of Gemma's fellow judges on *The Miracle Mile*, Sam Powell, the former PR and media executive, who found Josh—or, perhaps more accurately, definitively located him as lost. The Las Vegas Metropolitan Police called at Sam's hacienda-style home in Spanish Hills with a "routine enquiry" to see if he knew where Mr. Goldstone might be. There had been an accident, they said, but no details were being released as yet.

'Josh is with Gemma!' said Sam. 'I spoke with her this morning—when she was on her way back to Vegas from Phoenix. They were in the car together.'

'What time would that be, Sir?'

'About twelve, I guess.'

'And was Mrs. Goldstone driving?'

'Sure, it was her goddam Aston Martin! What's up? What's going on?'

The sergeant sighed. It was a big story and it was going to break soon whether they found the husband or not. Now it looked very much like they weren't going to find him alive.

'Mrs. Goldstone's car was in collision with a pick-up on the Hoover Dam.'

'What the hell was she doing there?' Sam bit his tongue and his tanned face lost colour as he realised what the officer had said.

'Oh my God! Is she alright?'

'Mrs. Goldstone's car went over the barrier and into the lake, Sir. We have no more than that right now.'

'Jesus Christ.' Sam fell backwards against the wall, sweat beads forming on his face. The whole world crashed and burned in his mind. '*Jeezus!*'

'And you are saying that her husband was with her? Are you sure, Sir?' the officer asked.

'Jesus Christ!' Sam's mind was reeling. 'What? Yes. She said so.'

'Thank you Sir.'

'Wait—wait. Have they found her?'

'A woman's body has been found, Sir. We have no formal identification as yet. We need to find someone who could identify her as soon as possible.'

'Oh God. You'd better take me there. Jesus wept. I can identify her. Oh Christ…'

'Thank you Sir. There's a car outside.'

Sam looked at the tiny, empty body, its cold, elfin face strangely blank, white and totally unscathed. She would have died swiftly, they said, from multiple injuries to the spine caused in the collision and, if not then, as soon as the car hit the water.

He nodded, curtly, holding back unexpected emotion. 'That's Gemma.'

They offered him terrible coffee from a vending machine. 'Don't you guys know that you can get machines now with coffee that tastes like coffee?' he said, irritated but craving the caffeine and throwing the obnoxious mix down his throat as though it were a shot of tequila. The grimace that followed was familiar to anyone who knew him—Sam Powell was known as much for his hard drinking and high life as for his TV personality. Tequila was his drink of choice and there was a running joke that when he bit the lime afterwards it was the fruit that reacted to the bitter taste of Sam.

'Jeez, I never thought I'd end up family,' he muttered as he ransacked his cell phone address book for people who needed to know the news before it hit the headlines. He gave seventeen names to the police to deal with; the remaining six he called himself.

Outside the mortuary, the press was already lining up. The accident itself was news but Sam's involvement and the cell phone footage of the Vantage were quite enough evidence with which to go live: the story was breaking all over the world.

The truck-driver, Frank Morrison, was dead too, his neck broken like a stick in the impact. Frank's truck didn't go over the impossibly high wall but its contents—boxes of chips and cocktail snacks—did. They floated pathetically over large areas of the lake all that day with all the accessible ones being salvaged by tourists before the police cordoned off the entire area. After that, they sank, slowly and dismally, to be investigated without much enthusiasm by fish and small crustaceans.

Police examined the truck and found that the brakes had failed for no apparent reason. It had the appropriate service history; the driver's body tested negative for alcohol and drugs; there was nothing to apportion blame. There was no logical reason why it or the Aston Martin were even on the dam. There was a goddam by-pass for Christ's sake! It was just a freak, impossible, stupid accident.

Gemma's face was on every front page in the Western World every day until the funeral and her presence lived on perpetually, across Internet forums, conspiracy sites and tribute websites. In the first week after her death, Josh was sometimes in the picture too. Gemma would have said herself that the coverage was the best she had ever had. She had never actually written the long-planned autobiography but her brother, Paul, arrived at the Goldstone's Los Angeles home from London within forty-eight hours of her death and rumour said he had brought in a team of researchers and ghostwriters. A multi-million dollar deal for the 'authorised' biography was a dead cert.

Gemma had been a phenomenon. She had risen from what most people chose to see as humble Jewish beginnings (but which were actually perfectly comfortable lower middle-class) in London to become a dancer, briefly a singer in an all-girl band, and then a talent agent. The girl bands she promoted were tacky, it's true, and hardly ever lasted more than one album containing three hit singles, but who minded that when the money kept rolling in and there were always more ingénues who were queuing up to become the next, greatest thing?

Gemma's great coup was to be the first one to take talent-seeking TV back to the tradition of vaudeville, opening doors to both old and new-fashioned acts alike, and the first to take the show to Las Vegas. The theatres and casinos in Vegas always needed new stars and *The Miracle Mile* provided them in bucket-loads. And Vegas had fallen on the idea of its very own talent-seeking show where nothing was too glitzy and nothing too outrageous. *The Miracle Mile* was followed up by *Miracle Camp* for teenagers each summer, touring shows and a year-long Las Vegas-based series of concerts, circus gigs and theatrical extravaganzas from that year's contestants. Gemma's company, Gemstone Inc, was now as integral a part of the Las Vegas profit-making machine as any of the casinos, its conscience salved by Gemma's billion-dollar children's charitable foundation.

Others, of course, followed her—the world was flooded with talent shows—but there was no one like Gemma and nothing with as much kudos as *The Miracle Mile*.

She was married, all the time, to her childhood sweetheart. Their 15th anniversary renewal of vows was featured in *Celebrity Star* magazine after a price-war between glossies and the five million dollar fee went directly to Gemma's charitable foundation. Gemma looked golden and glorious in a series of high-couture outfits with her husband in the background looking vaguely bemused and uncomfortable. He had been shoehorned into designer clothing that made him feel ridiculous.

Josh was always the boy next door, the son of an American who worked at the US Embassy in London. He was her rock, Gemma said, her best friend, her reality-check. Professionally, he was an academic and theologian and an expert in ancient languages. He had even written a textbook on Bible translations which was published by *Oxford University Press* and read by virtually nobody. He probably even had a PhD in something obscure but nobody ever called him Doctor.

Josh worked somewhere in UNICEF at the start of Gemma's fame but, once the roller-coaster of talent shows took off, he didn't need a job and Gemma wanted him by her side wherever she went. There was never a sniff of scandal on either side.

They dredged the whole of Lake Mead for his body but all they found was Josh's wallet, suitcase and cell phone.

Sam swore blind that Gemma told him he was with her; the hotel staff in Phoenix confirmed that they had left together in the car that morning and CCTV confirmed that a man looking very like Josh *was* in the car moments before the crash, raising a lot of understandably awkward questions as to why he hadn't been noticed the first time anyone looked. He had to be *somewhere*. But he was not.

The Miracle Man

IMAGINE THAT THE Messiah came today as TV talent show judge. Imagine that his healing powers made Medicare, drugs, drink, shopping and our other addictions redundant. *The Miracle Man* charts two years in the life of a modern day Messiah who is judge on *The Miracle Mile* (*America's Got Talent*). Living in the spotlight, every move he makes is splashed all over the media.

The book follows the exact chronology of the four Gospels of the New Testament, featuring every major character and updating every story to make it relevant for the secular world of today. Josh Gardener harnesses the world of the media to launch a celebrity-led peaceful liberation of Tibet and an extraordinary U-turn in Chinese policy. But a man this powerful is too much of a threat to the world order. Josh's PR guru Jude Isaacs (Judas Iscariot) believes that the greatest publicity coup would come from a live on air assassination.

After all, Josh will complete the story by rising again. Won't he?

Praise for *The Miracle Man*:

'Spellbinding. Josh Goldstone is an angel for the modern world.'—Jacky Newcomb, author of *Angel Saved My Life*.

'To my mind, it takes a lot of imagination, wisdom and skill to bring together biblical wisdom, metaphysics and contemporary spirituality and not end up with a dogs dinner. But then to create a fantastic story out of them that is funny, gripping and personally engaging takes genius. Well done Maggy, you pulled it off. Loved your book—please write another one quickly.'—Nick Williams, author of *Resisting Your Soul.*

The Miracle Man is published in paperback by O Books and is available from your local bookstore. There's a Kindle edition, too, from Tree of Life Publishing.

Lightning Source UK Ltd.
Milton Keynes UK
UKOW06f2159111116

287403UK00001B/51/P